BOUND TO THE BILLIONAIRE MAFIA BOSS

AN AGE GAP ENEMIES TO LOVERS SECRET PREGNANCY ROMANCE

ALPHA BILLIONAIRE MAFIA BOSSES

MORGAN S BLISS

Copyright © 2024 by Morgan S Bliss

All rights reserved.

Unauthorized reproduction, duplication, or transmission of any portion of this document, whether in digital or print form, is strictly prohibited and violates legal rights. Recording this publication is strictly forbidden, and storing this document is only permissible with explicit written consent from the publisher.

Copyrights not owned by the publisher are retained by their respective authors. All rights reserved."

❦ Created with Vellum

1

CHARLIE

I pace my living room, excitement fizzing through me as the reality of landing the Romano Holdings deal sinks in. They called me. They chose me. Grabbing my phone, I dial Katie—my best friend and my rock through every high and low. She picks up on the second ring.

"Hey, girl! What's up?"

"I got the job!" I nearly shout.

"What?!" Katie's voice rises, matching my excitement. "No way! The Romano deal? Charlie, that's insane! I'm so proud of you!"

"I know!" I laugh, the sound bubbling up from deep inside. "It's the Horizon City project—the biggest one in San Diego. Luxury residences, high-end retail, commercial spaces. A billion-dollar venture. And if this goes well, Katie...it could redefine my career."

Katie exhales, somewhere between amazement and pride. "You have to let me celebrate you."

I glance at the clock, torn. Meeting Dante Romano himself is surreal—I've heard about his presence, the way he commands a room. As thrilled as I am, I can't afford distractions. "I don't know...I have my first meeting with Romano tomorrow, and I need to be sharp."

"Just one drink. You've been working your butt off for this—you deserve it. Please?"

Her excitement is infectious, and a part of me can't resist. Maybe she's right—I have earned this. "Fine. But just one."

Katie squeals with delight. "You're the best! I'll pick you up in an hour. Wear something that screams 'I'm here to win!'"

The bar hums with soft jazz, a comforting counterpoint to the bustling nightlife outside. As Katie and I settle into our booth, I take a deep breath, trying to wrap my mind around this opportunity. I feel a thrill of anticipation, but beneath it, a thread of trepidation. This deal could change everything.

Katie's voice and laughter soon wrap around me like a familiar warmth, and I let myself relax for the first time in weeks. But then I feel it—a shift in the air, a presence that draws my gaze toward the bar.

There he sits, an older man with a rugged, chiseled look that sets him apart. Our eyes meet, and a strange thrill runs down my spine as he holds my gaze with a faint, knowing smile. There's an intensity to him, a quiet confidence that's impossible to ignore.

Katie's voice breaks through my reverie. "Everything okay?"

I turn back to find her on her phone, brow furrowed. "Client emergency. They're acting like the world's about to end. I hate to do this, but..."

I wave her off. "Go. Handle your crisis. I'll be fine." As she hurries out, I settle back into the booth, suddenly aware of how alone I am. A fresh drink appears at my table, and I look up, surprised.

"That's because I did." His deep, smooth voice sends a shiver down my spine. "I couldn't help but notice you from across the room. You don't see someone like you every day."

I raise an eyebrow, feigning indifference despite the flutter in my stomach. "Is that so? And what exactly makes me so unique?"

He leans forward slightly, his gaze steady. "Confidence, with something unspoken underneath. Like there's more to you than meets the eye."

A shiver runs down my spine, but I keep my voice steady. "Mystery, huh? You don't strike me as someone who enjoys guessing games."

He smirks, lifting his glass. "Touché. Maybe that's why you caught my attention."

Our conversation flows with an unexpected intimacy, and I find myself drawn to his charming, enigmatic nature. There's a pull between us, a simmering tension that has me constantly aware of his presence.

Eventually, he glances at his watch, then back at me with a small smile. "What do you say we get out of here?"

I hesitate, my heart racing. This isn't like me—I'm usually so cautious, so focused on my career. But tonight, something about him has me intrigued. I nod, feeling a mix of excitement and nerves. "Alright."

Outside, a sleek black car awaits, and he opens the door for me. As we drive through the city, the silence between us is comfortable, almost charged. I can feel his gaze on me, and when I meet his eyes, I see a hunger there that quickens my pulse.

When we arrive at the hotel, he leads me through the opulent lobby and into the elevator. The moment the doors close, the tension snaps. He pulls me close, his hands firm on my waist, and I lose myself in the heat of his kiss. It's intense, electrifying, a surge of emotions that have been building since he first approached me.

My body responds eagerly, my hands tangling in his hair as I press against him. I can feel the strength in his arms, the power in his touch, and it sends a thrill through me. This is so unlike my usual cautious self, but in this moment, I don't care. I want him, all of him.

He trails hot, open-mouthed kisses along my jaw, down my neck, making me shiver with anticipation. "Please," I whisper, the word barely audible, a plea for more of his touch.

He chuckles softly against my skin, the vibration sending tingles down my spine. "Impatient, are we?" he murmurs, his warm breath fanning over my sensitive skin. "We have all night, beautiful."

I whimper at his words, both frustrated and excited by his teasing. His hands continue their journey, tracing the straps of my dress, teasingly close to my breasts but never quite touching them. I squirm, seeking his touch, my body on fire with need.

"Easy, Charlie," he whispers, his lips brushing my ear, sending shivers down my body. "I want to take my time and savor every inch of you." His fingers finally slip beneath the fabric, grazing the bare skin of my shoulders, making me tremble. "You're so damn beautiful, did you know that?"

I can only nod, my words escaping me as his hands glide down, slowly, agonizingly so, until they cup my breasts. I arch into his touch, my nipples hardening beneath the thin fabric of my dress. His thumbs circle the sensitive peaks, sending jolts of pleasure through my body.

The elevator seems to take an eternity to reach our floor,

and I'm grateful for the slow ascent, allowing us to prolong this intense foreplay. His hands continue their exploration, sliding down my waist, over the curve of my hips, and then back up, leaving a trail of fire in their wake.

Just as I'm about to beg him to take me, to claim me, the elevator comes to a smooth halt.

"I've been wanting to do this since I first laid eyes on you," Dan whispered, his breath hot against my ear. His words sent a jolt of excitement through my body. I nodded, unable to form a coherent response, my mind clouded with desire.

With expert hands, he untied the sash of my dress, letting it slide off my shoulders, revealing my lace bra and the swell of my breasts. His eyes darkened with hunger as he took in the sight, and I felt a surge of power, knowing I had this effect on him.

"You want me?" he asks with hunger.

I nodded, breathless, and he pressed the button to keep the elevator doors open. With a swift motion, he lifted me, making me wrap my legs around his waist. I giggled, feeling playful and desired all at once.

"Impatient, are we?" I teased, running my hands through his hair.

"You have no idea," he growled, his voice husky.

Dan carried me out of the elevator, his strong arms holding me effortlessly. I felt like a prized possession, and I loved every second of it. As we entered our suite, he kicked the door shut with his foot, never breaking his stride.

The suite was luxurious, with a spacious living area and a large bed that beckoned to us.

Dan strode towards it, his eyes never leaving mine. He lowered me onto the soft mattress, his body hovering over mine. I could feel his heat, his desire, and it fueled my own.

"I want to taste you," he whispered, his breath fanning across my neck, sending goosebumps across my skin.

I arched my back, offering myself to him, and he trailed hot, open-mouthed kisses down my neck, pausing to suck and nibble on my sensitive skin. His hands tugged at my dress, and with a quick motion, he ripped it off, leaving me in nothing but my lace panties.

Dans eyes gleamed with satisfaction as he took in the sight of my naked body. He hooked his fingers into the sides of my panties and slowly slid them down my legs, his gaze never leaving my face. I felt exposed and vulnerable, but the desire in his eyes made me feel powerful.

"You're stunning," he said, his voice thick with admiration.

I reached for him, wanting to touch him as much as he touched me. I tugged at his shirt, eager to feel his skin against mine. Dan lifted his arms, allowing me to pull it over his head, revealing a ripple of muscles.

I leaned up, capturing a nipple between my lips, and suckled gently, earning a soft moan from him. His hands tangled in my hair, guiding me as I lavished attention on his nipple, alternating between teasing bites and gentle licks.

"Oh, god, that feels incredible," he breathed, placing his hardness at my entrance and making me arch my hips off the bed wanting to take him inside of me.

I smiled against his physique, delighted that he was the source of my pleasure. His hands roamed over my body, exploring my curves. "Please," I whispered, my voice hoarse with need. "I need to feel you."

I felt a rush of vulnerability, but Dan's intense gaze, filled with raw desire, gave me a surge of confidence.

"Charlie, you're breathtaking," he whispered, his voice deep and raspy. His eyes traveled down my body, taking in every curve and dip. I was aware of my plump breasts, the soft swell of my hips, and the delicate patch of dark hair between my legs, and by the look in his eyes, he appreciated every inch of me.

"**So beautiful,**" he murmured, his fingers trailing along my bare skin, leaving a trail of goosebumps in their wake. I shivered, not from the cold, but from the intensity of his touch. His eyes gleamed with a mixture of admiration and raw hunger.

My fingers traced the contours of his muscles, and I reveled in the feel of his warm, firm skin. I leaned in, my lips finding one of his taut nipples, and I captured it between my teeth, tugging gently. A soft gasp escaped his lips, and I felt his hands entwine in my hair, guiding me as I lavished attention on his sensitive flesh. I alternated between gentle suckles and light bites, driving him wild with pleasure.

"**Charlie, oh god...**" His words trailed off into a moan as I continued my sensual assault on his nipple. His hands tightened in my hair, urging me on, and I reveled in the power I held over him. I could feel his hardness pressing against my thigh, a silent testament to his desire.

With a final, lingering lick, I pulled away, a satisfied smile playing on my lips. I looked up at him, my eyes sparkling with mischief. "**Your turn to feel pleasure,**" I whispered, my voice laced with promise.

Dan's eyes darkened further, and he gently guided me towards the edge of the bed, his touch possessive. I felt the soft sheets beneath my knees as he positioned me on the edge, my legs slightly parted. He stood between my thighs, his erection pressing against my core, making me aware of how much I wanted him.

"**Please, Dan,**" I breathed, my voice hoarse with need. "**I want to feel you inside me.**" I reached up, running my fingers through his hair, pulling him down for a kiss. Our lips met in a hungry dance, tongues tangling as we devoured each other.

He broke the kiss, his breath coming in ragged gasps. "**I want to taste you first,**" he said, his voice strained. With that, he lowered his head, his lips finding the sensitive skin at the base of my throat. He kissed and nipped his way down my body, leaving a trail of fire in his wake.

As his lips hovered over my breasts, I arched my back, offering myself to him. He took one nipple into his warm mouth, sucking and teasing it with his tongue, while his fingers skillfully played with the other. I moaned, my hands gripping the sheets, my body on fire with pleasure.

His lips and tongue continued their journey, leaving no inch of my skin untouched. When he reached my navel, he dipped his tongue into it, making me squirm with delight. I felt his warm breath on the sensitive skin of my inner thighs, and I parted my legs further, inviting him to explore.

Dan's fingers gently stroked the insides of my thighs, making me shiver with anticipation. I could feel my wetness glistening, a clear indication of my desire. His breath hitched as he took in the sight of my glistening folds, and I reveled in the power I held over him.

"**You're so beautiful, Charlie,**" he murmured, his voice thick with admiration. With that, he lowered his head, his tongue finding the sensitive bud of my clitoris. I gasped, my body jerking at the intense pleasure he delivered with each flick and swirl of his tongue.

His fingers joined the dance, sliding into my wetness, stroking and filling me as his tongue continued its magic on my clit. I was lost in a sea of sensations, my body trembling on the edge of release.

"**Dan, I'm close,**" I whispered, my voice breathless. I

didn't want this moment to end, but my body was demanding its release.

He seemed to understand, for he increased the pace, his tongue and fingers working in perfect harmony. I cried out, my body arching off the bed as wave after wave of pleasure washed over me. I clutched at the sheets, my fingernails digging into the fabric as I rode out the storm of my orgasm.

Dan slowly brought me back down, his lips and fingers continuing their gentle ministrations until my breathing returned to normal. I felt boneless, my body sated and satisfied, but I wanted more. I wanted him.

I reached for him, pulling him up for a kiss, tasting myself on his lips. "**Now, Dan,**" I whispered against his mouth. "**I need to feel you inside me.**"

He needed no further encouragement. With a swift motion, he freed himself from his pants, revealing his impressive erection. He positioned himself at my entrance, his tip nudging my wetness. I was ready, more than ready, and I lifted my hips, urging him to take what was his.

With one smooth thrust, he slid into me, filling me completely. I gasped at the sensation of being stretched and filled, my body welcoming his invasion. He paused, giving me a moment to adjust to his size, before he began to move.

His hips moved in a slow, steady rhythm, each thrust sending ripples of pleasure through my sensitive body. I wrapped my legs around his waist, pulling him deeper with each stroke. Our bodies moved together in perfect harmony, our skin slick with sweat as passion consumed us.

Dan's hands gripped my hips, holding me firmly in place as he quickened his pace. His breath came in harsh gasps, and I knew he was close. I tightened my inner muscles around him, milking his length, wanting to bring him to the edge.

"Charlie, I can't hold on much longer," he groaned, his voice raw.

"Don't hold back," I whispered, my nails digging into his shoulders. "I want to feel you come inside me."

His thrusts became more urgent, his body slamming into mine as he sought his release. I matched his rhythm, my body moving in perfect sync with his. The pleasure was building again, a different kind of heat coiling low in my belly.

"Together, Charlie," he panted, his eyes locked with mine. "I want to feel you come with me."

His words were like a spark, igniting the fire within me. I felt my orgasm building, a delicious pressure gathering at my core. I cried out, my body trembling as the waves of pleasure crashed over me. Dan's name fell from my lips in a hoarse whisper as I shattered around him.

He gave one final, powerful thrust, and I felt him pulse and throb deep within me, his hot seed filling me as he found his own release. We clung to each other, our hearts pounding, our breath mingling, as we rode out the aftermath of our shared climax.

As our breathing slowed, Dan collapsed onto the bed beside me, pulling me into his arms. I snuggled against his warm, sweaty body, feeling utterly content. I could feel his heart still racing, matching the rhythm of my own.

"That was incredible," he whispered, his lips brushing my forehead. "I've never felt anything like that before."

As I lay there, wrapped in his arms, I knew this was just the start of our passionate encounter. This hotel had become our playground for the night, and I couldn't wait to discover what other delights awaited us.

The next morning, I wake to soft light filtering through the curtains, a lingering warmth in my body. For a moment,

I lie there, letting the memories of the night wash over me, a small smile tugging at my lips. But then reality sets in—I have a meeting with Romano today. A meeting that could define my career.

Quietly, I slip out of bed, gather my things, and dress, trying not to disturb him. Part of me wants to stay, to see where this could lead, but I know better. This was just a moment, a brief escape from reality.

With a soft sigh, I take one last look at him, still asleep, his face relaxed in the early morning light, and slip out of the room.

By the time I arrive at Romano Holdings, I've pushed the night's events firmly to the back of my mind. This is my career, my future, and I can't afford distractions. I smooth my skirt, take a steadying breath, and approach the receptionist.

"Good morning. I have a meeting with Mr. Romano."

She smiles and nods, checking her screen. "Yes, Ms. Harris. He's expecting you. If you'll follow me, please."

My heels click against the polished marble as I follow her down the hall, the weight of anticipation settling over me. This is the moment I've been working toward for years. But as she gestures to the door and I push it open, I can't shake the feeling that this is different.

My gaze lifts, and my breath catches.

Seated behind a massive, sleek desk, watching me with a look of calm interest, is the man from last night.

Except now, he's not Dan. He's Dante Romano, the billionaire who holds my future in his hands.

A quiet smile plays on his lips, unreadable. "Good morning, Ms. Harris. I trust you're ready to get started?"

2

DANTE

For a beat that stretches too long, I'm speechless. My stomach drops, but I force myself to recover, careful not to show it. I'm rarely surprised—practically never—but this... this takes the cake.

The woman standing before me is Charlotte Harris. "Charlie," she introduces herself with calm professionalism, as if last night's heat between us never happened. She extends a hand like we're meeting for the first time, under a new set of rules.

"Pleasure to meet you," she says, voice steady, though her eyes flicker, betraying a hint of recognition.

I hesitate, still too stunned, but take her hand firmly, keeping my expression neutral. She knows exactly who I am; I can see it in her eyes. She's here to keep things professional, setting the rules with a clean slate. I almost want to laugh. After last night, it's like she's doing me a favor by letting it go.

"Pleasure to meet you, too," I reply smoothly. I return to my seat across from her, keeping a calm I barely feel.

The room is large, impersonal, and quiet except for the

soft click of pens and shuffle of papers. Besides me and Charlie, there are a couple of aides and David, who came in with me. David sits to my left, eyes flicking curiously between us before settling on the files in front of him.

"Shall we get started?" Charlie says, smoothing her hands over her skirt—a nervous habit, maybe. Or something else. I can't help wondering if she's fighting her own memories of last night. I know I am. I hold her gaze, watching her cheeks color faintly.

She crosses her legs as she takes her seat—not overtly flirtatious, but I notice. It's inconvenient, to say the least. I need to focus.

She doesn't miss a beat, her tone brisk, all business. "I've prepared these," she says, sliding a stack of neatly bound files across the table. "They outline potential legal pitfalls for this project, both from consumer and user perspectives."

"Legal pitfalls." I flip through the file, barely absorbing the words. My mind's elsewhere. I place the document back on the table with a quiet sigh.

"That's it?" she asks, brows drawing together.

"Huh?"

"'Legal pitfalls,' and that's it?" Her voice sharpens.

I shrug, keeping my tone casual. "That's what you're here for, right? It's your specialty." I tap the file in front of me. "I doubt I'll understand the legal jargon without a headache, and I'd prefer to keep my head clear."

My smile seems to hit a nerve; I catch a flash of frustration in her eyes, tempered with a hint of amusement.

"I'd hoped to go over these with you in detail," she says, her voice a careful coolness.

"And you still can," I reply, meeting her gaze steadily.

She looks at me, and I swear I see a hint of exasperation in her eyes. I almost smirk, but I hold back, keeping my expression composed. Charlie takes a deep breath, her eyes flicking around the room, likely reminding herself we're not alone. Finally, she lifts the file and begins speaking in an even tone. "I'd like to address these issues with your input. Since nothing's finalized, your insights would be invaluable in helping us prevent potential complications."

"I'm all for fewer complications," I say lightly. "I'm a big believer in things running smoothly."

She opens her mouth as though to counter, then closes it, jaw tightening with a small click of her teeth. A flicker of amusement stirs in me, but I keep my face neutral.

She sighs. "I had some questions, if you've looked at this at all..." She holds my gaze, searching for a reaction. I maintain my even expression, not giving her an inch. "Since you haven't, we'll proceed regardless."

I raise a finger, silencing her mid-sentence. Her face flickers—annoyance, confusion—before settling on mild exasperation. I reach into my jacket and pull out my phone, which has been vibrating insistently. I already know who it is; very few people have access to this line.

"Yes?" I answer, keeping my tone low. Charlie's gaze hardens, but she stays silent, her expression carefully controlled.

"Boss, I just got word," Gabe's voice says on the other end, steady and measured. I wait, knowing he'll get to the point. I see Charlie's jaw tighten as she watches me, unimpressed by the interruption.

"Silas Kane was seen at one of Lorenzo's hotels," Gabe says, his tone pointed. He doesn't need to say anything else —the implications are clear.

I grit my teeth, managing a short, "I'm on my way."

Charlie's expression shifts, confusion mixing with irritation.

"I have to go," I say simply.

Her voice remains impressively even. "We're not finished. We haven't even begun, actually."

"Sorry, but I need to take care of this," I repeat, though a flicker of reluctance surprises me. Part of me would rather stay, see this through. But this can't wait.

She takes a deep breath, likely reminding herself not to snap. "So we'll reschedule, then?" Her tone is remarkably composed.

"Sure," I reply, standing. David follows my lead, already moving toward the door to bring the car around.

"Good," she says, her voice layered with a restrained calm that tells me she's gritting her teeth.

"Right. See you later," I say, turning to leave.

"Wait! When are we rescheduling to?" she calls, her tone carrying a slight edge.

I shrug, giving her a small smile. "We'll figure something out." Without waiting for a response, I exit, leaving her staring after me.

As the door swings shut, I think I hear a frustrated groan from inside the room, but I don't stop. My casual demeanor vanishes as I stride briskly down the hall, the gravity of Gabe's message gnawing at me. There are no coincidences in my line of work.

Outside, David has the car waiting. As I approach, the engine revs softly, sensing my urgency. I slide into the backseat, shutting the door harder than I intend.

David pulls out into the street, navigating with the speed and precision he knows I expect. I glance out the window, my mind churning with thoughts of Silas Kane and what this could mean.

Silas, supposedly committed, is meeting with Lorenzo—my oldest rival. He's supposed to be loyal—and above all, transparent. But he's at Lorenzo's hotel. Lorenzo, ruthless and shrewd, would never let this slide by chance. This doesn't sit right.

David catches my eye in the rearview mirror. "You think Silas is up to something?"

I exhale sharply, my gaze drifting over a row of office buildings. "Either he is, or he's become remarkably careless. And Silas has never been careless."

David nods, the tension settling between us like a heavy fog. If Silas is at Lorenzo's hotel, it's intentional. But his intentions are still a mystery.

"You want me to reach out?" David asks, his tone cautious.

"Not yet," I reply, running a hand over my jaw. "First, I need to know exactly what Silas has been doing over the last few days. I want to know who he's seen, where he's been. Get Gabe on it. I want a full report."

David nods and pulls out his phone, relaying the instructions to Gabe. As he speaks, I stare out the window, recalling every conversation I've had with Silas in recent weeks, searching for any detail that might hint at this. The project has faced its share of hurdles—financial negotiations, logistical setbacks, even a few legal concerns, which is why I brought in Charlie. I need someone sharp, someone who can anticipate and dismantle any legal traps lying in wait.

If Silas is aligning himself with Lorenzo, it complicates everything.

David finishes his call and looks back at me. "Gabe's on it. We'll have something by the end of the day."

"Good." I nod, relieved. If there's a flaw in Silas's loyalty, I need to find it—and fast.

The car slows as we pull up to one of my office buildings.

I've set up an off-the-radar meeting space here, just in case. David heads inside first, ensuring everything is in order. I follow a few minutes later, slipping through the side entrance and into a quiet, nondescript hallway.

My phone buzzes in my pocket. Pulling it out, I see a text from Gabe: Silas spotted at Lorenzo's twice this week. No other intel yet but working on it. Will keep you posted.

Twice in a week. That's enough to start unraveling this. If it's more than just a social call or a random meeting, Silas could be aligning himself with Lorenzo in a way that jeopardizes everything we're working on.

As I read the message, my thoughts drift back to the meeting room where I left Charlie. Her eyes flashed with irritation as I left, a mix of frustration and something else. Despite her calm professionalism, I sensed her impatience simmering beneath the surface, just as I feel a strange, unwelcome pull. Last night was a glimpse, a moment outside my normal life, something I hadn't anticipated.

But it can't be anything more. I shake my head, bringing myself back to the present. Charlie's role in the Horizon City project is critical, and I need her on her A-game, focused and unshakable. Whatever last night was, it stays firmly in the past.

Stepping into the meeting room, I check my messages again, hoping for another update from Gabe, but there's nothing new. I need answers soon. If Silas is working with Lorenzo, there's more at stake here than I initially thought.

David enters the room, his expression grim. "Gabe found a few connections between Silas and one of Lorenzo's offshore accounts. Small transactions, but enough to raise suspicion. Lorenzo could be using it as leverage."

"Damn it." I set my phone down, running a hand over my face. This is worse than I thought. Small transactions could mean anything—a favor, a setup, or something more deliberate. I can't tell yet if Silas is being manipulated or if he's testing the waters with Lorenzo. Either way, it's dangerous.

David watches me, his gaze steady. "What do you want to do?"

"Stay close to him," I say, my voice steely. "If this is just Lorenzo trying to sow discord, I won't bite. But if Silas is in on this, I want him to show his hand."

David nods. "Understood."

As we leave the building, slipping out the back, I try to push thoughts of Silas and Lorenzo from my mind, but it's impossible. Betrayal isn't easy to anticipate, and it can ruin everything—every step, every ounce of trust. I've seen it enough times to know the damage it can do.

As we head back to the main office, my thoughts drift briefly back to Charlie. Her insight could be critical in protecting the project, but our partnership will be complicated. I can't afford the distraction she brings—not now, not with this new storm brewing.

My phone buzzes, a message from Charlie herself: Regarding our earlier meeting, I need a new time to discuss the documents. Let me know what works.

I can practically hear the veiled frustration in her message, and a faint smirk tugs at my lips. She's as relentless as I am. She won't let me sidestep the details, and strangely, I appreciate it.

I type a quick reply: Tomorrow at 10 a.m. sharp.

David glances over, noticing the faint smirk on my face. "Everything alright?"

"Yes," I say, pocketing my phone. "Just a reminder that some people in this business still keep me on my toes."

"Charlie Harris, I assume," David replies with a knowing look.

I don't respond, but my silence confirms it. Charlie is sharp, relentless, and seemingly immune to intimidation tactics. I'm not used to that—not with someone brought in from outside my circle.

"Let's keep this close, David," I say, shifting back to the matter at hand. "The fewer people who know about Silas, the better."

"Understood."

As we return to the office, the urgency of Gabe's latest message spurs me forward. Silas's betrayal is deeper than I thought. Small transfers, some hard to trace but consistent enough to suggest intent.

I nod slowly, the pieces starting to fall into place. Silas has been planning this for months, and the Horizon City project must be the final move.

Gabe is waiting, his expression grim but determined. "We'll stay on him. You'll know the minute he makes a move."

"Good." I glance at my desk, seeing the documents Charlie left behind. For the first time, they feel like pieces in a larger game.

What Silas and Lorenzo don't know is that, in the end, I always make the final move.

3

CHARLIE

I storm out, fuming. My bag swings from my shoulder, files jammed under my arm. He walked out. In the middle of a meeting. No explanation. What the hell?

I march toward the parking lot, anger mounting with each step. Just as I reach my car, my phone rings. Juggling the files and my bag, I try to dig it out, but it's impossible. With a frustrated sigh, I drop everything, crouching over the scattered pile of my belongings on the pavement.

Triumphantly, I fish out my phone and glance at the screen: it's Katie, my best friend. "Hello, Katie," I say, more brusquely than I mean to.

"Hey! How did the big meeting go?" she chirps, as cheerful as ever.

I gather my things, cradling the phone between my shoulder and ear as I unlock the car door. "It was... frustrating. He just walked out. Mid-meeting."

Katie gasps. "No way! He just got up and left?"

"Well, he got a call first," I admit, recalling how Dante's expression had tensed before he turned and walked out without a second glance. "But still—no explanation. Just walked out."

"Maybe it was an emergency?" Katie suggests, always quick to give people the benefit of the doubt. "Maybe he has kids?"

"No." I pause, realizing how little I actually know about him. Dante Romano is my new client, a billionaire, and devilishly good-looking. Technically, this is our second meeting—if I count... that night. A hot blush creeps up my neck. "Oh my God, Katie, I didn't even tell you."

"Tell me what?"

I close my eyes, leaning against the car. "Katie, Dante is the guy from the bar."

There's a long pause, and I check the phone to make sure we're still connected. "Hello? Katie?"

She finally responds, her voice tinged with disbelief. "The guy you went home with? The one you couldn't stop talking about?"

"Yes!" I laugh a little, more out of disbelief than humor. "I walked into the meeting, and there he was, calm as anything, like he wasn't the same guy from the bar."

"And you didn't call me immediately?"

"I... forgot?" I say, sounding defensive even to myself. I'd been too thrown by Dante's dismissal, too irritated by his disappearing act, to even process the fact that my client is also the man I can't get out of my head.

Katie makes an exasperated sound. "Charlie, how do you 'forget' to tell me something this huge?"

"Love you, too," I say, cutting her off before she can start a full lecture. I toss the phone onto the passenger seat with a sigh, feeling a pang of guilt. Katie's right—I should have called her, but Dante's behavior had completely thrown me. After a day like today, the last thing I need is a lecture.

I start the car and pull out of the lot, steering toward the exit. Despite my frustration, my mind keeps drifting back to Dante. We hadn't even acknowledged what happened between us; we'd plunged straight into business, and he seemed unaffected. Though, more than once, I'd caught him looking at me with that same intense focus, something unresolved and silently potent.

When I get home, I drop my files and bag onto the coffee table and head straight to my bedroom, kicking off my shoes and peeling out of my work clothes. Twenty minutes later, freshly showered and in comfortable clothes, I feel a little more grounded.

Sinking onto the couch, I open my laptop. Katie's suggestion about an emergency lingers in my mind, and I find myself typing "Dante Romano" into the search bar, feeling a strange mix of curiosity and hesitation. He's a high-profile client—I should know more about him, especially after last night.

The first search results are predictable—business achievements, recent projects, charitable contributions. I scroll, scanning through corporate articles and interviews. On the second page, I finally find a biography, but it's brief: his title, a few company facts, and a stoic headshot. The same hard gaze, those eyes that seem to follow me, even through the screen. I shake my head, forcing myself to focus. Get a grip, Charlie.

The deeper I dig, the stranger it feels. For a man with such a public profile, Dante's personal life is hidden under layers of corporate polish. Even his business partner, Silas Kane, is equally vague—a few old mentions of family, maybe a pet. It's like they've both meticulously blurred their private lives from public view. I shut the laptop and sit back, feeling oddly unsettled. Last night had felt intense, vivid. I'd thought I'd seen something real in him. But today, it's like that man doesn't exist.

The TV's on in the background, and I glance up just in time to catch a breaking news story. A sleek black car, twisted and mangled, fills the screen, reporters crowding around the scene. I look down, only half-listening, until a name catches my attention.

"... Dante Romano. I repeat, the car involved in the accident belongs to billionaire Dante Romano..."

My heart lurches, the file slipping from my fingers. No. This can't be real.

I fumble for the remote, turning up the volume, but my pulse thunders in my ears, drowning out the reporter's words. My mind races, trying to piece together what I'm seeing, what it means. Dante had seemed urgent when he left the meeting, as though something was pulling him away. I'd been annoyed, but now... now I feel nothing but dread.

His name flashes on the screen, unrelenting. A pulse I can't ignore. I stare at the twisted metal of his car, barely recognizable, crumpled as if some monstrous force had crushed it. Reporters swarm the scene, cameras capturing every angle, every shard of broken glass glinting under the harsh lights.

I grab my phone, fingers shaking, and open a news site, scrolling for anything, some update, something to tell me he's okay. Every headline just makes my stomach clench tighter.

Dante Romano's car involved in accident. Condition unknown. Emergency crews on site.

The words feel cold and detached, as though they're describing someone else. Someone I don't know. But I do know him, don't I? Or I thought I did.

On-screen, they cut to an image of Dante, the same one from his bio. He stands in front of a sleek black car, arms folded, gaze piercing. But now, seeing him there, alive and intense, only deepens the ache in my chest. Who is he? A man whose gaze made me feel seen, who remains an enigma even as I tried to find answers. My client, a billionaire with his life hidden away from the world. And now, he might be gone.

I reach for my phone again, desperately needing to talk to someone. I dial Katie, my fingers trembling.

She answers on the first ring. "Charlie? What's wrong?"

"Katie… it's him. It's Dante." My voice cracks, the words coming out in a whisper.

Her voice sharpens, concern replacing her usual warmth. "What happened? Are you okay?"

"He was in an accident. His car—it looks bad. Really bad. They're saying he's in critical condition." The words feel foreign, as if I'm hearing them for the first time.

She gasps, the concern thick in her voice. "Oh my God, Charlie. I'm so sorry. Are you sure it's him?"

"It's his car." My voice is barely audible, my eyes glued to the screen. "They showed it on the news. It's unmistakable."

Katie's voice softens. "Listen, I know this is terrifying. I can't imagine how you're feeling, but don't jump to conclusions. He's tough, Charlie. We don't know the whole story yet."

"You're right." I try to sound steady, but my voice betrays me. "I don't know what to do."

"Maybe call the hospital? You're his attorney, after all. You have every right to check on him."

The suggestion jolts me out of my frozen state. She's right—I am his attorney. I take a shaky breath, feeling a new determination.

"Thank you, Katie," I say, my voice steadier now. "I'll call the hospital."

"I'm here if you need me, Charlie. Let me know as soon as you find out anything."

Hanging up, I pull up a list of local hospitals and dial the first number. My heart pounds with each ring, the weight of dread pressing on my chest.

"San Diego General Hospital. How may I assist you?"

"Hi, I'm calling about a patient, Dante Romano. I'm his attorney, and I wanted to check on his condition."

The line goes silent for a second. "Please hold while I transfer you to the emergency department."

The hold music feels distorted, almost mocking, as I sit there, gripping the phone tightly. The longer I wait, the harder it is to keep my panic at bay.

Finally, a tired but professional voice comes through. "Emergency department. How can I help?"

"I'm calling about Dante Romano. I'm his attorney, and I need to know his condition."

There's a brief shuffle, then silence. "I'm sorry, ma'am. We aren't authorized to give out patient information over the phone. If you're listed as an emergency contact, you'll be notified directly."

"Right." Disappointment seeps into my voice. "Thank you."

I hang up, feeling an odd calm settle over me—a quiet, bitter acceptance. I stare at the screen, where the reporters continue to speculate, the world spinning forward while I feel stuck in place, clutching at fragments. I think of his intense gaze, the way he'd looked at me like he could see every part of me, even the hidden parts. Now, he's somewhere beyond my reach, and I'm left with nothing but memories and an unshakable dread.

4

DANTE

I curse myself for not seeing this ambush coming. The signs were there—obvious in hindsight—but I didn't act fast enough. David's loyalty deserved better, and now he's slumped forward, unmoving, in the driver's seat. The gunfire has stopped, but the chaos it leaves behind is a deafening roar in my mind.

The car reeks of gasoline and blood as I shift to take control. My left arm burns, slick with blood, but I ignore it. There's no time for pain. Whoever orchestrated this is waiting for the kill.

As I shove the car into gear and reverse into the ambushers, I let fury take the reins. Metal crunches, screams echo, and the satisfaction is fleeting but sharp. The second vehicle attempts an escape, but I'm on them, relentless. When their car flips and lands in a heap of twisted metal, I'm already reaching for David's gun.

The rest unfolds in a blur. The driver dies with poison in his mouth before he can answer my questions. Gabe arrives, but his presence only confirms what I already know—this ambush wasn't random. It was precise, calculated, and personal.

The city's lights streak past as Gabe drives us back. My arm throbs, but I let the pain center me. I shouldn't be alive, yet here I am, plotting my next move.

My phone vibrates, pulling me from my thoughts. Charlie. Her name on the screen is a lifeline I didn't know I needed tonight.

"Hello?"

"Oh my God, Dante! I saw your car on the news—I thought..." Her voice breaks, a genuine mix of fear and relief.

"I'm fine," I reply, forcing calm into my tone. "Just a bad night."

She hesitates, then, "Can we reschedule? Maybe Wednesday?"

Her concern is palpable, cutting through the haze of violence. It steadies me, if only for a moment. "Wednesday works."

Her soft "Take care of yourself, Dante" lingers in my ear long after I hang up.

BACK IN MY PENTHOUSE, the quiet is oppressive, filled with shadows I can't trust. Gabe leaves with a terse nod, promising to find whoever orchestrated this. I sink into the leather chair by the window, staring at the sprawling city below.

Then the phone rings again. Charlie's name flashes, and a knot tightens in my chest.

"Charlie?"

"Dante... I don't know who else to call." Her voice is trembling, so unlike the confident woman I spoke with earlier. "There's someone outside my apartment. They've been there for over an hour."

The anger I've kept at bay all night flares hot and sharp. They're after her now.

"Stay calm," I say, my voice low and firm. "Lock your door, stay away from the windows. I'm coming."

The drive to her apartment is a blur. My wound screams with every movement, but it's nothing compared to the thought of her in danger. When I arrive, I don't even bother with the pretense of knocking. I unlock her door and step inside, gun drawn, scanning every shadow.

She's huddled in the corner of the living room, phone clutched in her hand. Her eyes widen when she sees me, relief and fear warring on her face.

"You're safe now," I say, my tone softer than I expect.

The tension in her shoulders eases, but she doesn't move from her spot. "There was a man... he was just standing there, watching."

I cross the room, placing myself between her and the window. "Did he try to get in?"

She shakes her head, wrapping her arms around herself. "No. He just... stared. It was like he wanted me to know he was there."

My jaw tightens. This wasn't random; it was a message.

As I secure the apartment, the silence stretches between us. When I finally sit across from her, her eyes flicker to my arm.

"You're hurt," she says, her voice barely above a whisper.

"It's nothing," I reply, brushing it off.

Her lips press into a thin line. "You're bleeding through your shirt. That's not 'nothing.'"

Before I can stop her, she's fetching a first-aid kit. When

she returns, she kneels in front of me, her hands steady despite the tension in her expression.

"Let me." Her voice is firm, brooking no argument.

I allow it, though every instinct tells me to refuse. As she peels back the fabric of my shirt, the air shifts. Her touch is gentle, yet every brush of her fingers sends a jolt through me.

Her focus is intent, but I can feel her awareness of me—of us.

Her fingers were cool against my heated skin, her movements careful and precise. As she cleaned the wound, I became acutely aware of her closeness, the scent of her perfume filling my senses. Her breath brushed against my skin, and I felt a tightening in my groin, a response I hadn't expected.

Charlie's focus was on the task at hand, but I could sense her awareness of me, of the electricity between us. Her touch was gentle, yet firm, and I found myself wanting more. As she applied the antiseptic, I hissed, the sting of the liquid mingling with the heat of desire.

"Sorry," she murmured, her eyes meeting mine. "Does it hurt?"

I shook my head, unable to find my voice. The pain was nothing compared to the storm of emotions raging within me. I wanted to pull her close, to feel her body against mine, to lose myself in her. But I stayed still, letting her finish her work.

With deft fingers, she bandaged the wound, her touch lingering a moment too long. I caught her gaze, my eyes holding a question, a silent plea. She bit her lip, the nervous habit returning, and I knew she felt it too—the tension, the desire.

"Thank you," I managed to say, my voice hoarse.

Charlie smiled, a shy, uncertain curve of her lips. *"Anytime, Dante. I'm glad I could help."*

The air between us crackled with unspoken words, unfulfilled desires. I wanted to kiss her, to taste the sweetness of her lips, but I held back, not wanting to scare her away.

When she finishes, the silence between us feels heavier. Her gaze lingers on mine, and for a moment, the chaos outside the apartment fades.

"Thank you again," I say, my voice quieter than intended.

She nods, but her eyes search mine, as if looking for something. "What happens now?"

"Now, I make sure whoever sent that man regrets it."

She shivers, and without thinking, I reach out, brushing a strand of hair from her face. The tension between us crackles, unspoken but undeniable.

My fingers trace along her collarbone, feather-light. Her breath hitches, and I feel her pulse quicken beneath my touch. The air between us grows thick with possibility.

"Dante," she whispers, her voice trembling slightly.

I cup her face gently, studying the flecks of gold in her eyes. She leans into my touch, and the simple trust in that gesture makes my chest tight.

When our lips meet, it's soft at first - hesitant, questioning. But then her hands slip into my hair, pulling me closer, and restraint becomes impossible. The kiss deepens, igniting something primal and protective within me.

I back her slowly against the wall, careful to keep my weight off her. Her fingers grip my shoulders as if anchoring herself, and I break the kiss to trail my lips along her jaw.

"You have no idea what you do to me," I murmur against her skin.

She tilts her head back with a soft gasp that sends fire through my veins. "Show me."

I FORCE myself to step back, grounding myself in the reality of the situation. "You'll stay somewhere else tonight. Somewhere safe."

"Dante, I can't—"

"It's not up for discussion." My tone leaves no room for argument, but the way her lips press together tells me she's already considering pushing back.

The knock at the door breaks the moment. Gabe steps in, his expression grim. "Boss, we found something."

I glance at Charlie, whose eyes dart between us. "Pack a bag," I tell her, my voice softening just a fraction. "I'll explain everything later."

She hesitates but nods, disappearing into the bedroom. Gabe steps closer, lowering his voice. "The ambush wasn't just about you. They're targeting her, Boss. Whoever's behind this knew you'd come for her."

The fury I've kept simmering boils over. They think they can use her to get to me?

As Charlie reappears with her bag, I motion her toward the door. "You're staying with me tonight."

Her eyes widen, but she doesn't argue.

As we drive into the night, the weight of what's happened settles over me. Whoever is behind this has made a grave mistake.

They've underestimated me. And they've underestimated just how far I'm willing to go to protect her.

5

CHARLIE

After our failed initial meeting—thanks to Dante Romano's abrupt decision to end it—I insisted on rescheduling. A project as big as Horizon City demands attention to every detail, and I won't move forward without knowing exactly what's expected of me.

Now, I sit across from him in his office, dressed in a pinstripe suit that conveys confidence. The morning sun filters through the floor-to-ceiling windows, casting his sharp profile in an almost ethereal light. His features are annoyingly attractive, the dark suit and white shirt emphasizing his immaculate, well-put-together appearance. There's nothing in this Dante that resembles the man I shared a night with, his hands and voice making promises he'd clearly forgotten.

I blink away the memory, a sharp reminder to keep my head in the present.

"Thank you for rescheduling," I say, breaking the heavy silence hanging between us.

He shrugs, his gaze steady and unyielding. "Since we're

both busy, we might as well get it over with. Especially since you wouldn't take no for an answer."

The dismissive tone stings, but I bite back a retort. We haven't even started, and he's already on edge. I have to keep this professional if we're going to work together effectively.

"Very well," I reply, keeping my tone steady. My fingers press into my palms, releasing some of the tension. Then, as he leans forward, his jaw clenches as if he's bracing himself to say something that pains him more than he wants me to know.

"I'd like to be very clear about something before we proceed." His gaze bores into mine, as intense as it was the night we met. "What happened the other night was... a fleeting incident. Nothing about our professional relationship will change because of it. I expect you to understand that."

The coldness in his tone is a punch to the gut, but I swallow the sting, keeping my composure intact. A few days ago, that night had felt almost dreamlike, filled with unspoken promises and electric chemistry. Now, he makes it sound trivial, meaningless. I force myself to breathe and hold his gaze as I respond.

"Crystal," I say flatly. "I wouldn't dream of it, Mr. Romano. I'm simply here to do my job, and that's all." I add, with an arched brow, "Besides, you're not exactly my type."

A flash of irritation crosses his face. Good.

For a beat, neither of us speaks. The air conditioning hums, underscoring the thick tension between us. He glances at his watch, clearly impatient. "Fine. Let's finish this meeting."

The next thirty minutes are a test of endurance. I force myself to focus, though it's hard to ignore the sting of his earlier words. Despite his obvious disapproval, I'm impressed with the scale of Horizon City. Objectively, it's an ambitious vision, a "city within a city," as he describes it, complete with retail, residential, and even its own police department.

Dante slides a thick file toward me, his fingers brushing against mine for the briefest moment. A shiver jolts through me. He notices too, pausing just slightly, his brows knitting together as our eyes meet. I pull my hand back quickly, heart hammering.

"I'd appreciate it if you could keep your interactions professional," he says sharply, his eyes narrowing.

"Mr. Romano, that was an accident. Nothing more." I keep my tone steady, refusing to let him rile me. His gaze shifts, something unreadable flickering there, but I dismiss it, returning to the file.

When I've reviewed the project plans, I slide the document back toward him, careful to avoid his hand this time. "The layout looks solid. I'll need a copy to review in more detail, especially for compliance with land use and zoning regulations."

He nods, barely looking at me as he files it away. "I'll forward it to your email after this meeting." His movements are tense, his jaw clenched as he shifts uncomfortably.

"Are you okay?" I ask before I can stop myself. "You look like you're in pain."

"I'm fine." He says it through gritted teeth.

"But… you're obviously not. Do you need me to call your secretary?"

His gaze turns icy. "I said I'm fine. It's just a minor injury from an accident a couple of days ago. If I remember correctly, you were adamant about rescheduling the meeting then, too."

I flush, defensive. "But you claimed you were okay."

"And I am. It's just a flesh wound." He shrugs as if it's nothing, though his face betrays a hint of discomfort. "My shirt pulls at it sometimes."

I'm incredulous. Here he is, pushing himself through meetings with a serious injury. As the CEO, surely he can afford a day of rest.

"Are you keeping it dry? Do you have someone helping you? A nurse or..." I trail off, realizing what I'm implying.

His stare hardens. "I manage fine on my own. And I don't appreciate the assumption that I need a wife or girlfriend to look after me. I don't cheat, Miss Harris, nor do I condone it. Loyalty matters to me."

I nod, realizing that I'd unconsciously feared he was married. The relief that he's not is swift, a realization I barely understand myself.

"My apologies. I only meant that it's wise to rest when you're hurt." I pause, choosing my words carefully. "But if my concern is out of line, I'll refrain."

"Good," he says, his tone clipped. "Let's stick to discussing the Horizon City project." He eyes me, a subtle challenge in his gaze. "Or Romano Holdings might need to explore other options for lead attorney."

I square my shoulders, matching his stare. "There's no need for that. I'm aware that Romano Holdings only works with the best, and I'm precisely that."

He gives a small, grudging nod, seeming almost amused. "I appreciate the confidence, Miss Harris."

The meeting wraps up shortly after, though I'm left seething at his arrogance. By the time I step outside, I'm muttering curses under my breath.

As I walk to my car, my phone rings. It's Katie, her voice bright and playful. "Charlie! Are you free for lunch?"

I glance at my watch. "I think I could use a break. Why?"

"Just because," she says, laughing. "I'll send you the address."

Smiling, I hang up and sink into my car, letting out a sigh of relief. I hadn't even realized I was holding my breath. Being around Dante is exhausting, in every way.

As I start the car, Katie's message pops up with the lunch spot. I take a deep breath and drive off, relieved to be leaving thoughts of Dante behind.

Or so I think.

6

DANTE

The ride is almost peaceful. Outside, scenery blurs past, a quiet reminder of how things appear one moment and vanish the next. We're in a cocoon, a world separate from the one rushing by.

I shake my head, pushing away the thoughts. Maybe it's the meds, or maybe something else.

"You okay, boss?" Gabe's voice snaps me back, his gaze holding mine from the front seat.

I nod, turning back to the view. Since the shooting, Gabe's been hovering—equal parts reassuring and relentless. I manage a faint smile; he means well.

"We're almost there," the driver says. Not David. *David is gone.* The thought settles, a weight pressing in my chest.

I set my jaw. "Get ready. We don't know what we're walking into."

Gabe nods, and I look out for one last glimpse of the fading green before we pull into a compound of lights and armed guards. The place radiates power, as if it's daring me to step inside. Fitting, I think.

The car halts, and a guard opens my door. "Welcome, sir."

I step out, careful not to strain my left arm beneath the suit. The doctor assured me it would heal, leaving only a scar—just one more memento.

One more scar for the collection.

Gabe falls into step beside me as the driver pulls away. "Did you remind him not to park too far off?"

"I did," he replies smoothly.

"What's his name, anyway?"

"David."

"No, the new guy."

Gabe's brow lifts. "His name's David." His voice is steady, but the name hits like a punch, igniting a quiet anger that simmers beneath my skin.

"What is this? Some kind of sick joke?"

Gabe's hands raise in defense. "I thought the same, but it's no joke. He was the best fit. There's no replacing David, not like that."

I take a slow breath, adjusting my cuffs, forcing myself to calm down. Gabe wouldn't make a decision out of insensitivity. If this is a joke, it's the universe's, not his. Apologizing crosses my mind, but I let it pass, turning and continuing toward the building. Gabe quickly falls into step beside me.

As we approach, the music from inside grows louder.

"I thought this was supposed to be a meeting," Gabe mutters.

I glance up at the sprawling building before us, lights spilling out into the night. "Meeting, party... same thing to them."

We ascend the steps toward the entrance. Guards in tactical gear and police officers stand alert, a mix that makes me wonder about the dynamics here. The bullet wound in my arm pulses, a reminder to stay cautious.

"I don't trust this setup," Gabe says quietly.

"Neither do I."

"We should've brought our own team."

"Would've looked weak." I know he's right, but I won't let them think they've rattled me. "If we look too cautious, they'll see we're on edge."

"But they *have* rattled us," Gabe replies, his voice low, eyes sharp. I see a flash of anger in them, which, strangely, brings a faint smile to my face.

"True. But showing up like this will keep them wondering." I give him a sidelong glance. "Who shows up with *less security* after being ambushed?"

"Only someone insane," he grumbles, a slight grin cracking through. "Or reckless."

I let a grim smile stretch across my face. "Exactly. Let them wonder."

We pass a group of elegantly dressed guests chatting on the steps. With Gabe on the side of my injured arm, his presence is reassuring, like a barrier against those trying to engage us. We brush by with only brief nods, maintaining a steady path toward the building's core.

Inside, the crowd thins as we near a man standing with two women who look like sisters. Silas Kane. His back is to me, but I recognize him instantly.

"Silas," I say, loud enough to catch his attention.

He turns, visibly startled. The women eye me curiously, assessing. I flash them a polite smile, then look back at Silas. "Mind if I borrow him for a moment?" I ask with a slight smile.

They frown but let go, Gabe closing in on Silas's other

side. I catch movement in my periphery—his guards, too far off to intervene.

"Silas, my friend." I steer him a step further from the approaching guards. He glances over his shoulder, a flicker of panic in his eyes.

"Lovely party, isn't it?" I say, as if oblivious to his discomfort.

"Yes," he stammers, wiping a bead of sweat from his brow. "Quite the spectacle."

I nod thoughtfully. "Expected more of a meeting than a show. But I suppose it's like a casino—set the right mood, and people are more willing to make bold decisions."

Silas forces a chuckle, shifting uneasily. "True, very true."

I tilt my head, eyeing him. "So, how've you been holding up? Health-wise. No issues?"

His face pales, his eyes darting to his champagne flute. "Health? No, no issues. Why do you ask?"

"No reason." I glance at his drink. "Just concerned. Too much of that," I gesture to the glass in his hand, "could lead to an early grave."

He peers into the flute as if expecting to see poison swirling in it. The guards inch closer, but Gabe and I steer Silas in a slow circuit, just far enough to keep his men from intervening.

"I heard you've been staying at hotels," I say. "What happened to the house?"

"Nothing—just remodeling," he replies hastily. "Thought a change of scenery would be nice."

I hold his gaze, noting his shiftiness. Either he knows exactly what I mean, or he's lying.

"Remodeling can be refreshing," I reply, a smile curving my lips. "Everyone needs a reset now and then."

Gabe's eyes flick toward the crowd, catching mine. I turn just as Charlotte steps toward us, gliding gracefully through the throng. My breath catches for a moment, and for the first time tonight, my focus wavers.

"Hello," she greets, a playful smile lighting up her face. "Fancy running into you here."

I manage a slight nod. "Who'd have thought."

Her grin widens, and the flicker of light in her eyes is almost enough to make me forget where we are. For just a moment.

"Well, Silas," I say, patting him on the shoulder. "I'm sure we'll be seeing each other soon."

Silas's gaze hardens, defiance sparking within the fear in his eyes. "Of course, Dante. Much sooner than you think."

I catch the challenge in his words. My smile widens, and I pat his shoulder once more, just as his bodyguards finally reach him. Letting go, I take Charlotte's arm and turn us away, moving as naturally as breathing.

"What was that?" Charlotte asks, her tone curious as we walk away.

"What was what?" I reply, feigning innocence.

"That," she says, glancing back toward Silas. "It was... strange."

I study her, amused at how quickly she picks up on the shift in tension—a skill most of the crowd here lacks. "Nothing you need to worry about."

We turn as the lights dim, signaling the event's start. The guests involved in the Horizon City project are ushered upstairs to a smaller room, where a row of chairs waits. Gratefully, I sink into one, the dull ache in my arm reminding me of my limitations. Charlotte settles beside me, Gabe on my other side.

The crowd here is smaller, quieter. I catch Silas's gaze

across the room and offer him a nod. He looks away, scowling.

When proceedings begin, I sit back, watching as Charlotte takes the lead in negotiations. She's a force to be reckoned with, dismantling each counterpoint with practiced ease. I realize now why she's earned her reputation—she's relentless. By the end, most of the room has conceded to her demands, her arguments leaving no room for doubt.

Gabe glances at me, and we share a knowing look. Best not to end up on Charlotte's bad side.

When negotiations conclude, waitstaff begin circulating with trays of drinks and hors d'oeuvres. I swipe two flutes from a tray, handing one to Charlotte.

"Impressive work," I say, genuinely admiring.

She sips her drink, her eyes gleaming. "Thank you."

"Boss," Gabe interjects, leaning in. "We should make our exit."

I glance around, then nod. "Good idea. Best to leave before the crowd."

"I'll have David bring the car around," Gabe says, slipping away.

I rise and extend a hand to Charlotte. She takes it, and together we move toward the exit.

At the end of the hallway, we stop by the elevator.

"Elevator?" I ask, noticing her eyeing the grand staircase.

"I'm too tired for stairs," she laughs softly.

We step into the elevator, and as the doors close, the sounds from the hall fade, replaced by the soft hum of the lift. Charlotte stands beside me, and the proximity stirs a restlessness I can't ignore.

A subtle shift, and our arms brush. I can feel the warmth radiating from her, a tempting contrast to the cool detachment I've forced myself to maintain.

Suddenly, the urge to kiss her—to pull her close—is overwhelming. I turn to her, my gaze locking on her lips. I know I should look away, but the thought of stepping back seems impossible.

I shake my head slightly, but the image holds. I look again, letting my gaze linger.

7

CHARLIE

I thought returning to work would clear my head, but I couldn't be more wrong. The tension from the car ride with Dante lingers, making it hard to focus. His intense gaze and the way his voice wrapped around those words, "Good girl," keep replaying in my mind. My cheeks warm just thinking about it, and I have to shake myself out of it.

The Horizon City project files spread out before me, demanding attention. I try to lose myself in the detailed plans and contracts, hoping they'll distract me from thoughts of Dante. There's a knock at my office door, pulling me from my thoughts.

"Come in," I say, steadying myself.

Katie steps in with a fresh stack of files and a knowing smile, clearly sensing my distraction. "You okay, Charlie?"

I manage a half-hearted laugh. "I'm fine. Just... a long night."

She raises an eyebrow, unconvinced but mercifully lets it go. "I thought you'd want to see this," she says, setting a file labeled "Kane Holdings" on my desk. "I dug up everything I could on Silas Kane. Figured it might be useful."

"Perfect timing," I reply, masking my surprise. After last night's unsettling research, I'd almost forgotten I asked her for this. "Thank you."

She nods and leaves, and I dive into the file, curious about what more I can uncover. My eyes skim through lists of assets and past projects, most of which are unsurprising —tech acquisitions, real estate investments, some vague references to international trade. But then, something unusual catches my eye.

There's a mention of an "Agritech Innovations Summit" in Country E, where he reportedly attended as a keynote speaker. The same event from the broadcast. My brows knit together, recalling how odd it was for Silas, a mogul with no known agricultural ties, to be involved in an event like that. I scan the document further, looking for clues, but it's filled with the standard jargon. The more I read, the less it adds up.

There's more to Silas Kane than meets the eye. Why would he attend a public summit in a field he's barely connected to unless he had something to hide? A prickle of unease stirs in my gut, an instinct urging me to dig deeper.

I reach for my phone, deciding to call Micah to see if he's found any leads on the information I'd asked him to gather.

He picks up after the first ring. "Hey, Charlie. Just the person I was about to call."

"Funny you asked about Silas Kane," he says, his tone serious. "He's involved with some high-stakes, less-than-legal trades."

A chill runs through me. "Go on."

"His deals in Country E connect with some unsavory

networks—political groups, underground trade. He funds certain agricultural projects as a front for moving assets. Very few people know it exists."

My heart races. "So, he's using agriculture as a cover. For what?"

"Hard to say, but likely for funneling money. These projects keep things off official records, especially in countries where regulations are lax."

I let his words sink in, questions flooding my mind. "Thanks, Micah. This... this really helps."

"Glad to help. Just be careful, Charlie. Silas isn't the type to play fair."

We hang up, and I sit back, my mind buzzing. The stakes just rose dramatically. If Silas is hiding something this big, working with him could be dangerous—not only for Dante but also for me.

My phone buzzes with an incoming message. It's Dante: "Available for a quick call?"

Just seeing his name lights something up inside me, but the weight of what I just learned tugs at my conscience. I glance from the "Kane Holdings" file to my phone. I type out a quick response, agreeing to the call, and within seconds, the line connects.

"Charlotte." Dante's voice is smooth, steady, yet there's a hint of something else—maybe curiosity.

"Hi, Dante," I reply, keeping my tone light.

"Hope I'm not interrupting. I wanted to get your thoughts on the Horizon City project after yesterday."

His professionalism is grounding, but I can't shake thoughts of our last encounter. "Of course. I was just reviewing the latest documents. Everything seems solid, though I may need to go over a few things in person."

"Silas Kane, for instance?" he asks, his tone sharpening.

I pause, not sure how much to reveal. "Yes. He's... an interesting addition."

"Interesting is one way to put it," he says, his voice laced with an edge. "Silas has a talent for complicating things. Is there anything I should know?"

His question is direct, almost as if he senses I'm holding back. My pulse quickens, but I keep my response neutral.

"Nothing specific yet. Just that he may be unpredictable. I'll keep you posted if anything comes up."

He hesitates, as though considering my words, before speaking again. "Let me know if there's anything I should be concerned about. I trust your instincts, Charlotte."

The sincerity in his words stirs something in me—a sense of responsibility and something else I can't quite name. "Thank you, Dante. I appreciate that."

"Good. Then let's meet later this week to go over the updates." There's a pause before he adds, "And, Charlotte?"

"Yes?"

"Stay sharp."

The call ends, but his words linger—a subtle warning that sends chills down my spine. I lean back in my chair, mulling over everything I've uncovered. Silas's hidden dealings are a serious risk, but telling Dante outright feels premature. I need more proof—more than a few suspicious documents and a news clip.

THE NEXT EVENING, I'm still knee-deep in research. Every lead on Silas only raises more questions, leaving my mind tangled in half-formed theories. Frustrated, I close my laptop, deciding a break is long overdue. I grab my jacket and head to a nearby cafe, hoping the change of scenery will help clear my head.

The cafe is quiet, and I find a table near the back, ordering a coffee as I settle in. It isn't long before I hear a familiar voice.

"Charlie?"

I look up, surprised to see Katie standing there, holding a tray with her coffee and a pastry. "Katie! What are you doing here?"

She shrugs, smiling. "I needed a break. Figured some caffeine might help." She takes the seat across from me, her eyes narrowing slightly as she studies me. "Are you okay? You look... tense."

I manage a smile, though I know it doesn't reach my eyes. "It's been a long week. The Horizon City project is... complicated."

She arches a brow, clearly interested. "Complicated how?"

I hesitate, weighing how much to say. Katie is one of my closest friends, but revealing too much could pull her into this mess. "Let's just say I'm dealing with some interesting personalities."

She laughs. "Sounds intense. But you've got this, Charlie. You always do."

Her confidence is reassuring, a reminder that I'm not as alone in this as I sometimes feel. I change the subject, steering the conversation away from work, and we chat for a while before she has to leave. As I watch her go, I feel a little lighter, grateful for the distraction.

On my way back home, my mind drifts back to Dante and the questions I can't shake. It's clear he's dealing with his own secrets, but how much does he know about Silas? And why does he trust me to navigate this alone?

. . .

THE NEXT DAY, I'm back at the office, but I can't shake the feeling that I'm being watched. It's subtle—a glance from someone passing by, a lingering look from a colleague. I remind myself that paranoia is the last thing I need, but the sense of unease refuses to fade.

Around midday, Dante stops by my office, his presence filling the room with an intensity that both steadies and unnerves me. He's dressed impeccably, as usual, and his gaze is sharp, assessing.

"Charlotte," he says, closing the door behind him. "I wanted to see how you're managing the latest developments."

I look up, trying to read his expression. "Things are... progressing. Slowly, but I'm getting a clearer picture."

He nods, crossing his arms as he leans against the door. "Good. I need someone I can rely on, especially with Silas involved. He's proven to be... unpredictable."

The way he says it, like he's choosing his words carefully, heightens my suspicions. I decide to take a small risk. "Is there something specific I should know about him? Any potential conflicts that might come up?"

Dante's gaze sharpens, and for a moment, I think he might evade the question. But then he sighs, a look of resolve crossing his face. "Silas has a history of bending rules. He's ambitious, but his methods are... unconventional, to say the least. It's why I keep him at arm's length."

The weight in his tone tells me there's more he isn't saying, but I let it slide, feeling that I've gotten as much as he's willing to share for now. "Understood. I'll be careful."

He nods, a faint smile curving his lips. "Good. Just remember, if anything seems off, I want to hear about it."

A comfortable silence settles between us, one that feels almost intimate. I realize, with a jolt, how natural it feels to be working alongside him, to share this mutual trust. And just as quickly, I remind myself that I can't afford to let my guard down—not with someone as complex as Dante.

As he heads for the door, he pauses, turning back to look at me. "Take care, Charlotte. I'll see you at the next meeting."

And with that, he's gone, leaving me to wonder just how deep the secrets between us really go.

Charlotte

Later that night, I pour over the information I've gathered on Silas, my eyes growing heavy from hours of reading. Patterns are starting to emerge—a web of connections that hint at something larger than I initially thought.

There's a knock at my door, and I glance up, surprised. It's late, far too late for visitors, and I feel a jolt of apprehension as I make my way to the door.

I open it cautiously, only to find a familiar figure standing there, his silhouette framed by the dim hallway light.

"Dante?" I whisper, shock mingling with an unspoken thrill.

"Charlotte," he replies, his voice low and steady. "We need to talk. May I come in?"

I nod, stepping aside to let him in. The door closes softly behind him, and the small space of my apartment suddenly feels charged, as if the very air around us is humming with tension.

He looks around, his gaze settling on the stack of papers and my laptop on the coffee table. "Still working, I see."

I manage a nod, though my voice catches. "It's... a lot to process."

He turns to face me, his eyes serious. "There are things I haven't told you. Things about Silas—and this project—that you need to know."

My heart pounds as I watch him, waiting, knowing that whatever he's about to say could change everything.

8

DANTE

Charlie's voice echoes in my mind, each careful word laced with suspicion. She looked at me in a way that felt too close to the truth, like she's already piecing together details she shouldn't. If she's even close to discovering Silas's secrets, it won't be long before she uncovers mine.

The car cuts through the city, streetlights casting intermittent shadows that dance over Gabe's face in the front seat. He glances back, as if sensing something's off, but I keep my gaze fixed outside. The view blurs in streaks of neon and darkness, reminders of the world I've built—a delicate house of cards where one wrong move could bring everything down.

"Boss?" Gabe's voice slices through my thoughts. He's careful, watchful. "Everything good?"

"Fine." My voice is clipped, my decision firm. "Stick to the plan."

As we pull into the underground depot, the familiar scent of metal and machinery fills the air, grounding me. This place—remote, secure, hidden—has kept operations running for years. I built it on precision and control. But today, the air feels tense, almost charged, like everyone senses something is shifting.

Inside, Gabe stands with a few men, issuing orders with his usual efficiency. When he sees me, he straightens, nodding in silent acknowledgment. His respect is unmistakable, as is his readiness—a loyalty I can rely on without question. He knows we're on the edge of something big, something dangerous.

"What's the status?" I ask, letting my command carry through the room.

"Lorenzo's upped his shipments," Gabe responds, his voice low. "He's pushing more product than usual. If we go ahead with the original release, we'll be facing steep competition."

His words settle like a weight. The room falls silent, every eye on me, waiting. Gabe watches me, too, his concern just barely visible. He wants to be sure I understand the stakes fully—as if there's a world where I wouldn't.

"We stick to the plan." My voice leaves no room for debate.

Gabe's eyes narrow just slightly, questioning. It's a look he reserves only for me, a silent request for assurance. "You're certain?"

"Yes. Lorenzo can flood the market if he wants to. We hold our ground," I reply, the steel in my voice unwavering. "The next shipment goes out on schedule."

Tension releases, an unspoken acknowledgment of the decision rippling through the room. Even Gabe relaxes, if only slightly. He's earned the right to question me, but he also knows I don't make decisions lightly. As the men disperse, I catch a few subtle glances, their silent trust as solid as stone.

Lorenzo's maneuvers are reckless. Flooding the market might cripple smaller players, but I don't run a small operation. He's adding fuel to the fire, and he's too arrogant to see the consequences.

In the far corner of the room, a murmur breaks the depot's controlled quiet. A man sits bound to a metal chair, dark hair falling messily over his face, his eyes darting around the room. Duct tape covers his mouth, but it hasn't stopped him from making noise.

"Take the tape off," I say, my voice low but carrying.

One of my men steps forward, ripping the tape away in a swift, brutal motion. A pained cry escapes the man's lips, filling the silence.

I step closer, meeting his bloodshot gaze. His eyes are defiant, a mix of fury and desperation. A few of his teeth are missing, his face bruised and swollen from earlier "persuasion." He's one of Lorenzo's men—a spy we intercepted. A lucky find, though I don't believe in luck.

"Ready to talk now?" My tone is calm, controlled.

The man spits, his face twisting in rage. "Go to hell," he sneers, straining against the ropes binding him. His eyes burn, as if he'd tear me apart if he had the chance.

I keep my gaze steady. "Chatty behind the tape. Now you've got nothing to say?"

He stares, the defiance still there. He's clinging to some misplaced loyalty, some futile hope of escape. I know that look—the refusal to give in. But I also know how to break it.

"You should consider talking," I say, voice almost gentle. "It's the only way this ends well for you."

When he remains silent, a grim smile tugs at my lips. I lean in, letting him feel the weight of my presence, the unyielding authority in my gaze. "Still nothing?"

He jerks forward, face contorting with the effort, and I

see it before he even moves. He's going to spit at me. The contempt in his eyes is unmistakable.

Before he can, I drive my fist into his face, the impact jolting through my arm. He coughs, choking on his own spit, a strangled sound echoing in the room. Blood drips from his mouth, staining his shirt, and he slumps back, head lolling to the side.

I glance down at my knuckles, noticing a fresh line of blood. It's not the first, nor will it be the last. A flash of Charlie's face crosses my mind, and for a fleeting second, I wonder how she'd react if she saw me like this. If she truly knew what I am.

The thought lingers for a second too long. But this is the world I built; there's no place in it for doubts or distractions.

"Boss," Gabe's voice cuts through, steady. He holds out my phone, his expression unreadable. "It's Charlie."

Surprise flickers in my chest. "Charlie?"

Gabe nods. "She wants to meet."

I take the phone, pressing it to my ear. "Charlie?"

"Dante," her voice comes through, steady but laced with urgency. "Can we meet?"

"What's this about?"

"It's... sensitive," she says, her tone low. "I'd rather discuss it in person."

Curiosity sharpens, mingling with a trace of something I can't quite name. I glance back at the man in the chair, beaten and bound, and then at Gabe, who's watching me with quiet understanding.

"Where?"

She names a small café on the city's west side, a place I've never been but that Gabe seems familiar with. He gives a nod as I repeat the name.

"I'll see you soon," I reply, before handing the phone back to Gabe.

He raises an eyebrow, intrigued but too disciplined to ask questions. I'm grateful for his discretion. What could she want to discuss face-to-face? Is she starting to see the edges of the truth? A sliver of worry wedges itself in my mind, but I quickly suppress it. I can handle this. I've handled far worse.

Turning back to the informant, I offer him one last, cold glance. "I have an errand to run," I say. "Sit tight. We'll finish this later."

The man's glare follows me as I walk out, Gabe close behind. Outside, the cool night air hits my skin, a stark contrast to the stifling heat inside. Gabe leads me to the car, where David waits in the driver's seat. I slide in beside him, Gabe in the front.

The drive is quiet, but my mind isn't. My thoughts circle back to Charlie, to the tension in her voice. She's always been sharp, perceptive, able to read between the lines. I just hope that whatever she's discovered isn't enough to pull her deeper. There's a part of me that wants to keep her at a distance—to protect her from the truth. But another part... doesn't want to let her go.

"We're almost there," Gabe announces as the car slows, pulling up to the small café she mentioned.

The place is understated, tucked away on a quiet street, with warm, dim lights spilling over the entrance. It's the kind of place people go to disappear, to talk without being overheard. Charlie chose well.

I step out, adjusting my jacket as Gabe follows, his gaze sweeping over the area. I consider telling him to stay back, but I know better. Gabe is my shadow, and I trust him with my life. Besides, I might need backup.

As we walk in, the scent of coffee and baked goods hits me, a stark contrast to the metallic tang of blood still lingering in my memory. The patrons barely glance up, lost in their own worlds, but I can feel the weight of eyes on me, subtle but present.

And then I see her.

Charlie sits near the back, face lighting up as she catches sight of me. She stands, her smile genuine, though there's a flicker of tension beneath it. I can tell she's nervous, but her resolve is unshakable.

"Thanks for coming," she says, voice warm but edged with urgency.

"Of course," I reply, taking the seat across from her. "It sounded important."

She glances around, ensuring we're alone, before leaning in, her voice dropping. "I found something. Something about the Horizon City project and the people involved... particularly Silas Kane."

I keep my expression neutral, but my mind races. Has she uncovered Silas's connection to the underworld? Or worse, a connection to me?

"What did you find?" I ask, tone controlled.

She takes a deep breath. "It's not just a business venture. Silas—he's involved in some things. Shady things. I think he's hiding a lot more than he's letting on."

A chill runs through me, but I force a calm smile. "Silas? That doesn't sound like him."

She leans back, watching me closely. "I thought you might say that. But Dante... I'm not sure we should trust him. There's something bigger going on here, and I think it could affect both of us."

Her eyes are dark, intense. She doesn't know the half of it, yet she's closer to the truth than I'd like.

"What are you saying, Charlie?"

Her voice drops to a whisper. "I'm saying we need to be careful. Because if Silas is hiding this, there's no telling what else he's capable of. Or who he might drag down with him."

I meet her gaze, feeling the weight of her words. The irony isn't lost on me—she's closer than she realizes, yet still in the dark. For now.

But as I sit there, watching her, a part of me wonders how long I can keep her safe from the shadows she's stepping into.

And more importantly, how long I can keep her safe from me.

9

CHARLIE

Looking up into Dante's face, I can't tell if he believes me. His lips are set, thoughtful, but his gaze holds a sharpness that makes me feel exposed, as though he's seeing something I'd rather keep hidden. I press my fingers together, fighting the restless twitch building beneath the polished tabletop.

"Look, Mr. Romano—"

"Dante," he corrects gently, the edge in his gaze softening.

"Dante." His name falls from my lips, and an unexpected warmth unfurls low in my stomach. I push it down, hard, and force myself back to the topic. "I understand it might be hard to believe, but while I can't say for certain that Silas Kane is a criminal, I think it's obvious he's at least... shady."

Dante makes a small, noncommittal sound, his eyes never leaving mine.

"And as your counsel," I press on, finding conviction in my voice, "I'm obligated to warn you. His associations could adversely affect you—and the Horizon City project. Even the smallest rumor of illegal ties could make other investors pull back."

He watches me in silence, his gaze steady but unreadable. Finally, he leans forward, his hands coming together on the table. "And if these rumors don't stay rumors? What happens then?"

It's not the reaction I expected, but it steadies me. I settle back, taking a slow sip of my coffee to compose my thoughts. "If they come to light, it could jeopardize the entire project," I say, choosing each word with care. "At best, it would raise questions about your judgment. At worst, it could bring law enforcement into the picture, risking everything you've built."

"Hmm." His voice is low, his expression unreadable. "You believe Silas's involvement could ruin more than just Horizon City?"

I nod, feeling my pulse quicken. "Absolutely. He's an unknown variable, Dante. And with a project as high-profile as Horizon City, anything could tip the scales."

A smile plays at the corner of his mouth, but it doesn't quite reach his eyes. "And here I thought I'd hired you to make my life easier, not add complications."

I swallow a strange thrill at his faint compliment. "I don't mean to complicate things. But... I thought you should know." I hesitate, then add, "It's what I'd want if I were in your position."

An unspoken tension stretches between us, thick and tangible. I realize he's scrutinizing me, as if weighing my words—and perhaps my motives. There's a flicker of something almost vulnerable in his expression before his face settles into the mask of control he wears so easily.

Finally, he says, "You've done well here, Charlie. Better than most would."

A sense of pride rises unexpectedly, but his voice shifts, the faintest challenge in it. "Would you like to see what it is you're so diligently protecting?"

I blink, caught off guard. "See it?"

He nods, his smile tugging faintly. "Yes. I could show you Romano Holdings—not the whole thing, of course. That would take days, and we only have an afternoon." His eyebrow lifts, his gaze inviting. "You up for it?"

The offer is so unexpected that, before I can overthink it, I hear myself say, "Yes." There's an eagerness in my voice that catches me off guard. I want to understand the empire he commands. More than that, I want to see him in his element.

His smile widens, crinkling the edges of his eyes, and he rises with a grace that speaks to a lifetime of command. He offers me his hand, and I take it, savoring the warmth and strength in his grip, a sensation that feels too intimate for this public setting.

As we step out of the café, his right-hand man, Gabe, is waiting by the car, door open. I feel the weight of curious stares as we pass, and there's a subtle thrill in knowing I'm beside Dante Romano. Just as I settle into the back seat, I hear the faint click of a camera. I glance around, startled, but Dante rests a calming hand on mine.

"Leave it," he murmurs, voice low and reassuring. "People will always look. Just ignore it."

I nod, though my heart thumps a bit faster at the thought. If people knew who I was with right now... But before I can dwell on it, the door shuts, cocooning us in the quiet luxury of Dante's world.

As we pull away from the café, the tension eases, replaced by a quiet anticipation. The cityscape glides past in muted colors, and after a moment, I ask, "What is it you're constructing?" I need something to focus on, something other than the way his presence fills the car.

He raises an eyebrow, a playful gleam in his eye. "You'll see. I like the idea of keeping you guessing." His eyes linger on me a beat longer. "You always seem to have everything figured out, Charlie. It's nice to have a chance to surprise you."

The intensity in his words sends a shiver down my spine, one I try to ignore as I return his smile. "Well, I suppose I can give you that much."

He chuckles, the sound deep and rich, and I realize with a start that I want to hear it again and again. As he points out various buildings his company has developed over the years, my admiration grows with each reveal.

Eventually, the car comes to a stop, and Gabe glances over his shoulder with a nod. "We're here, boss."

"Good work, David Two," Dante says with a faint smile, clearly in jest, and Gabe's smirk tells me he's used to it.

As we step out, I find myself looking up at a massive construction site. Scaffolding wraps around a half-finished skyscraper, workers in hardhats move among stacks of iron beams. I squint, trying to imagine what it will look like when complete, but all I see is an incomplete shell.

"Is this... a new project?" I ask, attempting to hide my skepticism.

Dante glances at me, amusement flickering in his gaze. "Looks like just another construction site, right?"

I nod, sheepish, but he smiles, gesturing forward. "Trust me. It may not look like much now, but when it's done, this will be one of the most luxurious office towers in the city. Think high-end executive suites, entire floors dedicated to single tenants. Offices for the elite."

I can hear the pride in his voice, and for a moment, I

glimpse the man behind the title. There's a childlike thrill in his eyes as he describes the details, and I'm drawn to it, captivated.

"And you just... envisioned all of this?" I ask, genuinely curious.

He nods, his gaze drifting up to the towering framework. "When you've been in this business long enough, you start to see things differently. Where others see risk, I see opportunity. A canvas."

There's a poetic quality to his tone, striking a chord in me, admiration mingling with an unsettling realization. I'm standing beside a man who sees the world not as it is, but as it could be—a quality both thrilling and dangerous.

Dante glances down at me, his eyes intense. "You want to see the top floor?"

My heart skips a beat at his suggestion, but I nod, feeling drawn by his curiosity, by the unspoken promise in his words. "Lead the way."

He chuckles, motioning to a makeshift construction elevator, caged and rusted but functional. As we step in, the doors clang shut, and the elevator begins its shuddering ascent. The city shrinks below, and I'm acutely aware of Dante's presence beside me, close enough that our shoulders brush.

The silence between us hums with tension, an electric charge prickling along my skin. I glance at him from the corner of my eye, catching the faint smirk on his lips, as if he knows exactly what he's doing.

The elevator jolts suddenly, and I instinctively reach out, my hand landing on his arm. I feel the warmth of his skin through his shirt, muscles tensed beneath my fingers. I pull back, embarrassed, but he catches my hand, holding it steady.

"Nervous?" he murmurs, his voice sending a thrill down my spine.

"A little," I admit, my voice barely above a whisper.

He squeezes my hand gently, his gaze steady on mine. "You don't need to be."

The elevator slows, then stops, and the doors slide open, revealing a vast, empty floor with a panoramic view of the city. The skyline stretches out before us, glittering in the late afternoon light, and for a moment, I forget to breathe.

"Beautiful, isn't it?" Dante's voice is soft, almost reverent, as he steps forward, eyes on the horizon.

I nod, speechless, taking in the view. "It's... breathtaking."

We stand side by side, the city sprawling beneath us. A sense of calm settles, a quiet between us that feels deeper than words. I feel his eyes on me, and when I glance up, I'm caught in the intensity of his gaze.

"Charlie," he says, his voice barely above a whisper. "There's something I need to tell you."

My heart races as he steps closer, reaching up to brush a strand of hair from my face. My breath catches, warmth unfurling deep within me, something I can't deny.

But as his hand falls away, the elevator jolts with a violent lurch, throwing us off balance. I stumble, and he catches me, his arms around me as the ground shifts.

"Are you all right?" he asks, voice tense, grip steady.

"Yes," I manage, my voice shaking. "I... I think so."

We're still for a moment, our faces inches apart, the tension palpable. His gaze flickers to my lips, and I feel a surge of desire, the pull that's been building since the beginning.

But before either of us can move, the elevator jerks again, and the lights flicker, plunging us into darkness. His grip tightens, body solid against mine, his voice an edge of calm. "Stay close, Charlie."

We're suspended in darkness, city lights a distant glow beyond the glass. My heart pounds as I cling to him, feeling the danger and, for the first time, wondering if I'm in over my head.

Dante's voice cuts through the silence, low and almost ominous. "Charlie... there's something you should know. Something that might change everything."

I look up, my pulse racing, his expression unreadable, gaze dark.

Suspended between floors, the city stretching below us, I realize I'm caught in something far more dangerous than I ever anticipated.

10

DANTE

The hoist jerks beneath us, the sudden motion throwing Charlie against me before I can brace myself. I instinctively wrap an arm around her waist, pulling her close to keep her steady. The heat of her body against mine catches me off guard, as does the faint floral scent that lingers in the air between us.

"Are you okay?" I ask, keeping my voice steady even as the platform sways again.

She glances up, cheeks flushed from the jolt, and lets out a shaky laugh. "Well, that was a rush. When I agreed to the tour, I didn't realize I'd be fighting gravity."

Her humor is forced, but I can sense the tension beneath it. She's out of her element here—high-rise construction sites, the gritty reality of my world. And yet, there's something in the way she stands her ground, even now, that pulls at me.

I tighten my arm around her, unwilling to let go just yet. "You're tougher than you look."

Her gaze flickers to mine, and for a moment, the chaos of the site fades away. There's something raw and unspoken in her eyes, something that sparks against the guarded parts of myself I rarely let anyone see.

The hoist jolts again, breaking the moment. She stumbles slightly, but my grip keeps her steady. The proximity is unavoidable, her breath warm against my collarbone as she steadies herself.

The elevator platform sways beneath us, forcing her closer. Her back presses against my chest, and I instinctively tighten my grip on her waist. The scent of her perfume fills my senses, making it hard to focus.

"Easy," I murmur, my lips brushing her ear. She shivers in response, her hands gripping the railing.

When she shifts, trying to find her balance, the friction sends heat coursing through me. Her breath comes quicker now, matching the rapid beat of my heart.

"Dante," she whispers, turning her head slightly. Her lips are inches from mine, and the temptation to close that distance is almost overwhelming.

I trace my fingers along her arm, feeling her pulse race beneath my touch. She leans back into me, a silent invitation that tests my control.

The elevator shudders again, and I pull her firmly against me, one hand splayed across her stomach. She makes a soft sound that sends fire through my veins.

"We shouldn't," I say roughly, even as my lips brush her neck.

She turns in my arms, her eyes dark with desire. "Then stop."

But we both know I won't. Not when she's looking at me like that, not when every fiber of my being craves her touch.

When we finally reach the ground, I release her reluctantly, the absence of her weight against me an unwelcome void. I help her step off the platform, my hand lingering on hers longer than necessary.

"Thanks," she says, her voice soft, her expression unreadable.

As we walk toward the site exit, Gabe approaches, a blueprint in hand. His gaze darts between Charlie and me, something unspoken in his expression, but he keeps his tone professional.

"Boss, a quick word."

I nod, glancing at Charlie. "Wait here. I'll be right back."

She steps aside, her gaze drifting to the sprawling cityscape beyond the site. The afternoon light catches the curve of her cheek, her posture straight but contemplative. I force myself to turn my attention to Gabe, but my mind keeps drifting back to her.

"She's still here?" Gabe asks, keeping his voice low.

"For now," I reply curtly.

He nods, handing me the blueprints. "Structural adjustments for the northwest tower. Nothing major, but worth looking at before final approval."

I skim the plans, but my focus is elsewhere. When I glance back at Charlie, she's leaning slightly against the railing, her fingers tracing the rough metal, her gaze still on the skyline. I hand the plans back to Gabe.

"Let's talk later."

I stride back to her, placing my hand lightly at the small of her back. The contact is brief but intentional, grounding me in a way I can't quite explain.

"Ready to go?" I ask.

She turns to me, her eyes catching the last glint of sunlight. "Yeah. Let's go."

. . .

THE RIDE back is quiet at first, the hum of the city surrounding us. I grip the steering wheel, my thoughts tangled in the memory of her warmth against me on the hoist.

"Thank you for showing me around," she says, her voice breaking the silence.

I glance over, catching the faint smile playing on her lips. "Did it meet your expectations?"

"Well," she teases, "I didn't expect to be thrown around like a rag doll. But otherwise, it was… enlightening."

Her fingers trace the edge of the armrest, a small, absent movement that draws my attention. There's something about her quiet confidence that intrigues me, a resilience that's both familiar and foreign.

"Do you always drive like this?" she asks, a playful edge in her tone.

"Only when the company's this interesting," I reply, my voice softer than I intended.

Her gaze sharpens, a spark of curiosity lighting her expression. "Interesting? Is that how you remember the first time we met?"

I catch myself gripping the wheel tighter as a vivid memory of that night flashes through my mind—her breath hitching beneath me, the way her lips parted with each sigh.

"I remember more than you might think," I say, letting my gaze linger on hers for a moment longer than necessary.

Her breath catches, and the tension between us tightens, the air thick with everything we're not saying.

I pull off the main road, parking on a quiet street away from prying eyes. Turning to face her fully, I let my guard drop just enough to say what's been on my mind.

"But if you're asking if I still find you fascinating? The answer's yes."

Her laugh is soft, nervous. "Well, that's something," she murmurs, but there's a flicker of uncertainty in her eyes.

The silence stretches between us. My hand slides to her cheek, and she leans into the touch. Her skin is soft beneath my fingers as I brush away a stray strand of hair.

"Charlie," I whisper, drawn closer by an irresistible pull.

She tilts her face up, her breath catching as our lips nearly touch. The air between us is electric with anticipation.

"We shouldn't," I murmur, even as my thumb traces her bottom lip.

She trembles under my touch but doesn't pull away. "Then stop," she challenges softly.

Instead, I close the final distance between us. The kiss starts gentle, questioning, but quickly deepens as years of restraint crumble. She sighs into my mouth, her fingers gripping my shirt to pull me closer.

My hand tangles in her hair as the other wraps around her waist, pressing her against me. Her lips part beneath mine, and I drink in her soft gasp of pleasure.

The intensity builds between us, threatening to consume us both. Only the knowledge of watching eyes keeps me from taking this further. With immense effort, I pull back, resting my forehead against hers as we catch our breath.

"We can't," I say roughly, though everything in me rebels against the words. "Not here. Not now."

She nods, but her eyes still burn with desire that matches my own.

Just as I'm about to close the distance between us, the distant rumble of an engine pulls me back. My gaze snaps to the rearview mirror, catching the glint of a sleek black car parked down the block. Its tinted windows hide the occupants, but the intent is clear.

"What is it?" Charlie asks, her voice soft but steady.

I shake my head, forcing calm into my tone. "Nothing. Just... a distraction I don't need."

But she's not fooled. Her gaze follows mine, and her expression shifts as realization sets in. This is my world—one filled with shadows and unseen threats—and she's starting to see it for what it is.

"Maybe this is a bad idea," she says quietly, her voice laced with uncertainty.

I reach for her hand, holding it firmly. "Charlie, I know this isn't easy, and I know it's dangerous. But I'm not someone who walks away. Once I start something, I see it through."

Her hand tightens around mine, and for a moment, the tension eases, replaced by something softer.

"What happens next?" she asks, her voice barely above a whisper.

I don't answer. Instead, I start the car, pulling us back onto the road, my focus shifting to the threat lingering behind us.

WHEN WE REACH HER BUILDING, I park and turn to face her, the weight of everything unsaid hanging between us. She looks at me, conflicted, her fingers curling around the strap of her bag.

"Dante..." Her voice trails off, but I can see the question in her eyes.

I don't have an answer for her—not yet. "Stay safe, Charlie," I say instead, my tone softer than usual.

She hesitates, then nods, stepping out of the car. I watch her until she disappears into the building, the echo of her footsteps fading.

My phone buzzes, pulling me back. Gabe's message is short and chilling.

"Someone's watching you. Be careful."

I glance at the black car still parked down the block, its engine idling. Movement inside confirms my suspicion—they're not done.

As I pull away, the weight of the night settles over me. Whoever's behind this knows about Charlie. And if they're willing to go this far, she's already in more danger than she realizes.

This isn't just business anymore. It's personal.

11

CHARLIE

The latch clicks shut behind me, the finality prickling my skin. Silas Kane—of all people—stands in my living room, his tall frame filling the space with a dark, looming presence. How did he find me?

My mind scrambles, grasping for calm. I glance toward Katie, hoping she senses the urgency to stay silent, but her wide eyes tell me she's as stunned as I am.

"Lovely place you've got here, Charlie." Silas's voice is a smooth, unsettling murmur. He steps further in, his gaze sweeping the room with slow, calculated interest. I swallow hard, trying to steady my breathing. My pulse hammers as his gaze settles back on me, lingering with an intensity that feels invasive.

"What... brings you here, Mr. Kane?" I manage, forcing my voice not to waver.

His smile is thin, almost surgical. "Just wanted to have a chat. Nothing too formal, of course. We're friends, aren't we?" His eyes glint with a dangerous edge, a clear signal that this is anything but friendly.

Katie shifts beside me, visibly thrown. I shoot her a

quick look, hoping to communicate a silent warning. Whatever happens, she needs to stay quiet and let me handle this.

"I don't think this is the best time for a chat," I say, keeping my tone even. "If you want to discuss business, you can schedule an appointment at my office."

Silas chuckles, the sound devoid of humor. "Ah, but some things can't wait for an appointment. I thought you'd understand that, especially after the way you've been so... involved." His eyes narrow, calculating, and the message is clear: he knows more than he should.

My stomach twists. He's referring to Dante, our involvement in the Horizon City deal. Somehow, Silas has learned too much—and he's here to make sure I know it. My instincts scream that this is no courtesy call.

"Why don't we have a seat?" he suggests, gesturing to the couch. His tone is polite, but the undertone says I don't have a choice.

I look at Katie, who hesitates, glancing between us, wary. I give her a slight nod, hoping she understands to stay calm and seated.

As we settle, I feel the weight of Silas's gaze on me. "You've been a busy woman lately, haven't you, Charlie?" His voice is silk over steel. "A lawyer in your position—so close to Romano. Quite an influential role."

"Is there a point to this visit?" I cut in, sharper than intended. Every instinct tells me to keep control, not to let him sense the fear simmering under my calm facade.

Silas's smile curves cruelly. "Straight to the point. I admire that." He leans forward, his gaze as penetrating as a knife. "The Horizon City project—it's ambitious. Lucrative. And you're positioned right at the heart of it, aren't you?"

My pulse spikes, the implication landing like a blow.

Silas knows about my role, likely more than he should. But I can't let him see that.

"My role as Dante's legal counsel involves logistics only," I reply smoothly, trying to deflect.

He gives a slow nod, his eyes darkening. "But logistics... can mean more than just paperwork, can't they?" His words are laced with insinuation that turns my stomach.

Beside me, Katie shifts, glancing between us, trying to make sense of the danger simmering in the air. I give her a slight, reassuring look. I can't let Silas see he's unnerved us.

Taking a breath, I force my voice steady. "I'm not sure what you're implying, Mr. Kane, but if you think I'm involved in anything outside the law, you're mistaken."

"Oh, I don't doubt your commitment to the law," he says, leaning back, his fingers tapping a slow rhythm on the arm of the chair. "But sometimes... even the most principled people find themselves in over their heads. Especially when the stakes are high."

I can't shake the feeling he's setting a trap, testing me with each word. I meet his gaze, refusing to let him see me falter. "If you have accusations, make them directly. Otherwise, I don't see the need for this conversation."

His smile tightens, his eyes narrowing slightly. "You're brave. I'll give you that. But bravery doesn't guarantee safety, especially when powerful people have... conflicting interests."

Katie tenses beside me, her hand gripping the edge of the cushion. I reach over, squeezing her hand, a silent reminder to stay calm. Silas's gaze flickers to the gesture, his interest piqued.

"It would be a shame if anything... disrupted your future, Charlie," he says, voice a low hum of menace. "A promising career, a well-earned reputation, ties to someone like Dante Romano. People might... misinterpret things."

I force myself to keep breathing evenly. He's circling his point, probing for cracks in my defenses. "Is that a threat, Mr. Kane?" I ask, my voice firmer than I feel.

"It's a reminder," he replies smoothly, his eyes gleaming with dark amusement. "One I hope you'll take to heart."

The tension is nearly unbearable, the air thick with unspoken threats. Katie's fingers tighten around mine, her presence bolstering me, but I know this isn't over. Silas Kane doesn't leave without making his intentions known, and I sense he's only just begun.

Silas stands, adjusting his jacket, his eyes locked onto mine. "Thank you for your hospitality, Charlie. I trust you'll make wise choices." With a chilling smile, he strides toward the door.

I exhale slowly, watching him leave, but I don't relax until the door clicks shut behind him. Only then do I release Katie's hand, my own fingers trembling as I process what just happened.

"What... was that?" Katie's voice is barely a whisper. "Who was that man, Charlie?"

I swallow, the weight of the encounter settling over me. "That was Silas Kane," I murmur, hardly able to believe it. "He's... a powerful man. And he's involved in things I can't even begin to explain."

Katie's eyes widen, fear settling over her face. "Charlie, what have you gotten yourself into?"

I don't have an answer. All I know is that I'm standing on the edge of something dark, something that threatens to pull me under. And I don't know if I can escape.

I close the door with a trembling hand, the click echoing in the silence. I stare at it, half-expecting it to open again, for

Silas's chilling voice to slip back into the room like poison. But the hallway remains silent.

Katie is the first to break the silence. "Charlie," she whispers, her voice barely steady. "What... What the hell just happened? Who is that man? And why does he know where you live?"

I meet her eyes, fear reflecting between us. But as I open my mouth, I realize there's no simple answer. There's no way to explain Silas without unraveling the web I'm caught in—without admitting just how far over my head I am.

"He's a... a powerful figure in the business world," I say carefully, even as my mind races, trying to piece it together. "He's connected to the Horizon City project, indirectly, through some of Dante's competitors. He's just... trying to intimidate me."

Katie's brows knit, disbelief etched on her face. "Intimidate you? Charlie, he just barged in here like he owns the place. He's got you backed into some kind of corner. This isn't normal. This isn't how your job's ever worked."

I can't deny it. She's right. Nothing about this feels like the controlled, predictable world of law I'm supposed to work in. This is Dante's world—a world of shadows and threats, of people like Silas who look at you like they already know your weaknesses. I'd felt a glimpse of it before, but now it's unmistakable.

Katie grips my arm, her eyes scanning my face. "Charlie, you need to get out of this. Whatever's happening here, it's not safe. You're not safe."

Her words strike a nerve, and for a moment, I let myself imagine walking away. Cutting ties with Dante, leaving the Horizon City project, maybe even finding a new job far from all this. But the thought feels impossible. There's something about Dante—a pull I can't explain, a feeling that, despite the risks, he's the one thing I can't walk away from.

I shake my head slowly. "It's complicated, Katie. I can't just... leave."

Katie's grip tightens, her eyes fierce. "Charlie, please. I don't know what you're involved in, but it sounds dangerous. This guy—Silas—he's not playing games. He's using fear like it's a weapon."

I nod, because I can't deny it. And as much as I want to reassure her, a part of me knows she's right. But I can't back out now. Not when Dante's already tangled in this, not when I've risked so much just to get this far.

"I'll be careful," I say softly, a promise to both of us. "I'll talk to Dante. He needs to know about Silas and what he's trying to pull."

Katie's expression turns skeptical. "And what's Dante going to do about it? From the sound of things, he's part of this whole... mess." She pauses, frustration in her face. "Maybe he's part of the reason why you're in this mess."

The truth stings, and I look away, biting my lip. "Dante's... complicated. But he's not a threat to me. I trust him."

Katie's lips press into a thin line, but she doesn't argue. She knows I've made up my mind. Still, her gaze doesn't soften, and I can tell she's not convinced Dante is someone I should be relying on.

A heavy silence falls, weighted by everything left unsaid. Finally, Katie lets out a sigh and pulls me into a tight hug, her arms wrapping around me like a shield. "Just promise me you'll be careful," she murmurs, her voice cracking. "I can't lose you, Charlie. Not over something like this."

I nod against her shoulder, swallowing the lump in my throat. "I promise," I whisper, though the words feel hollow.

Because deep down, I know that being careful might not be enough.

Katie pulls back, searching my face, as if trying to memorize it. "Good. Then maybe you should get some sleep. You look like you've been through hell."

A faint smile tugs at my lips, though I'm sure it doesn't reach my eyes. "Feels like it, too."

She squeezes my hand once more before gathering her things and heading for the door. I lock it behind her, bolting the latch this time, as if that could keep out the shadows lurking beyond it.

Once she's gone, silence settles over the apartment like a thick fog, pressing down on me, amplifying every creak and sigh of the building. The room feels too quiet, too empty. The weight of Silas's words lingers, echoing in the corners of my mind.

"People might... misinterpret things."

The way he'd looked at me, as if I were already compromised, tangled in the web he'd spun. He knew more than he should. About Horizon City, about Dante, even about me. And now he was here, making veiled threats to remind me just how close he could get.

I reach for my phone, hesitating only a moment before dialing Dante's number. The call rings twice before he picks up.

"Charlie." His voice is a low, familiar rumble, laced with something close to relief. "I was just thinking about you."

The warmth in his tone is a stark contrast to the chill that clings to me. "Dante, we need to talk. Now."

His tone shifts, sharp with concern. "What's wrong?"

"Silas Kane," I say, keeping my voice steady. "He came here. To my apartment."

Silence stretches on the other end, but I can almost hear his tension building. "He came to your home?"

"Yes," I reply, my heart pounding as I replay the encounter in my mind. "He was... implying things. About Horizon, about you. He knows more than he should."

A low curse escapes him, and I can tell he's already calculating. "I'll be there in twenty minutes," he says, voice hard, unyielding. "Don't open the door for anyone else."

The line goes dead, and I clutch the phone tightly, as if it could somehow keep me safe. I glance around my apartment, every shadow suddenly feeling like a threat. I walk to the windows, checking the locks, pulling the blinds tighter. The faint glow of streetlights seeps in, casting an eerie glow across the room.

Minutes tick by, each one stretching longer than the last. I can't shake the feeling that Silas is still watching, lurking somewhere close by, waiting to make his next move. The calm, calculated way he'd spoken, the way he'd smiled as if he held all the cards—I can't let him have that power over me.

The knock on the door makes me jump, my pulse spiking as I whirl to face it. I peer through the peephole, relief flooding me as I see Dante's familiar figure standing on the other side.

I unlock the door quickly, and he steps inside, his gaze scanning the room with a sharp, assessing look. He closes the door behind him, his presence filling the room with steady, grounding energy.

"Are you alright?" he asks, his voice low but intense as he steps closer, his hand brushing my arm in comfort.

I nod, though my heart is still racing. "I... I don't know what he wants. But he's after something, Dante. Something involving us. He mentioned Horizon City. And you."

His jaw tightens, a flicker of something dangerous flashing in his eyes. "I know what he wants," he mutters, almost to himself. "And he won't stop until he gets it."

I look up at him, the weight of his words settling over me. "What are we going to do?"

Dante's gaze darkens, his expression hardening with resolve. "We're going to make sure he regrets ever coming near you. But first…" He pauses, his eyes locking onto mine with an intensity that leaves me breathless. "First, I need you to tell me everything he said. Every single word."

The gravity in his tone sends a chill down my spine, and I realize that whatever is happening, whatever Silas has set in motion, is far bigger than I could have imagined. And there's no going back.

12

DANTE

I watch Charlie's reflection fade from the side mirror until she's just a memory against the backdrop of darkening streets. A hollow feeling settles in her absence, something unsettling. I shift in my seat, trying to shake it, but the quiet drive only amplifies the heaviness circling my mind, thoughts I can't quite shake. I glance in the mirror once more, half-expecting to see her there, wishing I hadn't had to let her go.

I told her we should keep things professional, convinced it was for the best. But her scent, the warmth of her smile, the clever glint in her eyes—all these linger, pulling at my resolve, making me question if I've made a mistake. There's a weight here, a feeling I'm not used to: doubt. I remind myself of the risks, of all that could go wrong if I let my guard down around Charlie. But the reminder does little to settle me.

A red light forces me to a stop, the silence pressing in. I tap my fingers on the steering wheel, wondering if Charlie feels the same uncertainty I do. Before I lose myself in those thoughts, my phone rings, shattering the quiet.

"Boss," Gabe's voice crackles through the speakers.

"Gabe. What's the status with our guest?" I ask, keeping my tone neutral. The man we picked up earlier—one of Lorenzo's men—has been left tied up in the basement. I'm hoping silence has worn down his resolve.

"He's behaving himself," Gabe replies, his voice carrying a dry amusement. "Not causing any trouble."

"Good to hear. I might stop by later."

"He misses you," Gabe adds, hinting that the man could use a little motivation. It's a subtle cue—our way of keeping things under wraps in case the call isn't secure.

"I miss him too," I reply, mirroring Gabe's tone.

We exchange a few more words before Gabe adds, almost as an afterthought, "Oh, and your uncles send their regards. They say they miss you."

My jaw tightens. Gabe's reminder about the family meeting hits with familiar dread. "Of course they do," I mutter.

The call ends, and I toss my phone onto the passenger seat, my earlier satisfaction fading, replaced by a weight I can't ignore. Family meetings rarely bring good news.

As I pull up to the Romano estate, the building's grandeur looms large, casting sharp shadows under the dim lights. It's always been a fortress, a symbol of power, but tonight, it feels closer to a cage. I park and take a breath, gripping the steering wheel a moment longer before stepping out.

Nicolai, the butler, appears at the door as I approach, his face lined with tension. "Your uncles are in the study, sir."

"Let me guess—helping themselves to the bourbon?" I ask, my voice carrying a touch of irritation.

He dips his head apologetically. "I couldn't stop them,

sir. But I managed to put aside the new bottles you wanted to save."

I chuckle, clapping him on the shoulder. "Good man."

The walk to the study feels longer than usual, the familiar path now thick with tension. My fingers tap against my keys, restless. Thoughts of Charlie keep pulling at me—her reaction when I suggested boundaries. She didn't bother hiding her displeasure, and part of me wonders if I'll ever see that spark again.

I pause outside the study door, gathering myself. Voices hum beyond it, low and tense.

When I enter, all conversation halts. The study is vast, designed to intimidate, its walls lined with dark wood and a massive desk at the far end. Normally, that desk is mine, but tonight, Uncle Stefano has claimed it, sitting there like he's the one in charge. The other four uncles are arrayed in armchairs facing the desk, turning to glance my way.

"If it isn't the favored son," one of them mutters.

I ignore the jab, shutting the door with deliberate calm. Stefano's choice of seat is a power play, a way to unbalance me. But I know better than to let it show.

"Hello, Uncle Stef," I say smoothly, knowing he hates the nickname. I catch his slight frown; good.

"Making yourselves comfortable, I see." I head to the bar, noting the half-empty bourbon bottle—one I'd been saving—sitting before Uncle Angelo. "Nice choice," I remark, nodding toward it. Angelo raises his glass, smirking.

I pour myself a drink and down it in one smooth motion, letting the burn settle my nerves. Turning back, I give them a casual smile. "Shall we get to business?"

"We called this meeting," Stefano snaps, annoyance lacing his tone.

I shrug, sinking onto a stool by the bar. "Well, I'm here now. What's so pressing?"

Stefano's expression hardens, and I catch a brief look of surprise from the others. They're not used to seeing me relaxed, immune to their attempts to rile me. Uncle Angelo throws back another drink, apparently unaware—or indifferent—to Stefano's simmering rage.

In many ways, my uncles are a divided front. Stefano and Mateo cling to tradition, valuing control above all else. Angelo and Alessandro, meanwhile, are willing to bend the rules, unafraid to challenge convention. Then there's Emiliano, who generally follows Stefano's lead, but even he has moments of independence.

I watch as each subtly shifts to face me, breaking the formation they'd set up. It's a small win, but one I savor.

Angelo's grin widens, amusement lighting his eyes. "He's so proud of this project of his."

I match his grin with a shrug. "If it goes as planned, we'll all have reason to be proud."

Stefano's voice slices through the room like a blade. "The Horizon City Project. We've heard a lot about it. We're here to discuss the consequences."

My focus sharpens. Horizon City has been months in the making, the venture that could secure our future foothold in the city. But I wasn't expecting them to confront me over it.

Mateo leans forward, his tone measured. "We've received information that could threaten the project."

I keep my expression neutral, but questions race through my mind. What could they possibly know that I don't? They rarely leave Italy, preferring the safety of their villas.

"What information?" My voice is steady, controlled.

Stefano's eyes narrow, scrutinizing my reaction. "Lorenzo," he says. "We're hearing that he's making significant moves. Aggressive moves. We're advising you to ease up, avoid drawing unwanted attention."

A scoff almost escapes me. Lorenzo's nothing more than a stubborn thorn, a rival too mired in outdated tactics to truly pose a threat. But he's persistent, and apparently, enough to worry my uncles.

"We need momentum to keep the capital flowing," I reply evenly. "And that requires action."

Emiliano speaks up, voice cautious. "If the money's not there, maybe it's best to put the project on hold."

"Horizon City isn't just a project," I say firmly. "It's the first step in a larger expansion. Once we're in, we'll control markets, front legitimate businesses that will grow our influence. It's a gateway to our future."

Alessandro's interest flickers, but Stefano remains unyielding. He sighs, long and pointed. "Grand ambitions," he mutters. "Like Icarus, bound to fly too high and fall."

I keep my gaze steady, swallowing my irritation. "With respect, Uncle, risk is often necessary for growth."

Stefano's glare sharpens. "Lorenzo has ties in Italy. Dangerous ones. If he feels threatened, he won't hesitate to retaliate."

A heavy silence fills the room, the weight of his words pressing down. I've always known Lorenzo's connections, but hearing my uncles acknowledge the danger hits harder.

After a beat, I nod. "I'll keep that in mind."

Stefano's expression tightens, sensing my reluctance. "Good. It's time you start listening to those with experience."

Mateo's tone softens. "We want what's best for the family, Dante. This project could bring success, but it's also a risk. Tread carefully."

"Understood," I reply, though my mind churns. Caution is one thing, but delay could cost us everything.

I lean forward, shifting the atmosphere. "If that's all, shall we move to dinner? I'm sure Nicolai has prepared something special."

They murmur reluctant agreement as I rise, feeling their eyes on me, a mixture of pride and frustration simmering beneath their gazes. As I head for the door, conflicting thoughts weigh heavily. Family, loyalty, power—each pulling in different directions.

But there's one thing I won't sacrifice: Horizon City. This project is everything I've worked for, the legacy I intend to build, something truly mine.

And despite their warnings, I know some risks are worth taking.

I close the study door behind me, heading toward the kitchen. My uncles' words echo in my mind, their warning about Lorenzo a barely visible fissure that could widen at any moment. But I can't turn back now. This project carries too much weight—for the family, for me.

Rounding the corner, I spot Nicolai overseeing dinner preparations. I gesture, and he steps over, sensing the gravity in my expression.

"Ensure we're undisturbed tonight," I instruct. "No interruptions, no calls getting through."

He nods. "Understood, sir. Dinner will be served shortly."

I nod back, my mind already elsewhere, when my phone buzzes. I glance down, irritation flickering until I see the name. Charlie.

Surprise tempers the tension knotting inside. I wasn't expecting her to call, not after our last conversation, not after the boundaries I insisted on.

"Charlie?" I answer, striving for an unaffected tone.

There's a pause, a hesitation on the other end that sets my instincts on high alert. "Dante, I... I had a visitor today." Her voice is tense, anger mingling with something vulnerable. "Silas Kane showed up. At my apartment."

My grip tightens on the phone, my pulse quickening. Silas has crossed a line—a calculated move meant to unsettle her, to send a message. His jaw clenches. "Are you safe?"

"For now," she replies, her voice steadier. "But he implied... he's watching. And it felt more like a threat than a warning."

I close my eyes briefly, anger hardening into a razor-sharp resolve. "I'm coming over."

"Dante—"

"No. I'll be there in twenty minutes. Lock everything until I arrive."

A resigned sigh drifts through the line. "Alright."

As I slip my phone back into my pocket, the simmering rage solidifies into cold determination. Silas has made a grave mistake, one I won't overlook. I'll play the game, but I'll be the one making the final move.

With one last look toward the dining room, I stride back to my car, a promise echoing in my mind: Silas Kane will regret ever coming near her.

13

CHARLIE

The door clicks shut behind Silas Kane, and the silence in my apartment crashes down like a wave. For a moment, I'm frozen, my heart pounding in the aftermath of his visit. The way he spoke, the threats laced into his charm—it's enough to make me feel as if the walls are closing in.

"Are you okay?" Katie's voice is soft, her concern tangible as she sits beside me on the couch.

I shake my head, trying to ground myself. "I don't know," I admit. "That man... Silas. He's dangerous."

Katie's brows knit together, her gaze flicking toward the locked door. "Do you think he's serious about what he said?"

I nod slowly, the weight of his threats sinking in. "Absolutely."

Katie reaches for my hand, squeezing it tightly. "You need to tell someone about this. You can't face this alone, Charlie. What about Dante?"

The mention of his name sends a shiver through me, a mix of fear and longing. Dante. The thought of him makes me feel safe, even now, but I also know the storm it might unleash if I bring this to him.

"I'll think about it," I say finally, though even as I speak, I know I don't have a choice. I have to tell him.

LATER THAT EVENING, I find myself standing in front of Dante's building, my fingers hovering over my phone. The message I need to send feels heavy in my hands, like a weight I'm not ready to carry.

Before I can overthink it, I press the call button.

"Charlie." His voice is steady, calm, but there's a note of something warmer underneath.

"I need to see you," I say, my voice firmer than I feel.

There's a pause, then, "Come up."

WHEN I STEP into his penthouse, the space feels different tonight—quieter, darker, as if it's holding its breath. Dante stands by the window, his silhouette framed by the city lights. He turns as I enter, his gaze immediately locking onto mine.

"What happened?" he asks, his voice low and controlled.

I hesitate, the words catching in my throat. But then he crosses the room, his presence grounding me, and I find the courage to speak. "Silas Kane came to my apartment tonight."

His expression darkens instantly, his jaw tightening. "What did he want?"

"He... he tried to bribe me," I admit. "He wanted information about you, about your business. And when I said no..." I trail off, unable to finish.

Dante's eyes narrow, his hands clenching at his sides. "He threatened you?"

"Yes." The word slips out before I can stop it.

For a moment, he's silent, the tension in the room palpable. Then, with a deliberate motion, he reaches for his phone, his fingers already dialing.

"No," I say quickly, stepping closer. "Don't. I didn't come here to escalate this. I just... I thought you should know."

His gaze softens slightly as he looks at me, the fire in his eyes dimming just enough to let something else through. "Charlie, you don't have to handle this alone. You shouldn't have to."

The warmth of his body behind me is intoxicating. His hands settle on my hips, steadying me as the platform sways. Each small movement brings us closer, until I can feel the solid wall of his chest against my back.

My breath catches as his thumb traces small circles on my hip. The touch is innocent enough, but it sends shivers down my spine. When I glance up at him, his eyes are dark with barely restrained desire.

"Charlie," he breathes, and my name sounds like a prayer on his lips.

I turn in his arms, drawn by some magnetic force I can't resist. His hand comes up to cup my face, and time seems to stop. For a moment, we're suspended in this fragile space between friendship and something more.

Then his mouth finds mine, and the world falls away. The kiss is gentle at first, almost reverent, but quickly grows heated as moments of denial crumble between us.

. . .

After a long silence, he speaks again, his voice softer this time. "I won't let anything happen to you."

I nod, the sincerity in his tone calming some of the fear still gripping me. "Thank you."

Dante moves to the couch, gesturing for me to sit beside him. "Tell me everything. Every detail."

I recount Silas's visit, the way he spoke, the way he looked at Katie, every word and action that set me on edge. Dante listens intently, his jaw tightening with each sentence.

When I finish, he leans back, his gaze fixed on the cityscape outside. "Silas has been pushing boundaries for months," he says finally. "But coming to you—threatening you—was his biggest mistake."

"What are you going to do?" I ask, my voice barely above a whisper.

His gaze shifts to mine, and for a moment, the intensity there makes it hard to breathe. "I'm going to make sure he never comes near you again."

The night stretches on, the conversation turning quieter as the adrenaline fades. At some point, I find myself leaning against the couch cushions, my body heavy with exhaustion.

"You should stay here tonight," Dante says suddenly, breaking the silence.

I glance up, startled. "What?"

"It's safer," he explains, his tone leaving no room for argument. "I can't guarantee Kane won't try something else. Not yet."

The logical part of me knows he's right, but the idea of staying here, in his space, so close to him—it's overwhelming. Still, I nod. "Okay."

Dante leads me down the hallway to the guest room, his hand resting protectively on my lower back. The touch sends warmth through me despite my exhaustion.

"You'll be safe here," he says softly, opening the door. The room is elegant but minimalist, clearly rarely used.

As I step inside, his hand lingers. I turn to face him, and the intensity in his gaze makes my breath catch. Without thinking, I reach for him, needing his steadying presence.

He pulls me close, one hand cupping my face while the other wraps around my waist. The kiss is gentle at first, almost hesitant, before deepening with shared need. I press closer, losing myself in his warmth, his strength.

When we break apart, he rests his forehead against mine. "Get some rest," he whispers, though his arms tighten around me. "I'll be right down the hall if you need anything."

HOURS LATER, the lights are dim, the penthouse wrapped in a comforting darkness. I lie on the couch, staring at the ceiling, but sleep refuses to come. The events of the day play on a loop in my mind, each moment sharper than the last.

"Can't sleep?" Dante's voice breaks the silence, and I glance up to see him standing in the doorway.

I shake my head. "Not really."

He crosses the room, sitting on the edge of the couch. "Do you want to talk about it?"

The question surprises me, his tone more open than I've ever heard it. "I don't know," I admit. "It's just... a lot."

He nods, his expression thoughtful. "You've been handling it well. Better than most would."

His words catch me off guard, the sincerity in them warming something deep inside me. "Thanks," I say softly.

For a moment, the darkness wraps around us, the only

sound the faint hum of the city below. Then, almost without thinking, I reach out, my fingers brushing against his.

The contact is brief, but it feels like a spark, lighting something between us. He looks down at our hands, then back at me, his expression unreadable.

"Charlie..." His voice is low, almost hesitant.

I swallow hard, unsure of what to say. But before I can respond, he shifts closer, his hand brushing against mine again, this time deliberate.

His fingers intertwine with mine as he moves closer. The darkness feels intimate, wrapping around us like a cocoon. My heart pounds as his other hand traces my cheek.

"Charlie," he breathes, before capturing my lips with his. The kiss is tender but urgent, filled with everything we haven't said. I arch into him, my fingers gripping his shirt.

He pulls me into his lap, and I straddle him, deepening the kiss. His hands roam my back as I press against him, drawing a low groan from his throat.

"Stay with me," he murmurs against my neck, sending shivers down my spine. "Not just tonight."

"Yes," I whisper, melting into his touch as his lips find mine again.

WHEN MORNING COMES, the heaviness in my chest has lessened, replaced by a quiet determination. Silas Kane may have brought his threats to my doorstep, but he won't win. Not with Dante by my side.

And as I glance over at him, still seated by the window, his gaze sharp and unwavering, I know one thing for certain —this fight is just beginning.

14

DANTE

The server's question barely registers as I wave him off. "No, that'll be all." I watch him bow slightly before he steps away.

From my corner seat, my gaze drifts over the cobblestone street outside. Upscale boutiques and chic cafés line the road, their window displays curated to pull in passersby. Here, inside the quiet lounge, the city's sounds are a softened hum, distant and faint, muted by the room's understated elegance. Velvet chairs and polished tables bask in the warm glow of chandeliers, creating a refined space that speaks of sophistication and restraint.

This isn't my usual spot for a business meeting, but that's intentional. Recently, my office has felt less like a workspace and more like a constant reminder of Charlie. Thoughts of her in that space linger far too long, conjuring images of her pressed against my desk, her mouth claiming mine. The woman has embedded herself under my skin. I need distance, control.

And here we are—neutral ground.

The rhythmic click of heels catches my attention, and I

glance toward the entrance. There she is, Charlotte Harrison, my sharp-mouthed attorney, moving toward me. She's wearing a silk blouse that clings just right, paired with a tailored skirt that hugs her every movement. Her hair is swept up, exposing her neck, and she meets my gaze with a polite, practiced smile—a smile I now know she reserves for clients.

I hate it.

She slips into the booth with practiced grace, places her bag beside her, and checks her watch before meeting my eyes. "I hope I didn't keep you waiting," she says, the smile still plastered on her face as she tucks a stray strand behind her ear. She does this when she's feeling uncertain, I realize.

Why am I noticing these things?

My face remains impassive, my tone cold. "Not at all. I just got here."

"Oh... good." Her smile falters slightly. She pulls out a notepad and file, flipping through them with brisk efficiency. Silence settles between us as she organizes her notes, and I can't stop my gaze from tracing the line of her neck, where my lips tasted her skin not long ago. Heat flashes through me, unbidden, and I quickly look away, schooling my face back to impassivity just as she looks up.

"After our last meeting, I reviewed a few details on the Horizon project," she begins, sliding a file toward me, her voice clipped and focused.

I flip open the file, scanning her notes. As usual, her work is thorough, and her attention to detail is impeccable. I'm about to turn the page when she suddenly asks, "How well do you know them?"

"Huh?" I glance up, surprised.

"The Horizon City partners," she clarifies, her tone firm. "How well do you know them?"

I shrug. "As much as I need to, I suppose."

She doesn't look satisfied. "What about Silas Kane?"

A slight pause. "What about him?"

"I'm asking how well you know him, Mr. Romano." A hint of impatience creeps into her voice, unusual for Charlie.

"I'm looking to do business, not make friends." My tone sharpens. "Why all the questions?"

Charlie rolls her eyes, letting her professional mask slip a bit. "Have you worked with him before? Is he trustworthy?"

I lean forward, hands resting on the small table between us. "In business, trust is a luxury. The kind that gets you burned. You do your part, and you watch your back."

She takes a deep breath, her gaze steady. "I understand, Mr. Romano. But you saw his reaction in the last meeting. He doesn't strike me as a man who'll take defeat lying down."

The way she says my name, cold and formal, feels wrong. But isn't this what I wanted? Keep things professional. No distractions.

"You're right," I say, keeping my tone even. "He won't. But don't worry. My team's handling it." I watch her closely. "Unless there's something you want to tell me?"

Her gaze drops, fixed on the table. Interesting. Charlie never avoids eye contact. Even when we're at each other's throats, she holds my gaze. Something's different.

"Is there something I should know?" I press, waiting for her to look up.

When she does, she looks torn, as if weighing her words. Then she sighs, the moment of openness closing as she mutters, "Nothing. I just have a bad feeling about Silas Kane."

I nod, disappointed. She's hiding something—something important. What does she know?

I take a slow sip of my drink as she continues her points. I listen half-heartedly, my attention drifting. That's when I spot him—a man in a dark suit seated in the far corner, partially obscured by the high-backed chair. His posture is too deliberate, too still, and I catch his gaze dart up from a book he's pretending to read.

I turn back to Charlie, but my senses are on high alert. This man isn't just a patron.

"Sorry, I missed that. Could you repeat it?" I say, shifting slightly to catch another glimpse of the stranger.

The man's posture is too calculated. He sits as if he's been waiting for hours, one arm draped casually over his chair, head tilted, book abandoned. A thread of unease coils in my gut as I track him out of the corner of my eye.

Charlie's voice pulls me back. "I said we need to take Kane's potential reaction seriously." Her tone is steady, but I can sense the tension beneath her words.

I glance away from the window, hiding my nerves. An idea strikes, and I decide to act on it. "What are you doing after this?"

She blinks, surprised. "I'm sorry?"

"Are you free after this?"

Her brow furrows. "Yes, but... why?"

A faint smile tugs at my lips. "I've got tickets to a play this afternoon. Thought you might like to join me."

She stares at me. "A play? Since when do you care about theater?"

"There's a lot you don't know about me." My eyes linger on hers, daring her to question me. "So, are you coming or not?"

She hesitates, clearly off balance. "This feels... strange. You're usually not this spontaneous."

I chuckle, keeping an eye on the man across the room. He's watching us closely, his head lifting slightly at our exchange. I need to move. "Consider it team building," I say, flashing her a pointed look. "Come on, we're not enemies, right?"

She studies me, a mix of confusion and reluctance in her gaze. Finally, she nods. "Alright. A play. Fine."

I stand, throwing a nod at the server as he clears our table. I catch a glimpse of the stranger, who's now leaning forward, watching us with open interest. He discards the book, rising as we head for the exit.

Yup. Definitely tailing us.

Outside, I hold open the car door for Charlie, then slip into the driver's seat, pulling out my phone as I start the engine. Quickly, I text Gabe: Get me two tickets to a play— VIP. And look into something for me.

I pull away from the curb, keeping an eye on the rearview mirror. The stranger is nowhere to be seen, and I ease up on the gas as we head toward the theater.

Beside me, Charlie shifts, her gaze sharp. "You seem tense. Everything okay?"

I consider telling her but decide against it. No need to worry her. "Just work. Waiting on some information from Gabe," I reply, the lie easy.

She's quiet for a moment, then asks, "Is this about Horizon City?"

I shake my head. "No, unrelated business."

I glance back in the mirror, and this time, I spot him—a dark sedan several cars behind us, keeping pace. My grip tightens, but I force myself to stay calm, flashing Charlie a reassuring smile. "We're fine."

Her gaze lingers, but she drops the topic. "Alright."

My phone pings just as we hit a red light. Gabe: Check your email, boss.

I quickly open my email at the light, scanning the ticket confirmation Gabe sent—VIP with a plus one. Perfect.

Charlie catches my slight smile. "Gabe?"

I meet her eyes, letting the smile linger. "Yes, it's Gabe."

She smiles back, and for a moment, I let myself relax. Her hand finds mine, fitting perfectly, as if it belongs there. The earlier tension eases as we near the theater.

Balboa Park is packed when we arrive. After a few laps, I find a parking spot close enough to keep an eye out. I hold out my hand to help Charlie from the car, and she hesitates, but she doesn't let go as we walk to the entrance.

"You've always been a fan of the classics?" she asks, breaking the silence.

I nod, keeping my tone light. "Always had a soft spot for timeless stories. Shakespeare, especially."

Her brows lift in surprise. "Really? I wouldn't have guessed."

I send her a sidelong glance. "There's a lot you don't know about me, Charlotte."

She laughs, a rare, unguarded sound. "Touché, Mr. Romano."

As we enter the theater, I reluctantly release her hand. A small frown crosses her face, but she doesn't say anything. Before she can step away, I reach for her waist, drawing her close. Her eyes widen, cheeks coloring, but she doesn't pull away.

"What are you doing?" she breathes, voice unsteady.

"Come on... unless you have one of these." I hold up my phone, displaying our tickets.

She flushes but nods. "Oh... alright."

We move toward the entrance, my hand on her waist as we pass the ticket check. "Enjoy the show," the usher says, and we step into the opulent theater.

The VIP section is set in intimate clusters, allowing for privacy. The faint scent of truffle oil and fresh pastries lingers in the air, a tempting reminder of the perks.

Beside me, Charlie's eyes widen. "This is incredible," she whispers, excitement lighting her face as she takes in the view. "Thank you, Dante."

We settle into our seats, and more than once, her hand finds my arm as she gasps or whispers during the play, her reactions genuine and unguarded. I can't help but be drawn in.

Halfway through, my attention sharpens. A familiar figure slips into the back—the same man from the lounge, watching us with a subtle challenge in his gaze.

I glance at Charlie, absorbed in the scene, and force myself to stay calm. Whatever he's here for, he won't get near her.

As we leave, I keep Charlie close, unable to shake the feeling of being watched. The man is nowhere in sight, but I feel his presence, like a shadow lurking just out of reach.

Charlie squeezes my hand. "Thanks for today," she says softly, her eyes warm.

Before I can respond, a voice interrupts.

"Oh, my goodness, it's you!" A man grabs her arm, his touch overly familiar.

I turn slowly, his hand on her sparking a cold fury. One thing is clear as I stare him down.

Hell is about to break loose.

15

CHARLIE

Dante's face is a thundercloud, his dark eyes fixed on the man gripping my arm. The tension crackles between them like a live wire, dangerous and electric.

The stranger, oblivious to the storm brewing, smirks at me. But his arrogance falters when Dante steps closer, his presence looming, every inch of him radiating menace.

"Let go," Dante growls, his voice low and lethal.

The stranger glances between us, clearly weighing his options. Whatever he sees in Dante's expression makes him pale. He releases my arm like it's burned him, raising his hands in mock surrender. "I didn't mean any harm. Just a misunderstanding," he stammers before turning and walking away, his steps quick and unsteady.

Dante doesn't move, his gaze following the man until he disappears through the door. His fists are clenched, his jaw tight, and his entire body hums with restrained fury.

"Dante," I say softly, hoping to pull him back. But part of me is captivated by this side of him—the raw, unapologetic protectiveness.

His head snaps toward me, his expression hard, though his eyes soften slightly when they meet mine. "Are you okay?"

"I'm fine," I say, my voice steady despite the flutter in my chest. The way he's looking at me now, as if ensuring every part of me is untouched, safe—it stirs something deep and thrilling.

He exhales sharply, the tension in his shoulders easing just a fraction. "No one touches you like that," he mutters, his voice still laced with anger.

I reach for his arm, squeezing gently. "It's over. Let it go."

Dante grunts, his gaze dropping to my hand on his arm. I can feel the heat of his skin through his sleeve, the coiled energy still radiating off him.

"Come with me," he says abruptly, his tone brooking no argument.

"Where?"

"Somewhere private," he replies, his hand lightly brushing the small of my back as he guides me out of the room.

DANTE LEADS me to a secluded lounge tucked away in the back of the venue. The staff member at the entrance nods and steps aside, clearly recognizing him. As the door closes behind us, the noise of the world fades, replaced by a cocoon of soft lighting and plush furnishings.

The intimacy of the space catches me off guard. It feels like we've stepped into another world, one where the rules are different.

"Drink?" Dante asks, moving to a bar in the corner.

"No, thank you," I reply, settling onto the couch. The

upholstery cradles me, its softness at odds with the storm still lingering in Dante's expression.

He pours himself a drink and sinks into the seat beside me, his movements controlled but tense. The silence between us is heavy, charged with unspoken words.

"You looked ready to start a fight back there," I tease lightly, hoping to lighten the mood.

His eyes meet mine, dark and intense. "No one disrespects you," he says firmly, his voice a low rumble.

The conviction in his tone sends a shiver through me, and I can't help but feel a rush of gratitude mixed with something deeper, something more dangerous.

His thumb traces my cheek as he leans closer, the protective fury from earlier transforming into something more intimate. I tilt my face up, drawn by the intensity in his gaze.

"Charlie," he breathes, before closing the distance between us. The kiss is fierce yet tender, a perfect reflection of his earlier protectiveness. His arms wrap around me, pulling me flush against him as I respond with equal fervor.

One hand tangles in my hair while the other presses firmly against my lower back. I arch into him, earning a low growl that sends shivers down my spine. His lips trail down my neck, and I gasp at the sensation.

"Dante," I whisper, clinging to his shoulders as he reclaims my mouth. The kiss deepens, speaking of possession and protection in equal measure.

DANTE'S HAND FINDS MINE, his fingers brushing over my knuckles. The touch is light, almost hesitant, but it sends sparks skittering across my skin.

"Charlie," he murmurs, his voice softer now.

"Yes?"

His gaze holds mine, unguarded for the first time tonight. "I can't promise to keep you out of danger. But I can promise I'll do everything in my power to protect you."

The vulnerability in his words catches me off guard. For a moment, I see beneath the layers of control and power to the man underneath.

"I know," I reply, my voice barely above a whisper.

The silence stretches between us, heavy with everything we're not saying. I find myself leaning closer, drawn to the warmth of his presence. His hand moves to my cheek, his touch firm but gentle, and I let my eyes drift shut as he pulls me into a kiss.

The kiss grows hungrier, more demanding. His hands frame my face as he pulls me closer, and I melt into him completely. Each touch, each breath between us speaks of need barely contained.

I straddle his lap, pressing against him as his hands roam my back. His lips trace a burning path down my throat, drawing a soft moan from me. When he finds that sensitive spot behind my ear, my fingers dig into his shoulders.

"Charlie," he groans, pulling back just enough to meet my gaze. The raw desire in his eyes matches the fire coursing through my veins. His thumb traces my bottom lip as we catch our breath.

The next kiss is slower but no less intense, filled with all the words we can't say. His touch promises protection, possession, devotion - everything I never knew I needed until him.

. . .

WHEN WE FINALLY PULL APART, the room feels different, as if the air itself has shifted. Dante leans back, his expression softer but still guarded.

"You're safe with me," he says quietly, as if reassuring himself as much as me.

I nod, feeling the truth of his words even as a flicker of doubt lingers. Dante's world is dangerous, and his protectiveness is both a comfort and a reminder of the risks.

THE DRIVE HOME IS QUIET, the tension between us lingering in the charged silence. I can't help but steal glances at him, his profile sharp against the glow of the dashboard lights.

"So... are we dating now?" I ask lightly, hoping to break the tension.

His hands tighten on the wheel, his expression unreadable. The pause stretches, and I feel my chest tighten with unease.

"Dante?"

"We're not," he says finally, his tone blunt.

The words hit like a blow, cold and final. I stare at him, trying to process the abrupt shift.

"What do you mean?"

He doesn't look at me, his focus fixed on the road. "We're not together. This isn't a relationship."

I feel my stomach twist, a mix of anger and hurt bubbling to the surface. "But what about tonight? What about everything we've been through?"

He exhales sharply, his jaw tightening. "Tonight doesn't change anything. It can't."

The finality in his voice leaves no room for argument. I turn away, staring out the window as the city blurs past, my chest aching with a mix of rejection and confusion.

When we arrive at my building, I step out of the car without a word. The cold night air bites at my skin as I make my way inside, the echo of his words replaying in my mind.

As soon as I shut the door to my apartment, the tears come, hot and unrelenting. I sink onto the couch, the weight of everything crashing down at once.

The man who had made me feel protected, cherished even, had just reminded me how fragile those moments were.

THE NEXT MORNING, I wake with swollen eyes and an ache in my chest that refuses to fade. As I stumble to the bathroom, a wave of nausea hits me, and I clutch the sink, waiting for it to pass.

Something feels off, and a thread of unease weaves through me as I try to piece it together.

Later that day, as I sit across from the doctor, her smile is kind but her words shatter my world.

"Congratulations. You're pregnant."

16

DANTE

The room is silent, held in the stillness of ticking thought. The clock ticks steadily, filling the space with a quiet rhythm that mirrors the unspoken tension between us. I sit at my desk, the weight of recent events pressing against my temples. Across from me, Gabe leans forward, his gaze locked on me, heavy with something unsaid.

I glance at the clock. We've been sitting like this for nearly an hour, dissecting the intricate workings of the business, detail by detail, each decision laden with consequence. There are so many moving parts it's hard to keep track, but Gabe's meticulous mind keeps everything steady. His presence grounds me, holding me back from the darker thoughts clawing at my mind.

There's a lull in the conversation as we retreat into our thoughts. The silence stretches between us, thick and tense, like the calm before a storm. My fingers tap a rhythm against the desk, the nervous energy in me finding release in this small, repetitive motion.

Gabe's gaze flickers to my hand, then back to my face. I

catch the look, and something in it stirs me to speak. "The other day..." I begin, my voice rough in the quiet. Gabe's eyes sharpen, and I look down, tracing the lines in my palm. "When we were at the theater, just as we were leaving... a man grabbed Charlie."

"You told me this," Gabe says, his brows drawing together. His tone is cautious, as if he senses I haven't told him everything.

"Yes, but there was something I left out." I look up, meeting his eyes. "The man had a tattoo on his neck. A fanged lizard."

Gabe's reaction is immediate. He leans back, his mouth tightening, and his eyes dart around the room as if expecting the man to materialize. "Are you certain?" he asks, his voice low.

I nod, a pang of unease stirring inside me again. "I saw it clearly."

"Do you think..." Gabe hesitates, then presses on. "Do you think Lorenzo's trying to send a message?"

I shrug, though the encounter left me rattled. That tattoo—it marked the man as part of Lorenzo's crew, a silent emblem of his reach, a reminder of the threat that shadows me even in moments meant for peace. My mind reels back to that second, the realization that something darker lurked beneath the surface, ready to strike.

"What did Charlie think?" Gabe's voice breaks through my thoughts.

"I didn't tell her," I admit, feeling the weight of that choice settle over me.

Gabe's expression remains neutral, though there's something probing in his silence. His nod isn't one of agreement but of acknowledgment, a silent witness to my decision. I wonder what he thinks of my choice. I still don't know if it was the right one.

"Should I have?" I finally ask, frustration simmering in my voice.

He regards me steadily, and his silence stretches longer than I expected. "I don't know," he says at last. "It might've been a good idea to tell her... or it might've just made things worse. Sometimes, information is a weapon. Other times, it's a burden." He shrugs.

I sigh, running a hand over my face. This indecision gnaws at me, tightening around my chest. "I just... I worry she's a target. Or that she'll become one."

Gabe considers this, his expression thoughtful. "I don't think so," he says finally, his voice steady.

I blink, caught off guard. "You don't?"

He shakes his head slowly. "She's outside of all this." He gestures broadly, taking in the room, the business, and the criminal threads woven into it all. "She's a lawyer, with no direct ties to the organization. I doubt Lorenzo would risk targeting someone that far removed."

"You think that's enough to keep her safe?" There's a flicker of hope in my chest, tentative and unsteady.

Gabe nods, though there's a shadow of doubt in his eyes. "I think it's likely. Lorenzo's ruthless, sure—but he's also strategic. Charlie isn't directly involved; he gains nothing from going after her."

I want to believe him. I want to cling to that hope. But a gnawing doubt lingers. Lorenzo is ruthless. Strategic, yes—but ruthless all the same. A man like him doesn't always need a reason.

"I don't know, Gabe," I murmur, the worry pressing heavy on my mind.

Gabe's response is a silent shrug. It's the same dilemma,

circling endlessly, eroding my nerves. My pen taps against the desk in a steady rhythm, an anchor as I try to steady my thoughts.

Finally, I push the thought aside and straighten in my seat. "We can't do anything about Lorenzo right now," I say, forcing myself to focus. "What we can control is our distribution. Let's make sure our products reach the right channels." My voice comes out firm, steady, a contrast to the turmoil within.

Gabe nods, rising to his feet with a sense of purpose. "I'll get going, boss," he says, his tone carrying the loyalty that has been my constant.

As he leaves, the silence in the room settles over me once more, thick and unyielding. My mind drifts back to the conversation with my uncle just days ago. He warned me, urged caution, advised abandoning my plans to avoid Lorenzo's wrath. They even mentioned that Lorenzo has backing from the Mafia in Italy.

Their concern is valid, but I can't stop now. I've come too far to retreat.

My thoughts hold me hostage, ambition and caution locked in a brutal clash within the quiet of the office. The pen's rhythmic tapping fills the room, a reminder of the relentless decisions that shape this life.

A buzz from my phone jolts me back to the present. I glance at the screen—a reminder for my meeting with Charlie. We're supposed to review the Horizon City project, finalizing the legal details she's been working on.

My heart kicks up at the thought of seeing her, but the memory of our last encounter dims that spark. I don't know what to expect. After how things ended, I doubt she's thrilled to see me.

Sighing, I push myself to my feet, stretching out the

tension that's settled into my shoulders. The office feels like it holds its breath as I leave, closing the door quietly behind me.

Outside, David Two waits beside the car, leaning casually against it. He straightens as I approach, nodding in acknowledgment. "Ready, sir?"

I nod, my mind thick with anticipation and a reluctant curiosity about the upcoming meeting.

The ride feels short, or maybe I'm too lost in thought to notice. We pull up to the office, and David gives me a nod as I step out. Inside, Stephanie meets me, her expression serious as she glances at her watch.

"She's already here, waiting in Conference Room B," she whispers.

I glance at my own watch, frowning. "Am I late?" My question comes out sharper than I intended.

Stephanie shakes her head, her expression softening. "No, she's just... prompt. Doesn't waste time."

She studies me for a moment, her gaze curious. "Are you okay, boss? You seem... off."

I force a smile, hoping to dispel the unease twisting inside me. "I'm fine."

The hallway feels too quiet as I make my way to the conference room, my mind a storm of conflicting emotions. Stephanie's words echo in my head—"off." Maybe I am. Maybe it's the uncertainty gnawing away inside me, or maybe it's something I don't want to name.

Charlie looks up as I enter, her expression unreadable. She glances at her watch, then back at her notes. I swallow down a flare of irritation—I'm not late.

"Good afternoon, Mr. Romano," she says, her tone polite but distant.

"Afternoon, Charlie," I reply, trying to catch her gaze, but she doesn't look up.

She dives into the documents in front of her, all business. "These are the city's permits, and the requirements we'll need to meet for approval," she says, passing me a stack of papers. "It's not much, but it's critical for Horizon City."

I glance at the pages, familiar with most of the codes, though some of the finer details are new to me. The project's sheer scale demands extra caution.

"Please go through them thoroughly," she adds, eyes fixed on her laptop. "Some of these might be new to you, and they'll prove important later."

I hold the paper, feeling the cool detachment in her tone. Her professionalism is impressive, yet there's a wall between us—a barrier that feels nearly impossible to breach. She's keeping her distance, every gesture, every clipped word reinforcing it.

"Alright," I reply, trying to focus on the document, though my attention keeps straying to her. Her focus is unwavering, her posture rigid, almost painfully formal.

The silence stretches between us, broken only by the soft tapping of her keys. I glance at her, taking in the quiet intensity she exudes, the calm resolve that clashes with the turmoil brewing inside me.

Clearing my throat, I hand back the first document. Without looking, Charlie reaches for the next set of papers, her gaze never leaving her screen.

"If you're done with that, here's the next set," she says coolly, passing it over.

Her indifference stings, yet I can't look away. Her perfume lingers in the air, faint but maddeningly familiar. My focus slips, drawn to her despite myself. Since walking into the room, an unspoken tension has settled over us, pressing on my chest, unyielding.

The silence grows heavier, thick with words unspoken. Finally, I can't stand it anymore. "Charlie—" I start, my voice barely above a whisper.

She cuts me off, her tone icy. "Look, Mr. Romano. Let's focus on the task at hand. The sooner we finish, the sooner we can both get back to our lives."

Her words are a slap, her cold demeanor slicing through my faltering resolve. I want to say something—to bridge this gap between us—but she's put up a wall I'm not sure I can—or should—cross.

I turn my gaze back to the paper in front of me, though the words blur as my thoughts spiral. Each inch of distance between us feels like a chasm, widening with every second. I tell myself it's better this way, that I made the right choice.

But deep down, a gnawing uncertainty lingers, whispering doubts I don't want to hear.

17

CHARLIE

The knock at the door pulls me roughly from the arms of sleep, yanking me from a hazy dream. Disoriented, I blink, trying to remember where I am. For a fleeting second, panic surges—I think I've fallen asleep at my computer in the middle of a meeting with Dante. But that was yesterday.

Slowly, memories return, settling in my mind like dust. The meeting hadn't been easy. Dante was his usual composed self, though more distant, more intense than usual. He'd tried to bring up the other night—when he'd turned me away. I'd cut him off, slipping into my professional armor, relying on the one thing I know. I managed to stay composed, and part of me is proud of holding my ground, of not letting him see the impact he has on me.

The knock sounds again, sharper this time, pulling me fully awake. I press my fingers into the sheets, grounding myself. I'm in my bed, in my apartment. Sunlight filters through the blinds, casting faint patterns across the room.

I remember waking up earlier, going through my usual

routine. Breakfast was simple: eggs and toast. Today, I'd decided to stay home. For a brief moment, the thought made me smile. Then I remembered why I was staying home, and the smile faded.

After my shower, I'd stood before the mirror, scrutinizing every inch of my reflection. My fingers grazed my stomach, and I swore I saw something different—some small shift in the gentle curve of my belly. Maybe it's too early for changes, but I feel different. I can't explain it, but I feel it in my bones. A life is growing inside me, fragile and new. And with it, uncertainty, blooming in equal measure.

I'm jolted from my thoughts by the knock, now more insistent. I hear voices, low but unmistakable, murmuring outside my door. My pulse quickens, and a chill crawls up my spine. What is going on?

Rising from bed, I pull on my slippers and step quietly toward the door. The knocking stops as I approach, and silence falls, thick and heavy. Maybe they left, I think, pausing just a few feet from the door, half-relieved, half-nervous.

But then a voice—a familiar voice—breaks the silence, soft yet cold.

"I know you're in there, Ms. Charlotte. I'd advise you to open this door. I'm not a very patient man."

Silas Kane.

My heart leaps to my throat, pounding hard. I glance around the room, my eyes darting from one potential escape to the next, though there's nowhere to go. The fight-or-flight instinct kicks in, and I feel the urge to grab something, anything, to defend myself. But what good would it do?

The silence hangs for a beat longer, giving me a moment to gather myself. I take a deep breath, willing my hands to stop shaking, and step closer to the door. There's no escaping this.

With a final exhale, I unlock the door and pull it open. Silas Kane stands on the threshold, his gaze sharp and assessing, a deceptive smile curving his lips.

"Hello, Ms. Charlotte," he drawls. "I thought you didn't want to see me anymore."

"I was asleep," I reply, my voice barely steady. I swipe the back of my hand over my mouth, feeling oddly exposed under his gaze, as if he can see through me.

He studies me for a moment, then chuckles. "You look like you needed it." His words are casual, almost friendly, but there's a chilling undertone.

"Okay..." I mutter, unsure how to respond.

His grin widens. "May I come in?"

I hesitate, but it's clear I don't have much choice. "Sure." Stepping aside, I let him in. He crosses the threshold, and as he does, I glance into the hallway, finding it empty. There's no one with him. For a brief moment, I wonder why. Does he trust me that much? Or is he simply that confident?

Silas's presence fills the room as I close the door behind him. I stifle a yawn, irritation simmering beneath my nerves. He's pulled me from the one space I felt I had some semblance of control. And I can feel the headache building, a dull throb at my temples.

"I won't be long," he says, his tone mild. "I'll be out of your hair in a minute." He sounds almost accommodating, but I know better. I get the distinct impression that I'm more valuable to him alive than dead. For now, anyway.

He removes his sunglasses, and I find myself staring into his eyes—dark, calculating, glinting with something dangerous. It feels like hot oil against my skin, a searing discomfort I can't escape.

"You should turn the heat up in here," he remarks, his gaze flicking over me. "You look... chilled."

I force a smile. "What can I do for you, Mr. Kane?" I ask, trying to keep my voice even.

He chuckles, slow and deliberate, and the sound sends an involuntary shiver down my spine. "Always so formal. Charlie," he says, savoring the name like a threat. My years of training hold back the disgust simmering beneath my expression.

"Charlie, Charlie... Can I call you that? I've enjoyed our talks," he continues, ignoring my question. "You're... refreshing. A breath of fresh air."

"Thank you, Mr. Kane." I manage, my patience fraying. "About—"

"You know what I like most about you, Charlie?" he interrupts, his tone almost playful.

I clamp my mouth shut, barely restraining my annoyance. He waits, eyes gleaming with expectation.

"What is it?" I ask finally, my voice clipped.

He nods, his smile widening. "You're smart."

"Thank you..." I murmur, unsure of where he's going with this.

"Because you're smart, I trust you'll make the right decisions. Like now," he adds, his tone soft but firm.

A chill creeps into my bones, and I instinctively pull my arms around myself. His words are veiled, but the meaning is clear enough. He's reminding me of his offer, the one I had flatly turned down.

"Yes, Mr. Kane, I remember," I say, forcing my tone to remain calm. "And as I told you before, I can't be involved in anything illegal. It's... it's against my principles. And the law."

He leans in, his eyes narrowing. "It's only illegal if you think it is," he says, his voice dropping.

"That's not how the law works," I retort before I can stop myself.

His smile vanishes, replaced by something darker, more calculating. His gaze pierces through me, unblinking, and I feel an instinctive shiver. I can't read his thoughts, but the menace is unmistakable.

"Ms. Charlotte," he says quietly, his voice edged with steel. "I've approached you several times now, with what I believed to be… mutual interests. Each time, you've turned me down. That's not smart."

A cold, creeping dread settles over me. I swallow, my mind racing with possibilities. Suddenly, I realize just how foolish it was to think I had any control over this situation.

"I hope you don't regret this," he murmurs, the words laced with a quiet finality.

Silence stretches between us, thick and suffocating. I try to rub warmth into my arms, but the chill refuses to leave.

Then, just as suddenly as it disappeared, his smile returns, and he slides his sunglasses back over his eyes. "Have a good day, Ms. Charlotte," he says, his tone almost cheerful as he turns and exits, leaving me alone with a storm of emotions.

I lock the door behind him, my hands trembling. I slump against it, trying to calm the panic clawing its way through me. Silas Kane had delivered a threat without saying the words, and it echoed in my mind like a curse.

He made it clear—I was to comply, or face the consequences. My hand instinctively drifts to my belly, seeking the comfort of the tiny life growing inside me. But there's no solace here, only more fear.

Finally, I force myself to stand, crossing to the bathroom. The reflection that stares back at me in the mirror looks haunted, shadows under my eyes, fear etched into every line of my face. I splash cold water onto my cheeks, steeling myself.

I have to tell Dante. He needs to know—about the pregnancy, about Silas, about everything. I don't know what he'll do, or if he'll even care, but the weight of this secret is too much to bear alone.

Half an hour later, I step out of the taxi and look up at Dante's building. It looms above me, imposing and impassive. My nerves are a tangled mess, and for a second, I consider turning back. But I can't. Not now.

I take a steadying breath and walk through the lobby, catching sight of Stephanie at the reception desk. She glances up, surprise flickering in her eyes.

"Ms. Harris," she greets me. "I didn't realize you had an appointment today."

"No... I don't," I admit, feeling oddly exposed. "But I need to see Mr. Romano. It's... urgent."

She studies me, then nods. "He's between meetings. Let me take you up."

I follow her to the elevator, trying to ignore the knot of anxiety tightening in my chest. We reach Dante's floor quickly, and Stephanie gestures toward his office.

"Go on in," she says, giving me an encouraging smile. I manage a weak smile in return and approach his door, my heartbeat thundering in my ears.

I knock softly, and his voice calls out from within. "Come in."

I open the door and step inside. He looks up from his desk, and for a moment, something flickers in his eyes—

something that almost looks like surprise or even relief. But it vanishes, replaced by his usual calm expression.

"Charlie," he says, his voice steady but guarded.

"Mr. Romano." I try to match his tone, but my voice wavers. "I... I need to tell you something."

He watches me, his gaze unwavering. "Go on."

I open my mouth, but the words stick in my throat. I force myself to breathe, to push through the fear. "I'm... I'm pregnant," I blurt out, the words escaping in a rush.

The silence that follows is absolute, filling the room with a tension so thick it feels like a physical weight pressing down on me. I search his face, desperate for some reaction —anything.

Finally, he speaks, his voice barely above a whisper. "Whose is it?"

The question hits me like a slap. My breath catches, and a wave of hurt rises in my chest, sharp and unrelenting. Did he really think that little of me? Did he believe I'd betray him so easily?

Without another word, I turn and walk out, ignoring his voice calling my name. I reach the elevator, my vision blurring with tears, and press the button, willing it to arrive faster. The doors finally close, and I feel my heart shatter as I descend, the weight of his accusation crushing me.

I step out into the lobby, barely holding back the sobs threatening to escape. My head is down as I cross to the exit, fumbling for my phone. I just need to get away, far away.

As I step outside, the roar of an engine fills the air. I look up, confused, just in time to see a flash of red.

The impact is sudden, jarring, sending me sprawling onto the pavement. Pain radiates through me, sharp and unforgiving, as a warmth spreads across my side. I realize, dimly, that it's blood, staining my clothes, pooling beneath me.

A voice shouts nearby, but it's muffled, distant, as if underwater. My vision swims, and I feel my consciousness slipping.

My hand drifts to my belly, cradling the tiny life within, a tear slipping from the corner of my eye as darkness pulls me under.

18

DANTE

The sharp crack of gunfire pierces the night, shattering the fragile calm. My instincts take over before the sound even registers. I'm out of my chair and into the hallway, my pulse racing as I barrel toward the elevator.

Behind me, Stephanie's startled cry barely reaches my ears. My thoughts are already racing ahead, piecing together the implications. Gunfire at this hour, in this place—it's no coincidence.

The elevator crawls as though mocking my urgency. My fingers twitch around the grip of the pistol I grabbed on my way out, the cold metal grounding me. Every second that ticks by sharpens the edge of my rage.

The doors open to reveal chaos. The lobby is scattered with employees crouching behind furniture, their wide eyes fixed on the glass entrance. The scene outside stops me cold.

Charlie.

She's lying on the ground, her jeans torn, her tank top darkened with blood.

A scream tears through the fog of my panic. It takes me a moment to realize it's my own voice.

"Has anyone called an ambulance?!" My words echo, but the crowd remains frozen.

"Boss!" David's voice cuts through the tension as he rushes forward.

"Car! Now!"

David doesn't hesitate, sprinting outside to pull up to the curb. I drop to my knees beside Charlie, cradling her head in my hands. Her skin is too pale, her body too still. My voice shakes as I lean close.

"Charlie, stay with me. Please."

Her eyelids flutter faintly, and I catch the barest whisper of a breath. It's enough. It has to be.

David skids to a stop beside me, throwing open the car door. I lift Charlie carefully, her limp body pressing against me, each step toward the car an eternity.

THE DRIVE to the hospital is a blur of red lights and desperate prayers. Charlie's blood seeps into my shirt, warm and sticky, a cruel reminder of how fragile she feels in my arms.

"We're almost there!" David shouts, weaving recklessly through traffic.

I keep my focus on her face, willing her to hold on. "Stay with me, Charlie. I need you to stay."

THE HOSPITAL STAFF descend like a swarm the moment we pull up. They take her from my arms, their movements swift and efficient.

"She's pregnant!" I yell after them, my voice hoarse.

A nurse nods, her expression grim. "We'll do everything we can."

I watch helplessly as they wheel her through the double doors, the warmth of her blood still clinging to my hands.

Time stretches unbearably. Gabe arrives with the reinforcements I demanded, and they take up positions inside and outside the hospital. But even their presence does little to ease the storm raging inside me.

I pace the waiting area, my mind replaying the scene in an endless loop. Lorenzo's name surfaces again and again, a poison that fuels my fury.

The nurse returns at last, her face a mixture of exhaustion and relief.

"She's stable," she says softly. "The bullet missed any vital organs, and she's out of danger."

"And the baby?" I manage to ask, the words sticking in my throat.

She smiles faintly. "The baby's fine. Both mother and child are lucky."

Relief slams into me, making my knees weak. I nod, struggling to hold onto the fragments of composure I have left.

"Can I see her?"

"For a moment," she says. "She's sedated, but she'll wake soon."

The room is quiet, the hum of machines the only sound as I step inside. Charlie lies pale and still, her chest rising and falling in a steady rhythm.

I sit beside her, brushing a strand of hair from her face. Her warmth grounds me, a lifeline amid the chaos.

"Charlie," I whisper, my voice rough. "You're safe now. Rest."

My thumb strokes her cheek as tears I didn't know I had blur my vision. "I almost lost you," I whisper, the words raw and painful. "Both of you."

Her skin is warm beneath my touch - proof she's alive, breathing, here with me. I lean down, pressing my forehead to hers as emotion overwhelms me.

"I love you," I confess quietly, the words slipping out before I can stop them. "I've loved you for so long, Charlie. I was a fool to ever push you away."

My lips brush her forehead, her cheek, so gently. Even unconscious, she stirs slightly at my touch, turning toward my warmth.

HOURS PASS IN A HAZE. Gabe's updates about security measures barely register. My focus remains on Charlie, on the steady beat of the monitor that keeps time with her breaths.

When she stirs, her lashes fluttering open, relief floods me. I lean closer, my voice low.

"Charlie? Can you hear me?"

She blinks slowly, her gaze finding mine. "Dante..." Her voice is barely audible, but the sound is enough to crack the walls I've built around myself.

"You're okay," I murmur, brushing my thumb over her knuckles. "You're safe."

Her fingers tighten around mine as I lean closer. "Dante," she breathes again, her voice stronger now.

I cup her face gently, my thumb tracing her cheekbone.

When her eyes meet mine, they're filled with such trust it makes my chest ache.

"I thought I'd lost you," I murmur, before capturing her lips in a soft, careful kiss. She responds weakly but eagerly, her hand coming up to grip my shirt.

I break away reluctantly, pressing my forehead to hers. "Rest," I whisper, though I can't bring myself to pull back completely. "I'll be right here."

She nods, settling back against the pillows but keeping her fingers intertwined with mine. The simple touch grounds us both.

CHARLIE'S EYES CLOSE AGAIN, her exhaustion pulling her under. I watch her sleep, my mind a whirlwind of rage and determination.

This attack wasn't random. Lorenzo made this personal, and he'll regret it. I've given him too much room to act, too much freedom.

I rise, my movements deliberate, and step into the hallway where Gabe waits.

"We need to move fast," I tell him, my voice cold and steady. "I want Lorenzo found. No more warnings. No more second chances."

Gabe nods, his expression grim. "Understood, boss."

As I return to Charlie's side, a new resolve settles over me. She's alive, and so is our child. But the line between my world and hers has been obliterated, and there's no turning back.

Whoever threatened her safety will learn that I don't forgive—and I don't forget.

19

CHARLIE

My eyes open slowly to blinding overhead lights and stark white walls. For a long moment, I lie still, my mind pushing through a fog of disorientation. Everything feels foreign—the smell, the sheets, the faint beeping of nearby machinery. Where am I?

Memories drift back in fragments. I was at Dante's office. I'd gone to tell him about the pregnancy. My hand moves instinctively to my belly, pressing down as if needing proof of the life still growing within me. The memory sharpens, and then... the gunshots. My breath catches. I was shot.

A shudder runs through me as I glance around. The sharp tang of antiseptic fills my lungs, the unmistakable scent of a hospital. I'm on a hospital bed, surrounded by monitors and IV lines, confirming the surreal feeling I'm trying to shake.

Part of me wants to move, but caution holds me back. I'm here—alive somehow—and I don't want to tempt fate before I understand what's happened. Another reason I haven't moved becomes clear: Dante, slumped in the chair beside my bed, looks as though he hasn't slept in days.

Even in sleep, he's restless. His hair is disheveled, going every which way, and his arms are crossed over his chest. His jaw, tense even as he rests, clenches and unclenches, his eyes moving beneath closed lids. He looks as though he's carrying the weight of something unbearable. I watch him, unsure what to make of it.

Part of me considers slipping out quietly, leaving him to sleep. Maybe it would be fair to let him worry, given everything. But as I shift, trying to find a more comfortable position, Dante's eyes snap open. He bolts upright, his hand instinctively flying to his hip, where I now notice a bulge under his shirt.

"Is that a gun?" I blurt out before I can think.

Dante's gaze sweeps the room for any danger before settling on me. He looks relieved, but an intensity flickers in his eyes. "Yes," he replies simply, reaching for the gun and showing it to me.

"Put that away!" I hiss, glancing at the door. "We're in a hospital, Dante. Someone could walk in!"

He gives a dismissive wave. "No one's coming in. We're not to be disturbed."

My eyes shift to the doorway, and sure enough, I catch sight of a man stationed just outside, clearly keeping guard. "Put it away anyway," I murmur.

Dante obliges, sliding the gun back into his waistband, though he looks mildly amused as he settles back into his chair, stretching his legs out. I watch him, gathering my thoughts, bracing myself to ask the question that's been lingering too long.

"Are you… a criminal?" The words slip out softly, more a statement than a question. But I need to hear him say it.

Dante freezes, his gaze locking onto mine. His eyes go wary, calculating, as if assessing what answer to give. He studies me for a long moment before finally nodding. "Yes."

I'm surprised at how little his answer bothers me. Just days ago, the thought would have shaken me to my core. Silas Kane had shown me photos, meant to plant doubt, to make me wary of Dante. I'd felt a flash of anger then, maybe a touch of fear. But now? I don't know what to feel.

Dante seems to notice my lack of reaction. "Who told you that?"

"Silas Kane," I reply, watching for any shift in his expression. His eyes narrow, his face hardening.

"What are you doing, meeting with Silas?" His tone has an edge I've never heard before.

"He visited me. Twice."

Dante lets out a low curse, running a hand over his face, his worry palpable. That worry sends a chill down my spine. He finally looks back at me, his voice firm. "Silas is dangerous, Charlie. You need to stay away from him. And you need to tell me everything that happens to you, every interaction. Understood?"

"Okay," I murmur, feeling his intense gaze linger. I lean back against the pillows, my body and mind exhausted.

Dante's eyes don't leave me. I feel the weight of his concern, his protectiveness, and beneath it, a tension simmering just below the surface.

After a long silence, I finally ask, "What happened? After I... I was shot."

"You were shot," he says quietly, as if saying it aloud is difficult. "You were shot." He repeats it, his eyes distant, the memory pulling him somewhere dark. I watch him, and it's as if he's somewhere else, reliving every second. I want to reach out, to break the silence, but his focus shifts back to me.

"I brought you here," he says finally, though his tone makes it sound far more complicated than the words suggest.

"By yourself?" I ask, hoping he'll tell me more. "Did you throw me over your shoulder and jog to the hospital?" The hint of a smile tugs at his lips, softening the tension.

"No," he replies, his voice lighter for a moment. "I had the car. David Two drove." He pauses, as if struck by a sudden thought. "I should give him a raise."

"David Two?" I ask, confused. "You've called him that before. I thought I misheard."

The fleeting smile reappears. "My previous driver was also named David."

He doesn't elaborate, and something in his tone suggests I shouldn't ask. I nod, letting the silence stretch out, strangely comfortable in his presence.

Dante finally breaks the silence. "How are you feeling?"

I shift, testing the aches in my body. "Sore. But the medication is handling most of it."

Dante's expression tightens. "I thought you were dead," he murmurs, the vulnerability in his voice striking me deeply. He stares at a spot on the wall, lost in thought. I reach out, squeezing his hand.

"Do you remember anything?" he asks, tentatively.

"Only bits and pieces. I remember the gunshots, the pain, and then... darkness." My voice falters, and Dante's grip tightens on my hand as if grounding me.

Then a sudden realization hits me, and I sit up with a gasp, gripping my stomach. "Oh my God, Dante. The baby..."

His face softens, his hand covering mine. "The baby's fine, Charlie. You didn't lose it."

Relief crashes over me, leaving me weak and grateful.

Tears spill from my eyes, the release of weeks of tension and fear. Dante doesn't let go of my hand, his thumb rubbing small circles, calming me in a way I didn't know I needed.

A soft beep from the bedside table draws my attention. It's my phone, blinking with unread messages. I pick it up, scrolling through notifications. Most are missed calls from friends and colleagues, but one message catches my attention, the timestamp recent.

My heart hammers as I open it.

Dante, noticing my expression, leans in. "What's wrong?"

Wordlessly, I turn the phone toward him. The text is from an unknown number, and I see his face darken as he reads it.

"Leave Romano Holdings. Leave the city."

A shiver crawls up my spine, and I cling to Dante's hand, feeling a deep sense of dread seep through me.

He doesn't react at first, his face a mask of icy calm. But his grip on my hand tightens protectively, and I can feel the controlled fury simmering beneath the surface.

"This isn't over," he says, his voice a quiet promise. He places my phone back on the table and meets my gaze, his eyes fierce. "They think they can intimidate you. But they don't know who they're dealing with."

The intensity in his gaze sends a shiver through me, and for the first time, I realize the full scope of what it means to be with someone like Dante. The world he moves in is dark, layered with threats and shadows I can't even begin to understand. And yet, there's a strange reassurance in his presence, as if his very existence wards off danger.

But I can't ignore the unease creeping through me. "Dante," I whisper, "are we safe?"

He doesn't answer right away, his jaw clenched. Finally,

he speaks, each word deliberate. "As long as I'm here, you're safe. I won't let anything happen to you or the baby. I promise you that."

I want to believe him, but the message's threat lingers in my mind, a reminder that I've willingly stepped into a world I barely understand. I wonder if Dante truly can keep that promise, if he can hold back the darkness closing in around us.

The silence between us feels thick, charged, as Dante's words settle over me. The weight of his promise is comforting, but I can still feel the chill of the message sinking in, its words like shadows stretching over us. I squeeze his hand a little tighter, needing the connection, needing him to ground me.

"You don't have to worry about them, Charlie," he says quietly, his voice low and resolute. "I've dealt with threats like this before. Whoever's trying to scare you doesn't understand what they've gotten themselves into."

He says it with such confidence, and for a moment, I almost believe him completely. I almost forget the message, the fear. But the memory of Silas's cold eyes lingers in the back of my mind. I can't help but wonder if Silas is behind this—or worse, someone even closer to Dante's world.

"Dante... I need to know. Are you really sure it's safe for me to stay?" My voice is softer than I intended, barely audible over the steady beeping of the heart monitor beside me. "I mean, I understand that you're used to this, but... I'm not." I glance down, avoiding his gaze. "What if whoever sent that message tries something worse?"

Dante's hand tightens around mine, drawing my attention back to him. His eyes, dark and intense, are filled with a fire I hadn't expected to see. "Charlie, listen to me." His voice is steady, unwavering. "No one is going to hurt you. Not while I'm here. They can threaten all they want, but they won't get close. I'll make sure of it."

I want to believe him, but there's a part of me that still feels the lingering echo of fear. The world he's part of is so much darker than I'd ever imagined. And now, I'm tangled in it too.

"Who do you think it was?" I ask, my voice trembling slightly. "Do you really think Lorenzo would go this far?"

His jaw clenches, and I can see the muscles working beneath his skin. "Lorenzo... he's capable of a lot. But threatening you like this—sending messages?" He shakes his head. "It feels more like something Silas would do. He knows how to get into people's heads, to make them feel vulnerable." He pauses, as if choosing his next words carefully. "He wants something, Charlie. And until I figure out what that is, I'm not letting you out of my sight."

The intensity in his gaze is both reassuring and unsettling. I know Dante would do anything to protect me, but the lengths he might go to—it's almost too much to think about.

"I don't want this to change my life," I say quietly, more to myself than to him. "I don't want to live in fear, Dante. I don't want to wonder if someone is watching me or waiting for the chance to..." My voice trails off, but Dante seems to understand.

He reaches out, gently brushing a strand of hair from my face. "It won't come to that," he says, his voice soft but firm. "I won't let it. You'll live the life you want, without looking over your shoulder. But to do that, we have to face this head-on. And that means staying close, being vigilant." He pauses, his eyes locking onto mine. "Are you ready for that?"

Am I? I don't know. But with Dante here, his presence steady and reassuring, I feel a little braver, a little less lost. I nod, hoping he can't see the doubt lingering in my eyes. "I think so," I say, my voice barely above a whisper.

His hand cups my cheek, warm and grounding. "I'll keep you safe, Charlie. And the baby. I promise."

There's something about the way he says it that makes my heart ache. I can feel the sincerity in his voice, the intensity of his vow. And for a fleeting moment, I let myself imagine a life where we're free of all of this, where threats like Silas and Lorenzo don't exist.

But reality has a way of shattering even the smallest hopes. My phone buzzes again, jolting us both out of the moment. I glance down, dread pooling in my stomach as I see the notification. Another message from an unknown number.

Dante's hand tightens on mine as he reads the words over my shoulder.

"If you don't leave now, you'll regret it. This is your last warning."

My heart pounds, each beat echoing the growing fear in my chest. I can feel Dante's anger radiating beside me, his jaw clenched, his eyes narrowing as he stares at the words. The room feels colder, as though the message has brought a chill with it, settling around us like a heavy fog.

"Charlie." His voice is low, almost a growl. "They don't get to threaten you. Not like this." He pulls his phone from his pocket, his fingers moving quickly as he types out a message, his jaw set with steely resolve.

"Who are you texting?" I ask, my voice shaky.

"Gabe. I want more security, here and at your apartment. We're not taking any chances." He looks up, his eyes meeting mine. "We're going to find out who's behind this, and when we do…" His voice trails off, but the hard glint in his eyes tells me everything I need to know.

A part of me wants to argue, to tell him that I don't want a small army following me everywhere I go. But another part—a larger part—is grateful. Because the truth is, I don't feel safe. Not anymore.

Dante finishes his message and slips his phone back into his pocket. He turns to me, his expression softening as he takes my hand again. "I know this isn't what you wanted," he says quietly. "I know you didn't sign up for any of this. But you're here now, and I'll be damned if I let anyone hurt you."

I swallow, the weight of his words settling over me. "I don't want to live like this, Dante," I say, my voice small. "I don't want our child to live like this."

He squeezes my hand, his gaze fierce and unwavering. "Then we won't. I'll make sure of it."

We sit there in silence, the gravity of our situation pressing down on us. I can feel the fear lurking at the edges, threatening to consume me. But with Dante here, his hand warm in mine, I find a sliver of courage. Because despite everything, I know he'll do whatever it takes to keep us safe.

The minutes tick by, each one heavy with unspoken fears and unmade promises. But even as the uncertainty looms, there's a part of me that feels a strange calm. Because in this moment, with Dante by my side, I feel like maybe, just maybe, we'll be okay.

But as I glance down at my phone, the words from the last message still glaring up at me, I can't shake the feeling that we're on borrowed time—that this peace, however fleeting, is only the calm before the storm.

And something tells me that once the storm breaks, nothing will ever be the same again.

20

DANTE

I hand over a couple of bills and wave the taxi on. The cab lumbers away, spitting and coughing, leaving behind a faint cloud of exhaust. I watch until its taillights vanish around the corner. The resort before me is pristine, a paradise for vacationers with money to spare. I was here years ago, when life was simpler and my purpose less clouded by obligation. Now, this place feels tainted by what I'm about to do.

I take a steadying breath and walk through the gate toward the private areas, eyes scanning the crowd of relaxed faces basking in the sun. No one stops me—I must look like I belong, like any other rich guy in a floral shirt and shorts. The weather is perfect, warm enough to settle in your bones and whisper, *stay awhile*. But I'm here for business, not pleasure.

I scan my surroundings, searching for familiar landmarks. According to my intel, my quarry should be near the pools, where guests lounge and sip overpriced cocktails. As I round the corner, a heavily accented voice stops me in my tracks.

"Ah, Mr. Romano! It's been a while."

I turn to see Boro, the resort manager, beaming at me like I'm a long-lost friend. I force a smile, hoping it looks genuine. I hadn't expected anyone to recognize me, but I underestimated Boro's memory.

"It has been, hasn't it?" I reply, shaking his hand. I never remembered his real name—'Boro' was a nickname that stuck.

He clasps my hand warmly. "Why so long away?"

"Work." I shrug, letting out a sigh as if the weight of responsibility were crushing me. "You know how it is."

Boro nods sagely. "But with work, one must also rest," he says, patting my arm in a fatherly gesture.

"True enough, Boro." I feel a twinge of impatience but keep my tone light. "Hopefully, I'll be back soon to enjoy it properly."

His face lights up with a grin. "I look forward to it, Mr. Romano. Take care, and do rest." He bows slightly and heads back inside.

Once he's gone, I shake off the last traces of our conversation and focus. I glance toward the pool, searching for my quarry, but the poolside is empty. A cold knot tightens in my gut. Did he spot me? Is he onto me already?

My hand drifts instinctively to my waistband, where a gun rests just beneath the hem of my shirt. My thumb grazes its handle as my gaze sweeps the area. Staff in blue uniforms move around, clearing glasses and adjusting lounge chairs. Just then, I spot a flash of orange disappearing around a corner.

An orange uniform? None of the staff wear that color. My quarry had been lying on an orange towel. I start forward, pulse quickening. Was it the towel I saw, or something else? I can't afford to waste time debating. I slip into a brisk walk, following the streak of color through a doorway.

As I turn down a narrow corridor, my steps slow. The hallways in this section are tight, just wide enough for three abreast, lined with hotel suite doors. I consider drawing my gun but dismiss the thought—too risky in a public place. This part of the resort is quieter, and I want to keep the advantage of surprise.

Ahead, a flash of orange flickers around another corner, and I pick up my pace. The rage simmering beneath the surface threatens to boil over. He went after Charlie. The audacity it took tightens my grip into a fist.

Focus, Dante. Stay in control.

I push forward, crossing into another hallway lined with private suites. Finally, I see him, and this time there's no mistaking it—my quarry is hunched by a door, fumbling with a key card. He has a guard with him, but only one. They're keeping a low profile, just like I am. I lower my hat over my eyes and walk casually, blending into the relaxed atmosphere.

The door clicks open. My quarry shoves the door and slips inside, his guard trailing. I close the distance, my heartbeat in my ears. With three quick strides, I'm on them, grabbing my quarry by the back of his head and slamming him face-first into the door. He lets out a strangled cry, stumbling inside. I follow, kicking the door shut behind me.

He sprawls onto the floor, clutching his face. I pull my gun, quickly assessing the room. The guard charges around the corner, weapon drawn, but he's a second too late. I intercept his wrist, wrenching the gun from his hand, then slam the butt of my pistol into his neck. He crumples to the ground with a grunt.

The room goes quiet, except for my quarry's ragged

breathing as he scrambles to his feet, the orange towel around his shoulders now slipping to the floor. I level the gun at him, my voice low and cold.

"Don't even think about moving."

He freezes, hands raised in surrender. "Dante, wait," he stammers, eyes darting around the room, calculating his options.

"Shut up, Silas," I growl. My hand trembles with restrained fury, every muscle tense.

I motion for him to sit. He stumbles to the chair, clutching his nose, which is bleeding from the impact with the door. I retrieve the guard's weapon, tucking it into my waistband, then kneel to check the guard's pulse. He's still alive. Lucky him.

"You went after Charlie," I say, my voice barely above a whisper but laced with venom. "That was a mistake."

Silas's eyes widen. "Look, it wasn't personal. It's just business. You know how it is."

I grit my teeth, cocking the gun. "Business?" The word tastes sour. "Charlie's off-limits. You knew that."

He flinches, hands up in a placating gesture. "Wait! It wasn't me. I mean, technically it was, but it wasn't my idea."

I lean in, gun aimed at his chest. "Then whose idea was it?"

He hesitates, visibly swallowing, the calm he wore a moment ago fraying at the edges. "If I tell you... I'm as good as dead."

"You're already in my scope, Silas. Talk."

He lets out a shaky breath. "Lorenzo. He's the one behind it all. I'm just... a minion. This goes way above me."

The name hits me like a cold slap. Lorenzo. Silas's words echo in my mind as the weight of his revelation sinks in. Lorenzo, manipulating things from the shadows. It feels like the ground beneath me has shifted. How deep does this run? How much of what I thought I knew is a lie?

I stare at Silas, the fear in his eyes as real as the blood dripping from his nose. He looks defeated, deflated.

"Please, Dante," he begs, his voice cracking. "I told you what you wanted. Let me go."

I hold his gaze, searching his face for any sign of deceit. I step closer, the cold, lethal calm settling over me.

"Good night, Silas." I bring the butt of my gun down hard against his neck. He slumps over in the chair, the orange towel slipping to the floor beside him.

For a moment, I just stand there, breathing heavily, surveying the wreckage of the room. Silas lies unconscious, his guard sprawled beside him, the room eerily still.

Then my phone buzzes, and I pull it from my pocket. Only one person would be calling me right now.

"Boss," Gabe's voice is sharp, tense, the urgency clear even through the static. "We've got a situation."

I brace myself. "What happened?"

"Someone hit the stores. Smashed everything up, took whatever they could carry."

I clench my jaw, heart pounding. Lorenzo. He's not just pulling strings from a distance; he's moving in close.

"Is that all?" I ask, though something in Gabe's tone tells me there's more.

Gabe hesitates. "No, boss. It gets worse." There's a pause that stretches too long. "Someone entered Charlie's room dressed as a doctor. They... took her."

The words punch the air from my lungs. For a moment, I can't breathe, my vision narrowing, thoughts spiraling. Charlie—taken from under our noses, from her room.

"Boss?" Gabe's voice pulls me back to reality.

"I'm on my way," I say, voice tight, fighting to keep the

dread from seeping through. I pocket the phone and head for the door, my steps quickening, anger coiling tighter within me.

Charlie's been taken. Lorenzo has escalated this to a new level. My blood turns to ice as I exit Silas's suite, breaking into a run. The stakes have never been higher, and as fury blazes through me, only one thought remains crystal clear.

I'll make them all pay.

As I race through the resort's hallways, my mind is a storm of plans, each one harsher and more ruthless than the last. I need to keep my head clear, but the thought of Charlie in Lorenzo's grasp is tearing through my focus. It's not just that he took her. It's the way he did it—a violation, slipping into her room like he's untouchable. Every detail of the plan I'm forming has one purpose: making him regret this, making him suffer.

I exit the resort through a back hallway, avoiding the lobby. Out here, the noise of the ocean crashing against the shore does little to settle the anger coursing through me. I don't even care if I'm spotted; the whole place could be watching, for all I care. I'm beyond caution now. The only thing that matters is getting to Charlie, ripping her away from Lorenzo, and making sure he knows he messed with the wrong person.

A flash of movement catches my eye as I head toward the parking area. A tall, wiry man in dark clothes lingers near the entrance, watching me with casual interest. I recognize him as one of Lorenzo's men—one I'd dealt with before, someone who knew better than to cross me. Yet, here he is, bold enough to make eye contact, to smirk as I approach.

I'm on him in seconds, grabbing him by the collar and

shoving him against the side of a nearby car. His eyes go wide, surprise quickly replacing that smug grin.

"Where is she?" I demand, voice low and venomous.

"Who?" He tries to keep his voice even, but I see the flicker of fear there. He knows exactly who I mean.

"You think I don't know you work for Lorenzo? Don't play stupid. Where did he take her?" My grip tightens, my fingers digging into his collarbone.

"I don't know what you're talking about, man," he stammers, trying to pull away, but he's trapped. "I'm just here for security."

"Lorenzo sends you to tail me?" I ask, my voice as cold as the steel pressing into his neck.

His gaze darts around, his confidence evaporating. "Look, I was just supposed to make sure things went smoothly. I don't know anything about the girl."

I let go of his collar, only to slam him against the car again, hard enough to knock the wind out of him. He coughs, gasping for air. "Then call him," I order, holding his gaze. "Call him, right now."

He hesitates, then slowly reaches into his pocket, pulling out his phone. I keep my eyes on him, not giving him a single inch. He dials a number, his hands shaking as he holds the phone to his ear. He waits, and then his face pales as someone picks up on the other end.

"Boss," he says, his voice barely more than a whisper, eyes flicking up at me. "It's… it's me. Yeah, I've got a situation here."

I lean in, making sure I'm close enough to hear every word. The man swallows hard. "Uh… yeah, Mr. Romano wants to know where the girl is." His voice shakes, his nerves completely unraveled.

There's a pause, and I can just barely make out the faint

murmur of Lorenzo's voice on the other end of the line, though the words are muffled. The man's eyes dart to me, then back to the ground as he listens, nodding slightly. He starts to speak again, but I grab the phone from his hand before he has a chance, pressing it to my ear.

"Lorenzo."

There's silence on the other end, then a slow, mocking laugh that sends a fresh wave of fury through me. "Dante. I was wondering when you'd get in touch. Enjoying your vacation?"

"Where is she?" I cut him off, voice like ice.

"Ah, Charlie," he says, dragging out her name as if tasting it, relishing in the fact that he has something I want. "Such a lovely young woman. So full of spirit. You really have an eye for talent."

"Tell me where you're holding her, or I swear I'll—"

"Or you'll what?" he interrupts, sounding almost amused. "You're not in any position to make threats, Dante. I'm the one holding all the cards here. You're the one running around, chasing shadows."

"You don't know who you're dealing with."

"Oh, but I do," Lorenzo says, his tone slipping into something darker, more menacing. "I know you better than you know yourself, Dante. I know how far you're willing to go for those you care about. And I also know you won't risk her life just to get to me."

His words hit harder than any punch. He's right—I can't afford to gamble with her safety. But he doesn't know what I'm willing to do to get her back.

"What do you want, Lorenzo?" I ask, keeping my voice level, despite the rage simmering beneath it.

He chuckles, the sound like nails scraping across glass. "What I want... is for you to feel exactly what I felt. The uncertainty. The helplessness. The pain of knowing that no matter what you do, you can't save her. I want you to watch your world crumble, one piece at a time, until there's nothing left but ash."

I grit my teeth, gripping the phone so hard it's a wonder it doesn't shatter. "Let's skip the theatrics, shall we? You know I'll come for her."

"Oh, I'm counting on it," he says, voice dripping with satisfaction. "But I'll make sure you find me on my terms, when I'm ready for you. In the meantime, I'll take good care of Charlie. She's safe... for now."

The line goes dead. I stand there, staring at the phone in my hand, feeling the full weight of his threat settling over me. Charlie is somewhere out there, alone, vulnerable, in the hands of a man who would use her as a pawn just to get to me.

I hand the phone back to the man, who's still leaning against the car, watching me with wide, terrified eyes. Without a word, I turn and head for my car, my mind already racing, every part of me focused on one thing.

I will find her. And when I do, Lorenzo will pay—no matter what it costs me.

21

CHARLIE

The small room feels oppressive, shrinking with every passing minute. It's been hours since I escaped the nightmare of that hotel, but the memory of it clings to me like smoke—thick, suffocating, impossible to escape.

The images replay in my mind on a relentless loop: the ambulance, the masked men, Lorenzo's voice dripping with calm malice. Even now, I can hear his words, feel the chill they left in their wake.

I wrap my arms around myself, shivering despite the warmth of the room. I'm safe now—Gabe made sure of that when he picked me up—but safety feels like a fragile illusion.

The door creaks open, and I glance up to see Dante stepping inside. His presence fills the space instantly, his sharp gaze sweeping over me. He looks the same as always—calm, controlled—but there's an edge to him tonight, a tension that ripples beneath the surface.

"Are you okay?" he asks, his voice low but steady.

I nod, though the tears threatening to spill betray my answer. "I'm fine. Just... trying to process everything."

He steps closer, his movements deliberate, his eyes scanning me as if searching for unseen wounds. When he reaches the couch, he sinks down beside me, his proximity both grounding and disarming.

"I should have been there," he says, his tone tight. "This never should have happened."

The guilt in his voice catches me off guard. "It wasn't your fault," I reply softly.

His jaw tightens, his gaze dropping to his hands. "You don't understand. I underestimated Lorenzo. I thought I could protect you, keep you safe. And now..." He trails off, the weight of unspoken words hanging heavy in the air.

I reach out, my fingers brushing against his hand. The contact is brief, but it sparks something between us, a flicker of connection that cuts through the haze of fear and uncertainty.

"Dante," I whisper, my voice trembling. "You did protect me. I'm here because of you."

He looks at me then, his eyes dark and searching. For a moment, neither of us speaks, the silence stretching taut between us.

His hand slides to my cheek, wiping away a tear I didn't realize had fallen. Without a word, he pulls me into his arms, and I bury my face in his neck. His warmth surrounds me, steady and safe.

When I lift my head, his lips find mine. The kiss is desperate yet tender, filled with relief and need. His fingers tangle in my hair as I press closer, seeking more of his warmth, his strength.

"I thought I'd lost you," he murmurs against my mouth before claiming it again, deeper this time.

. . .

The air feels heavier now, thick with everything we're not saying. Dante shifts closer, his knee brushing against mine, the faint contact sending a jolt through me.

"You don't have to face this alone," he says, his voice barely above a whisper. "I'm here. Always."

His words wrap around me, steadying the storm inside me. I meet his gaze, and the intensity there steals the breath from my lungs.

"Dante..." My voice catches, the weight of his presence pressing down on me in the most unexpected way.

He leans in, his face inches from mine. The space between us feels charged, electric, every second stretching into eternity. I can feel his breath on my skin, warm and steady, and my heart pounds in response.

Our breaths mingle as he leans in, his hand cupping my face. Time seems to slow, the air between us electric with anticipation. His thumb traces my bottom lip, drawing a soft gasp.

My fingers grip his shirt, pulling him closer as his forehead rests against mine. "Charlie," he breathes, my name a prayer on his lips.

Just as our lips are about to touch, a sharp knock at the door shatters the moment. We pull apart, the spell broken, and I'm left breathless, my skin tingling with the memory of his proximity.

Dante rises, his movements stiff, and strides to the door. Gabe stands on the other side, his expression grim.

"We have a problem," Gabe says, his tone clipped.

Dante's jaw tightens, his hand gripping the edge of the door. "What is it?"

"Lorenzo's men are moving," Gabe replies. "We intercepted a message. They know where we are."

The words send a chill down my spine, and I rise from the couch, my legs unsteady. "What does that mean?"

"It means we need to leave," Dante says, his voice hardening. He turns to Gabe. "Get the car ready. We're leaving in ten minutes."

Gabe nods and disappears down the hall. Dante closes the door and turns to me, his expression unreadable.

"Pack what you need," he says, his tone firm. "We can't stay here."

The urgency in his voice spurs me into action, and I move quickly, grabbing my bag and stuffing it with essentials. The entire time, I can feel Dante's gaze on me, steady and unyielding, a silent promise that he won't let anything happen to me.

THE DRIVE IS TENSE, the silence between us broken only by the hum of the engine. Dante's grip on the wheel is tight, his knuckles white, and I can feel the weight of his thoughts pressing down on him.

"Where are we going?" I ask, my voice quiet.

"Somewhere safe," he replies without looking at me.

I nod, trusting him despite the fear gnawing at my chest. The memory of Lorenzo's voice lingers in my mind, a constant reminder of the danger we're in.

His hand finds mine across the center console, our fingers intertwining naturally. The touch anchors us both in the darkness. When a sharp turn forces me closer, he wraps his arm around me protectively.

I lean into his warmth, letting my head rest on his shoulder. His lips brush my temple, the gesture impossibly tender given the tension thrumming through him.

"Rest," he murmurs. "I've got you."

When we finally arrive, it's at a secluded villa, hidden away from prying eyes. The sight of it is both a relief and a reminder of how far Dante is willing to go to protect me.

"We'll be safe here," he says, his voice steady as he steps out of the car.

I follow him inside, the weight of the past day settling heavily on my shoulders. The villa is quiet, almost eerily so, but its warmth offers a small comfort.

Dante turns to me, his expression softening. "Get some rest. We'll talk in the morning."

I nod, exhaustion pulling at me, and make my way to the bedroom he's pointed out. But as I lie in bed, staring at the ceiling, I can't shake the memory of how close we came to crossing a line.

And how much I wanted it.

22

DANTE

Hearing Charlie's voice brought me a relief I hadn't known I needed. Days of tension slowly began to unwind, but not entirely—not until I had her in my arms. I'd been holding my breath, strung so tight I could barely think, waiting for confirmation of her safety. When it came, I nearly collapsed with the release.

After leaving Silas at the resort, Gabe and I launched into a full-throttle search. We contacted every informant, mobilizing a network we usually kept hidden. Finally, one of our sources came through—Charlie was being held in one of Silas's own hotels. It was absurdly bold, clever in a twisted way. Who'd expect to find a hostage in plain sight?

But knowing where she was only solved half the problem. The next challenge was getting her out.

Storming the place was out of the question; it was a luxury hotel, filled with witnesses and potential casualties. A raid would draw too much attention. Simply walking in wasn't feasible either—Lorenzo controlled this operation, and he wouldn't hesitate to take down anyone in his way. He was leagues colder and more calculating than Silas. With

Lorenzo involved, even sending a team was risky; we didn't know who or what we'd be up against.

The tension on the flight back was suffocating. I barely spoke to Gabe, my mind racing through plans, contingencies, anything that might work. Finally, Gabe suggested we use some of our informants to create a diversion. It was a desperate move—using insiders in a direct operation could blow their cover. But for Charlie, I'd take the risk.

As the plan unfolded, there were moments I was certain we'd miscalculated. It felt like we were moving blindly, powered by sheer faith and desperation. But in the end, it worked. I was gripping my phone, barely breathing, when Gabe's voice finally came through: "It's done. She's safe." Moments later, I heard Charlie's voice.

I exhale, still savoring that relief. As I glance at my watch, I know we're nearing our descent. Soon, I'll be on the ground, and she'll be there. I sink back into my seat, hoping for a moment of rest, but my mind races. Since Charlie was shot, I've been running on fumes, too wired to sleep.

In the days since, I'd barely left her side at the hospital. Then, I tracked Silas across oceans, landing at the resort where I got the news of her kidnapping. Anger, helplessness —it all catches up to me now. I close my eyes, just for a moment, and when I open them, the flight attendant is gently shaking my shoulder.

"We'll be landing soon, sir."

"Thank you, Mary." I stretch, feeling a dull ache from sleeping in the chair, but that discomfort fades as the plane begins its descent. I'm about to see Charlie. My hand tightens on the armrest in anticipation, and I hardly notice when the wheels hit the tarmac.

The doors open, and I step toward the exit. Outside,

Gabe leans against a sleek black car, and beside him, there she is—Charlie. A smile spreads across my face.

I descend the stairs carefully, unable to look away as she approaches, mirroring my pace. When I reach the ground, she's there, and I pull her close, lifting her off her feet as we hold each other. We're laughing, crying, and a tear I didn't know I'd held back escapes.

"I thought I'd lost you," I murmur against her ear, the words slipping out before I can hold them back. I've been so focused on finding her, staying strong, that I hadn't allowed myself to acknowledge the fear. Not until now.

She clings to me, her voice soft. "I didn't know what to think." Her face pressed to my shoulder, she trembles slightly, fingers gripping me like she'll never let go.

Finally, I step back, wrapping my arm around her as we walk over to Gabe, who's been watching patiently.

I nod, giving Gabe a grateful smile. "Well done."

He shrugs, brushing it off. "All in a day's work."

Charlie rolls her eyes. "You two and your macho act." Her voice holds a lightness that makes me smile.

"We'll be leaving soon," I tell Gabe. "You'll keep things under control?"

"Always," he says simply, his expression calm and steady.

I extend a hand, and he grasps it firmly. Charlie groans. "Oh my God. Just hug, will you?"

Gabe and I exchange amused glances. "Maybe another time," I say, to which she rolls her eyes again.

In no time, the plane is refueled, and Charlie's belongings are loaded. We're taking off from a small, private airstrip we control, far outside the city, away from prying eyes. We're both more than ready to leave.

As we board the jet, I see Gabe wave from the ground. I know he'll handle things, but for now, I need distance—

from the chaos, from Lorenzo's threats, from the world that nearly stole Charlie from me.

The flight to the villa passes with her by my side. When we arrive, we head to our suite, and I close the door behind us. We're safe, we're together, and I don't want to think about anything else.

We kiss slowly, savoring the relief, the comfort of being close again. Soon, we're shedding layers, our hands tracing familiar paths over each other, and I'm lost in her warmth, her softness. We're a tangle of limbs and whispered promises—a silent celebration of everything we nearly lost.

Later, as we lie together, a haze of exhaustion and satisfaction wraps around us. My arm drapes over her waist, and she nestles into me, content in this cocoon we've made.

"I really like you," I say softly, almost to myself. I want her to know she's a part of me I can't let go.

She's silent for a long moment, and I wonder if she's fallen asleep. But then, she shifts, looking up at me with a serious expression. "If you really do, you'll tell me what's going on."

"What do you mean?"

She wriggles out of my embrace, propping herself up to meet my gaze. "Dante, I want to know why this happened. Why me? Why now? I've been dragged from one danger to another with barely a word of explanation."

Her intensity takes me off guard. I knew this moment would come, but I hadn't fully prepared for it. With a sigh, I sit up, running a hand over my face as I try to gather my thoughts.

"Charlie," I begin, choosing my words carefully, "this world I'm a part of—it's not straightforward. What happened wasn't random. You were targeted because you're close to me. Lorenzo—he has power and a network that's hard to track. He saw an opportunity to get to me."

She frowns, processing my words. "But why would he do that? What does he gain from hurting people around you?"

"Power," I say simply. "Influence. Control. I have assets he wants, networks he can't get on his own. This vendetta isn't new, but involving you was his way of testing how far I'd go to protect what's mine."

Her brow furrows, and she tugs the sheet up around her shoulders. "And you thought keeping me in the dark was the best way to protect me?"

"It's complicated." I can hear the defensive edge in my voice. "I thought it was safer if you didn't know everything."

"Dante," she says, her voice soft but insistent, "I need to understand. I need to know what I'm facing if I'm going to keep up with this life."

There's a strength in her gaze that gives me pause. I've always admired her resilience, but I realize now that it's more than that—she's not asking for protection; she's demanding respect.

"All right," I concede. "I'll tell you what I can. Lorenzo... he's a man who thrives on control. He tried to manipulate me once, years ago, through alliances and shared investments. I refused. Since then, he's used any means he can to break into my world. This isn't the first time he's threatened people I care about, but it's the first time he's gone this far."

She absorbs this, her gaze unwavering. "So, what now?"

"Now, we keep our guard up. We take precautions. I've put things in motion to protect us and limit his reach. And you have every right to know what's happening from here on out. I won't keep you in the dark."

A hint of a smile touches her lips. "Good. Because I'm not running from this."

Her resolve is unexpected, but it settles something in me. I can't deny the pride swelling in my chest. She isn't afraid of the challenges ahead; she's ready to face them by my side.

We sit in silence, letting the weight of our conversation linger. I reach out, threading my fingers through hers, and we sit like that for a long time, bound by something deeper than the threats that surround us.

In the quiet moments that follow, I know we're stronger together, and that's something Lorenzo will never break.

I nod, absorbing the intensity of her gaze. Her words hang in the air, and I feel an unfamiliar vulnerability in the realization that Charlie knows everything now. She's chosen to stand by me despite the dangers, despite the forces lurking around us. And somehow, that trust she's given me, her willingness to stay, feels like more responsibility than any deal or negotiation ever could.

But my thoughts circle back to Lorenzo. He's out there, and I know his game isn't over. Knowing him, he's biding his time, setting up his next move.

"Dante," Charlie's voice breaks through my thoughts. She's watching me, her face softened yet serious. "If Lorenzo is this dangerous... if he's really out there, what do we do now? We can't just stay hidden away forever."

She's right. We can't run, and we can't hide. And even as I sit here, I know that every moment I wait to act is a moment Lorenzo could be using to outmaneuver me. It's a game of patience, strategy, and timing—a dangerous game where the stakes have become higher than ever.

"I've made arrangements," I say finally. "When we get back, there'll be more security, more people watching out for us. I'll have my team tighten things up. I want you protected at all times, even if I'm not around."

She frowns at that, shaking her head. "That's not what I mean, Dante. I don't want to live in fear, surrounded by security guards. I want to be part of whatever happens next. You're not doing this alone. I'm with you."

There's a fire in her eyes, a determination that's impossible to ignore. But as much as I admire her resolve, the thought of involving her in the tangled, often brutal world of my business fills me with unease. I swore to myself I'd keep her safe, shield her from this darkness that surrounds me. But she's right here, daring me to let her in, demanding to share the burden. And I realize I can't say no.

"Okay," I say, nodding. "But if we're going to face this together, then you follow my lead. If I tell you to stay back, you stay back. This isn't a game, Charlie."

She meets my gaze, unflinching. "I understand. I won't hold you back, but I won't be left behind either."

A weight lifts, the tension that's been simmering between us for so long softening in the clarity of this shared understanding. She's not here just as an observer or a protected treasure. She's here as my partner, and I feel something shift between us—an understanding that's deeper, solid, a shared resolve that strengthens with every passing second.

"We'll get through this," I say, my voice low, conviction anchoring every word. "Lorenzo thinks he has the upper hand, but he's wrong. He doesn't know what we're capable of."

Charlie's hand tightens around mine, and she gives a small, determined nod. "Let's show him."

We sit together in the silence, the weight of the decision settling over us. I can feel a new kind of resolve building in me, sharpened by the knowledge that this isn't just about survival anymore. It's about reclaiming our lives, our future.

Finally, I let out a breath. "I don't know what he'll try next, but whatever it is, we'll be ready."

For a moment, we just sit there, letting the reality of what's to come sink in. The tension isn't gone, but there's a shared strength now, a unity I hadn't anticipated. I place a light kiss on her forehead, a silent promise that whatever comes, I'll protect her with everything I have.

And as we sit in the quiet, wrapped in the warmth of each other's presence, I know that this—us—is the one thing Lorenzo can never touch.

But as I look past her, at the darkening sky through the villa's window, a thought lingers, unshakable, an echo of doubt at the back of my mind.

We're ready for whatever comes next.

But are we ready for him?

23

CHARLIE

Dante falls silent, his gaze drifting to some distant point. I wait, the quiet stretching between us until he finally speaks, his voice low and hesitant.

"Romano Holdings... it's not what it seems," he says, his words weighted with a truth I hadn't expected.

"What?" I blink, trying to make sense of what I'm hearing. "I don't understand."

Dante looks up, his expression somber. "Romano Holdings exists, but it's only a front, a decoy. The company everyone knows—the one you researched, the one that takes contracts and pays taxes—that's not the real business."

"But... you have offices, clients, employees," I stammer, struggling to reconcile his words with everything I know. "You're registered. I've seen the documents. Everything seems so—"

"Legitimate?" he interrupts, a bitter smile tugging at the corners of his mouth. "It's all designed to look that way. My father set it up like that. Romano Holdings was built to give our family a facade of legitimacy, a cover story for the world."

Dante pauses, letting the weight of his words sink in, watching as I piece it together.

"So... Romano Holdings is a shell?" I ask quietly.

"Yes, in a sense. The real business is hidden. The real profits come from products and services that would never show up on an official ledger." His eyes meet mine, steady but pained.

I stare at him, feeling the ground shift beneath me. "What... what kind of services?" I finally ask, though part of me isn't sure I want to know.

He sighs, running a hand through his hair. "Weapons, mostly. The kind people don't like to talk about. Distribution channels, underground networks. My father and his partners established this web years ago, using Romano Holdings as a mask."

I swallow, my thoughts churning as I try to keep up. A thousand questions rise to the surface, but only one makes it out. "And Lorenzo... what was his role?"

Dante's jaw tightens, and his gaze hardens. "Lorenzo was my father's closest partner. Nothing moved on this continent without their approval. My father trusted him completely. It was... his biggest mistake."

He trails off, looking away, and I feel the weight of what he's saying settle heavily between us. Gently, I reach out and touch his arm. "What happened?"

"They had a deal with some Cubans," he begins, his voice steady but edged with something dark. "It was supposed to be straightforward—a shipment of arms. But things went horribly wrong. I wasn't there, but I saw the aftermath. The Cubans claimed my father had double-crossed them, that he'd tried to cheat them out of their share."

Dante pauses, his hands clenched in his lap, tension

radiating from him. "My father got out with my uncle's help. But it was Lorenzo who was supposed to be with him that night. Instead, he claimed he had car trouble, said he couldn't make it."

I hold my breath, the pieces falling into place. "So... Lorenzo set him up?"

Dante's gaze shifts to mine, his eyes dark and haunted. "My father didn't think so. Lorenzo convinced him it was just a misunderstanding, an unfortunate incident in a business full of risks. But I never believed him. I saw the look in Lorenzo's eyes when he spoke. There was no remorse. No regret."

My heart aches for the boy Dante must have been, forced to watch a trusted friend betray his father. "What happened after?"

"Six months later, my father was killed in what the police called a 'robbery gone wrong.' But we knew better. The Cubans had come for revenge."

He pauses, his expression hardening. "Not long after, Lorenzo disappeared. He cut all ties with our family, and the next thing we knew, he was setting up his own arms operation—the same weapons the Cubans accused us of cheating them out of."

The enormity of it all leaves me speechless. Dante's world is darker and more twisted than I'd imagined. I reach for his hand, squeezing it. "I'm so sorry, Dante. Your father... he didn't deserve that."

He nods, but his face remains stoic, his gaze distant. "I learned a lot from him. But I also learned that in this world, trust is a weakness."

His words settle over me like a heavy fog, and I realize he's been carrying this pain for years, hiding it beneath layers of strength and resilience.

After a moment, I gather my courage. "Dante... if Lorenzo's back, what does he want from you now?"

He shakes his head, a grim smile tugging at his lips. "Control. Influence. Power. The same things he's always wanted. And this time, he's willing to use anyone close to me as leverage."

A chill runs through me as I consider the implications. "Then we have to do something. I can help. I have a friend whose boyfriend works for the FBI. Maybe he could look into Lorenzo, give us something to work with."

Dante's eyes narrow slightly, his tension palpable. "The FBI?" He hesitates, the conflict clear in his expression.

I reach for his hand, speaking softly. "It's just an idea. I know it's risky, but we need allies. If there's a way to gather information without drawing too much attention..."

He watches me, and slowly, the tension eases from his shoulders. "Alright. But be careful. The fewer people who know, the better."

Nodding, I reach for my phone, feeling a surge of resolve mixed with trepidation. My hand hovers over the screen as I think about the story Dante has just told me, the darkness surrounding us both. I know that if I press this number, there's no going back.

I hover my finger over the contact list, thinking about the implications of calling in outside help. FBI involvement is a line neither Dante nor I have crossed before. It could expose everything—Romano Holdings, Dante's entire world, even me. But Lorenzo's reach and ruthlessness don't give us much choice. We need to understand the enemy we're up against, and if Dante's right, Lorenzo's game is far from over.

Taking a steadying breath, I look up at Dante. "If we're

going to do this, we need to be smart. No one can know it's connected to us."

He nods, his gaze steady. "We'll handle it carefully. Use whatever connections you trust, but keep my name out of it. Lorenzo has a way of finding out things that should stay hidden." A muscle tightens in his jaw, and I can see he's as unsettled as I am. For Dante, involving the FBI must feel like breaking an unspoken code—crossing a boundary he's spent years reinforcing.

I scroll through my contacts, feeling the weight of his gaze. My hand shakes as I pull up my friend Alicia's number. She's one of the few people I trust completely, and while I've only met her boyfriend, Mark, a few times, he seemed reliable enough. Still, my chest tightens at the thought of involving them in this mess.

I put the phone down and meet Dante's eyes, finding strength in his steady presence beside me. "I'll message Alicia first, feel her out before diving into details. That way, we can gauge whether Mark can be discreet."

"Good idea." Dante shifts closer, his hand brushing mine, grounding me. "If you can frame it as curiosity or concern for a friend in trouble, she's less likely to suspect anything else."

I nod, composing a message that sounds casual but will get Alicia's attention. As soon as I hit send, I feel the weight lift slightly from my shoulders. I turn back to Dante, and though he's watching me with that intense, guarded look, there's a softness in his eyes that I didn't expect.

"You've been through so much to protect your father's legacy and shield the people close to you," I murmur. "But you're not alone anymore, Dante. I'm in this with you."

He takes my hand, his grip warm and reassuring. "Charlie, being with me... it's not easy. You've already paid a high price just by being close. It's something I hoped to keep you from."

"I know. But I choose to be here," I say, my voice firm. "I can't walk away from this, from you, just because it's dangerous. I won't let Lorenzo or anyone else scare me off."

A faint smile touches his lips, and he raises my hand to his mouth, pressing a light kiss to my knuckles. "You're stronger than I deserve," he whispers, and for a moment, I glimpse the vulnerability hidden beneath his hardened exterior.

Before I can respond, my phone buzzes. It's Alicia's reply, quick and to the point: Everything okay? You sound worried. Want to talk?

I show Dante the message, and he nods in approval. "Keep it simple. She's perceptive—give her just enough to make it believable, but nothing too specific yet."

I type out a response: Just found out an old friend might be in trouble. They're mixed up with a guy named Lorenzo. Ever heard of him?

I press send, my heart pounding as we wait for her response. Each second stretches longer than the last, and I can feel Dante's quiet tension beside me. He's a man used to handling things alone, used to carrying the burden of his family's empire and the weight of his father's mistakes. But now, he's let me in, and I can sense the vulnerability it brings him, the risk he's taking in trusting me with his past.

Finally, the phone buzzes again. I take a breath and open her reply: Lorenzo... as in Lorenzo Moretti? Mark's mentioned him before. Dangerous guy. What kind of trouble is your friend in?

The name sends a jolt through me. Moretti. Of course, it would be Lorenzo Moretti. The name has power, the kind that sends a chill through even the bravest people in Dante's world. I glance at him, and he gives a slight nod.

Not sure yet, I reply. Just trying to gather info without raising any red flags. If you and Mark can help, it'd mean a lot.

This time, her reply is swift: Let me talk to Mark. I'll see what he can dig up. Just... be careful, okay? This guy isn't someone you want to mess with.

I show Dante the message, and he releases a quiet breath, relief and resolve flickering across his face. "We'll wait to see what they find. In the meantime, I'll have my people monitor any unusual activity around Lorenzo's contacts. If he's making moves, we'll see it."

The tension between us eases slightly as I put my phone down, but an unease still lingers in the air. As we sit in silence, processing everything that's just happened, I find myself wondering how far this will go, how deeply Lorenzo's influence has already seeped into our lives.

Dante's voice pulls me from my thoughts. "Charlie, you don't have to be involved in this if it's too much. I can handle it."

I shake my head. "No, Dante. I'm in this with you. And if we're going to stop him, we have to do it together."

A flash of admiration crosses his face, and he takes my hand again, his touch warm and steady. "I don't know what I did to deserve someone like you," he murmurs.

"You didn't have to do anything," I reply softly. "I'm here because I want to be."

He leans closer, his gaze searching mine. I feel the pull between us, stronger than ever, a force that binds us together, despite the darkness closing in around us. His hand comes up to cup my cheek, and he leans in, his breath warm against my skin. Our lips meet in a slow, tender kiss, a promise of trust and strength that we'll hold onto, no matter what lies ahead.

The quiet is broken by another buzz from my phone. I pull away reluctantly, glancing down at the screen. It's a message from Alicia.

Mark wants to meet. Says it's better to talk in person. Are you up for that?

I show Dante, who nods thoughtfully. "It could be risky, but if Mark's willing to talk, he might have information that would be harder to convey through messages."

I nod, feeling a mixture of relief and apprehension. I text Alicia back, agreeing to the meeting and setting a time for the following day. When I put the phone down, Dante is watching me, his expression a blend of pride and concern.

"You're sure about this?" he asks, his hand resting on my shoulder.

"I am," I say, meeting his gaze with determination. "We have to know what we're dealing with. If Lorenzo is coming after us, we can't afford to be in the dark."

He nods, a spark of resolve igniting in his eyes. "Then we'll do this together."

We sit in silence, letting the gravity of the situation settle between us. Tomorrow will bring new challenges, new risks, but for now, we have each other, and that's enough.

That night, as we lie tangled together, a sense of calm settles over me despite the uncertainty. Dante's presence beside me is solid and grounding, a reminder that no matter how dark the path ahead may be, we'll face it side by side.

24

DANTE

The villa is deserted, just for us. The quiet fills the space, broken only by my footsteps echoing against the stone floors. It feels strange, yet comforting. I can't remember the last time I had this kind of quiet, this freedom to just... exist. I find I quite like it. I'm rarely alone.

The kitchen is as pristine as the rest of the house, free of any human evidence. The cleaning staff has clearly been through, leaving every surface spotless. Without them, this place would likely be a forgotten relic, gathering dust and cobwebs. A faint grimace crosses my face at the thought of the state it would be in if they didn't come. Without them, it would have been nearly uninhabitable for Charlie and me when we arrived.

I open the fridge, the cold light illuminating a well-stocked range of items. For a moment, I wonder if Gabe had it all prepared before we arrived. Everything's here: milk, cheese, eggs. Simple, quiet comforts. I pull out a few items, setting them on the counter. Among them are eggs, which I'll base the meal around. I hope they haven't gone bad.

"Ama! How do you know if eggs have gone bad?" I call out, raising my voice over the sound of the shower running down the hall.

"What?" Her voice floats back, muffled by walls and water.

"Bad eggs!" I repeat, louder.

"What?!"

"Never mind!" I shake my head, a faint smile playing at my lips. Some questions just don't need answers. Holding an egg to the light, I turn it over slowly and shrug. There's only one way to find out.

I crack the egg into a bowl and nod. It's good. I crack a few more, focusing on the simple rhythm of cooking. The kitchen fills with the soft sounds of whisking and the sizzle of butter on the stove. These are sounds of comfort, of home —things I didn't know I missed.

Footsteps pull my attention, and I glance up as Charlie enters, fresh from the shower, her hair wrapped in a towel and her cheeks flushed pink. She looks radiant, a sight that still has the power to stop me mid-motion. She walks toward me, barefoot and beaming, and as she leans up to kiss me, my heart does an unexpected, unfamiliar lurch. Her smile pulls one from me in return.

"That smells amazing," she says, glancing at the pan.

"Wait till you taste it," I reply, grinning as I make up a plate for her.

She sits at the kitchen table, lifting her fork with a look of amusement and anticipation. Her eyes close as she takes the first bite, and a soft, satisfied sound escapes her. "That's... so good."

I can't help but grin a little wider, pride settling somewhere warm in my chest.

Her eyes open, and she looks at me with a playful glint. "I didn't know you could cook like that."

I shrug. "It's just eggs and toast."

"Well, I didn't think you could even manage that." She laughs, the sound light and genuine, and something in me softens.

"There's a lot you don't know about me," I say quietly, meeting her gaze.

She tilts her head, curiosity softening her expression. "Why is that?"

I don't respond right away. Instead, I focus on my own plate, the act of chewing giving me a moment to gather my thoughts. Not many people know much about me—least of all the parts I'd rather stay buried.

She studies me, her gaze unwavering. "Why are you always so guarded?"

A soft chuckle escapes me, breaking the tension. "You know my job, amore mio."

"Yes, but something tells me you've always been this way —long before you became who you are now."

I pause, letting the food settle as I think. She's right, of course. And for reasons I don't fully understand, I want to tell her. "My father was the capo before me," I begin, choosing each word with care. "A ruthless boss, the kind who made enemies with a handshake and a smile. I was his first son. So, naturally, I was involved from a young age."

Charlie's gaze holds steady, but I notice the subtle way her hand tightens around her fork.

"He made sure I learned early," I continue, "brutal as it was. It was... necessary, in his eyes."

A flicker of uncertainty crosses her face, her voice barely a whisper. "You... did things?"

I nod, letting a heavy silence settle between us. "Yes.

Many things." I won't say more—if she wants details, she'll have to ask. Thankfully, she seems to sense the boundaries because her next question shifts the subject.

"What was your father like?"

"He was tough. Hard. A demanding taskmaster, even from his own son." Bitterness tinges my words, unbidden and sharp. "There was no room for coddling or mistakes. He taught me to be careful—always. What I say, who I say it to, what I do... because missteps could cost lives."

I let the words hang in the air, glancing at her to gauge her reaction. Her eyes are somber, a glimmer of something deeper—pity, maybe—softening her gaze.

"Hey," I say, trying to lighten the mood with a faint grin. "It all worked out, didn't it?"

She returns my smile, but it's a sad one. Her hand reaches across the table to mine, her fingers warm and reassuring. The weight of her touch lingers, grounding me.

I look out the window, watching the sunlight cast shifting shadows across the trees outside. I'm not used to this—sharing these pieces of myself, even with someone as close as Charlie. But with her, it feels different. Safe.

The words slip out before I can stop them. "I want a quiet life, with a happy family."

Silence follows, and I turn back, surprised at myself. "I've never told anyone that."

Charlie's face brightens, her smile a gentle reassurance. She squeezes my hand. "Your secret's safe with me."

We eat in silence for a while, each lost in thought. The quiet is comfortable, peaceful, and I find myself wishing it could stay like this. A part of me, I realize, longs for this ordinary simplicity, far from the chaos that usually follows me.

But peace is fleeting, and reality waits for no one. My

phone vibrates on the table, snapping me back. I glance at the screen. Gabe.

"Tell him I said 'hi,'" Charlie says, getting up to clear the dishes.

I pick up the phone, watching her as she moves around the kitchen, humming softly to herself. "Hello, Charlie says hi."

"Send my regards," Gabe replies, his tone as brisk as ever. "How's it going?"

"It's... quiet," I admit, leaning back. "Surprisingly so."

"You like that?"

"It's growing on me." I take a sip of my coffee, savoring the bitterness.

"How's Charlie?"

I glance her way. She catches my eye and smiles, and I can't help but return it. "She seems to be enjoying herself."

"Good for you," Gabe says, but his tone shifts. "Because I have updates."

"Doesn't sound like good news."

"It isn't."

I sit up, tension sharpening my focus. "Go on."

"All business is halted. We're hemorrhaging money. Everything's at a standstill."

I exhale, rubbing a hand over my face, the momentary peace dissipating. "We knew this would happen."

"I know, but it's not pretty. I don't like it."

"Neither do I, Gabe," I mutter, feeling the familiar weight of responsibility settle on my shoulders.

A pause, then Gabe's voice drops. "Boss, there's something else. It's about Silas."

I clench my jaw, already sensing trouble. "What has that snake done now?"

"Nothing. He's dead."

The words hit like a punch. Despite everything, I hadn't expected this. Images of Silas flash through my mind: the smug smirk, his endless posturing. Then, the image shifts to him pleading for his life, beaten and broken, wrapped in an oversized orange towel.

"His body was found on the beach. Tortured," Gabe adds, his voice grim.

A cold nausea twists in my stomach. Torture... the image is too vivid. I picture him writhing, begging. A man like Silas doesn't die easy, and I know exactly the kind of people capable of such brutality. Part of me feels sick, but another part whispers, he deserved it.

I clear my throat, pushing down the emotion. "Thanks for letting me know, Gabe."

We end the call, and I set the phone down, staring at my coffee, now lukewarm. The silence feels different now, weighted with memories, regrets, and too many questions.

Charlie watches me from the sink, her brows furrowing. "Everything alright?"

I nod, though the words taste hollow. "Just... business."

She walks over, placing a hand on my shoulder, grounding me once more. For a moment, I let myself lean into her warmth, savoring the simple, steady presence she offers. Maybe, just maybe, there's a chance at something beyond all this.

I lean into her touch, allowing the comfort of her warmth to pull me out of my thoughts. But the silence between us has shifted, no longer as light as it was only moments ago. I know she's reading the weight on my face, trying to decipher what's left unsaid.

Charlie's hand slides down to my arm, giving it a gentle squeeze. "You don't have to tell me," she says softly, "but you don't have to carry it alone, either."

Her words stir something fragile inside me, and I almost say more than I should. Instead, I just nod, giving her a weak smile that I know doesn't quite reach my eyes. I'm too used to carrying this alone; opening up feels as foreign as it is tempting.

"It's nothing I can't handle," I say, keeping my voice steady, though I'm not sure I believe it myself. The truth looms heavy in my mind—Silas's fate could easily become mine, a reminder of how quickly things can turn.

She searches my face, and for a second, I wonder if she can see through the mask. But she doesn't press me, sensing the boundaries I'm barely holding up. "If that changes," she says quietly, "I'm here."

Before I can respond, her phone vibrates on the counter. She picks it up, glancing at the screen with a frown. "It's my mother," she murmurs, a hint of tension in her tone. "I should take this."

I nod, watching as she steps out of the kitchen, her voice soft but tense as she answers. Even from a distance, the faint sound of her words drifts back to me, a reminder that we each carry our own burdens.

Alone, I stare down at the remnants of breakfast, the empty plates and half-finished coffee seeming like relics of a simpler world—a world slipping away, piece by piece. I want to hold onto this quiet, this fragile peace, but I can feel the storm looming, an inevitability I can't ignore.

My phone buzzes again, and this time, I don't have to look to know who it is. Gabe's message is brief, but the words are enough to twist the knife just a little deeper: *They know where you are.*

The cliff edge grows sharper beneath my feet, and I realize I was right about one thing—peace was never meant to last.

25

CHARLIE

"What?!"

The word escapes me before I can stop it, my voice sharp and cracking with disbelief. Dante doesn't flinch. His expression remains impassive, stone-cold and unyielding, as if he didn't just casually drop a bomb that has me reeling.

"What do you mean he's dead?" I ask, my voice trembling.

"Dead," Dante repeats, the word landing like a gavel. Final. Absolute.

The air between us feels electric, charged with too many questions and not enough answers. I push myself upright, clutching the blankets for balance as the room seems to tilt.

"You saw him two days ago," I manage, my mind racing to make sense of this. "You said you found him, Dante. On that island."

"I did," he says evenly, sitting at the edge of the bed. "And now, he's dead."

The simplicity of his tone chills me.

I force myself to hold his gaze, searching for something—remorse, regret, anything to soften the edges of his words. But his expression remains unreadable, a mask I can't penetrate.

"How?" I whisper.

"Does it matter?" His voice is clipped, his eyes narrowing as if daring me to press further.

"Yes, it matters!" I snap, surprising even myself with the force of my words. "He wasn't just some random person. He was—"

"He was a liability," Dante interrupts, his tone razor-sharp. "And in this world, liabilities don't get to stick around."

The words hit me like a slap, and I suck in a breath, trying to steady myself. "You don't know it was Lorenzo," I argue, grasping for logic. "It could've been anyone—"

"It was Lorenzo," he says, his certainty like a wall I can't break through. "He had the means, the motive, and the message was clear. Silas crossed the wrong person, and he paid the price."

I shake my head, frustration bubbling to the surface. "And what about us, Dante? What does this mean for us?"

He stands abruptly, towering over me as his voice drops to a dangerous low. "It means we stay vigilant. It means you trust me to handle this. And it means you stop questioning every damn thing I do to keep you safe."

The heat in his voice makes my pulse quicken—not just from anger, but from something deeper, something primal that I can't ignore. I stand too, refusing to let him intimidate me.

"I'm not questioning you," I shoot back, stepping closer. "I'm trying to understand why you keep shutting me out. You say you want to protect me, but you won't let me in.

How am I supposed to feel safe when you treat me like an outsider?"

His eyes flash, and for a moment, I see something raw and unguarded beneath the surface. "Because letting you in would mean putting you even closer to danger. And I won't do that."

"Then what am I supposed to do, Dante?" I ask, my voice rising. "Just sit here and hope you don't get yourself killed while I wait for the next attack?"

"Yes," he says firmly, his hands balling into fists at his sides. "That's exactly what you're supposed to do."

We're inches apart now, the tension between us crackling like a live wire. My chest rises and falls with each ragged breath, and I can feel the heat radiating from his body, a stark contrast to the icy fury in his voice.

The anger crackles between us until suddenly his mouth crashes against mine. The kiss is fierce, desperate, all our frustration and fear pouring into it. His hands grip my waist as I press against him, matching his intensity.

I tangle my fingers in his hair, drawing a low growl from his throat. He backs me against the wall, his body caging mine. The kiss deepens, turning from anger to raw need.

"I can't lose you," he breathes against my lips, his voice rough with emotion.

THE SILENCE that follows is deafening, charged with everything we haven't said. Dante's gaze locks onto mine, his eyes dark and unreadable, and I feel a shiver run down my spine.

"Charlie," he says softly, his voice low and rough. "You don't understand what this world is like. What it does to people. To me."

"Then show me," I whisper, my voice trembling. "Stop shutting me out and let me in."

He exhales sharply, his jaw tightening as he looks away. But I reach for him, my fingers brushing against his hand, and the contact sends a spark through both of us.

"Please," I murmur, my voice breaking.

His eyes meet mine again, and this time, there's no mistaking the war raging within him. He's fighting something—his instincts, his fears, his desire.

Slowly, almost hesitantly, he steps closer, his hand lifting to cup my cheek. His touch is warm, grounding, and I lean into it despite myself.

"Charlie..." he breathes, his voice filled with a mix of longing and restraint.

Our faces are inches apart, our breaths mingling in the charged silence. I can feel the heat of his skin, the roughness of his calloused palm against my cheek, and my heart pounds in response.

His thumb traces my bottom lip as he holds my gaze. The tenderness in his touch contrasts with the storm in his eyes. My hands slide up his chest, feeling his heart race beneath my palm.

"Charlie," he whispers, leaning in until our lips nearly touch. His breath fans across my face, sending shivers down my spine. The moment stretches, electric with possibility.

His lips brush mine, feather-light, testing. My fingers curl into his shirt, pulling him closer as the kiss deepens with shared longing.

Just as our lips are about to meet, a sharp knock at the door breaks the moment. We both freeze, the spell shattered, and I step back, my cheeks burning.

Dante's expression hardens instantly, and he strides to the door, his hand already reaching for the gun at his waistband.

Gabe stands on the other side, his face grim. "We have a problem."

"What is it?" Dante asks, his voice cold and controlled.

Gabe glances at me before turning his attention back to Dante. "Lorenzo's men are on the move. They're closing in on our location."

The words send a chill through me, and I wrap my arms around myself as fear tightens its grip. Dante's jaw clenches, and he nods sharply.

"Get the car ready," he orders. "We're leaving in ten minutes."

Gabe nods and disappears down the hall. Dante turns to me, his expression unreadable but his eyes burning with intensity.

"Pack your things," he says, his voice low but firm. "We're not staying here."

I nod, my mind racing as I move to gather my belongings. The fear and adrenaline coursing through me are almost too much to bear, but I focus on the task at hand, clinging to the one thing I know for certain: Dante won't let anything happen to me.

As we step out into the night, the air feels heavy with the promise of what's to come. And for the first time, I wonder if we'll make it through this war unscathed.

26

DANTE

The sky burns orange as the sun dips, its edges blurring into the horizon. It should be a beautiful evening, one I'd usually savor, but tonight, peace eludes me. I pace the length of the living room, back and forth, like a caged animal. It's only been a few days since Charlie and I arrived here, and already, the walls feel too close, pressing down on me. I hate being trapped, especially on someone else's terms.

Lorenzo. His name grates on my mind like nails on glass. I can see his smirk, his face practically reveling in my confinement. My fists clench; I want to wipe that look off his face—for good. Going back would be foolish, but the longer I stay here, the more rage churns within me.

"Earth to Danny."

Her voice snaps me back to the present. I look up to see Charlie leaning in the doorway, watching me with that half-worried, half-amused look she gets when I'm too far lost in my head. I don't know how long she's been there.

"Hey," I say, attempting a smile to reassure her.

She steps closer. "You okay, Danny?" Her use of the

name I gave her when we first met brings a flash of warmth. It grounds me, reminding me of who I am with her. I put a little more effort into my smile.

"I'm fine, just going over some things in my head. Making sure there aren't any mistakes." I force my tone to sound casual, though the truth is anything but.

She studies me a moment longer, sensing there's more beneath the surface. "I get that way before a big case. If I don't prepare for every scenario, I can't sleep." Her hand slides up to my cheek as she leans in, pressing a soft kiss to my lips, her gaze lingering. "Are you sure you're okay?"

"Positive." It's half-true. There's nothing to worry about... yet. But I can't shake the feeling that our time here, our illusion of safety, is fleeting.

"Alright," she says, a hint of brightness returning. "I'm heading to the pool. Thought I'd swim for a bit and watch the sunset." She looks back toward the sliding doors, and that's when I notice her outfit.

She's wrapped a towel around her shoulders, a deep blue that highlights her bathing suit beneath. She clutches a book, and her hot pink flip-flops add a splash of color against the polished floor. She turns to me with a teasing smile.

"Will you join me?"

I want to, more than anything, but I can't. Not now, not when my mind is tangled in strategies and threats. If I go with her, I'll just end up pacing by the poolside, restless as ever.

"No, but thanks, honey. I need to make a phone call."

She raises an eyebrow. "Gabe?"

"My uncles." I sigh. The words feel heavy even before I've spoken them, knowing the conversation I'm about to initiate.

She gives a sympathetic look, her humor fading into concern. "Good luck with that."

"Thanks."

As she turns to leave, I reach over, giving her a playful slap on her bottom. She gasps, glancing back to shake a finger at me, though her smile betrays her amusement. I watch her until she disappears outside, the image of her carefree stride a small comfort amid my unease.

With a sigh, I pull out my phone. I wasn't bluffing when I said I'd call my uncles; it's time we had a conversation.

The phone rings, each tone amplifying the tension knotted in my chest. Finally, the ringing stops, and silence fills the other end, faint background noise filtering through. Dread slips in. Are they in danger?

"Hello?" My voice is sharper than I intended.

"Stop shouting, boy. I'm not deaf." The cranky tone of my Uncle Stefano floods me with relief, his voice laced with its usual impatience. He sounds solid and steady, so any thoughts of danger dissipate instantly.

"Are you okay?"

"Of course, I'm okay," he grumbles, as if the question were an insult. "Kids these days, always worried about things they don't need to be."

"Yeah, just checking." I suppress a grin, reminded of how he's always been: a gruff guardian, quick to criticize but dependable to a fault.

A second voice filters in, slurred and unmistakable. "How are you doing, Dante?" Uncle Alessandro. I stifle a groan—he's likely been drinking again.

"Just great, Uncle. Just great."

"Wonderful. Being 'just great' is underrated, you know," he says, his words blurring together.

"I agree." Before he can continue, I interrupt. "I called the group. Are you the only two here?"

"Matteo's with me," Stefano replies, his tone still edged with irritation. "We're spending this 'forced vacation' together. Thanks to you." His accusation is clear, and though I expected it, his words sting.

Another voice chimes in, "I'm here with Alessandro," Uncle Angelo says dryly. "Somebody's got to keep an eye on him."

"I don't need babysitting," Alessandro mutters, missing the sarcasm.

I almost chuckle but hold back. "Anyone know where Uncle Emi is?"

"He was on a flight. He should be fine. We'll know more in a few hours," Stefano says dismissively.

I nod to myself, reassured. "Good. I'm glad we're all safe for now." I start pacing again, gathering my thoughts. "I made this call to strategize. We've all been affected by Lorenzo's latest move—"

"Issues you caused, boy," Stefano cuts in sharply.

"Uncle—"

"No, let me finish." Stefano's voice hardens. "We told you to leave Lorenzo alone. We told you to leave that Horizon project alone. It was bad news from the start. But did you listen? No."

"No, he didn't," Matteo chimes in.

"Of course he didn't," Stefano continues, his voice dripping with disdain. "The golden child has to get his way. And now, because of you, we're being hounded from our territories, our businesses are under attack, and everything's in turmoil. For what?"

I clench my jaw, letting his words sink in like stones.

Stefano's anger isn't new, but this bitterness—this accusation—is sharper than before.

"Now you call us," he goes on, his tone dripping with disdain, "for what? To gloat? To tell us we were right? Or maybe to rub it in? Maybe this was your plan all along, hm?" His voice drops, muttering curses in Italian that sting.

Silence follows, as thick as smoke. Finally, Uncle Angelo clears his throat, breaking the tension.

"Dante, your uncle isn't wrong. The quickest solution is to let this go."

I sigh, pulling the phone from my ear and setting it on speaker. Uncle Angelo's voice fills the room.

"Just give Lorenzo what he wants, and we're all good."

"He attacked my factories," Alessandro adds, frustration barely hidden. "Nothing's coming out of those places for a while. I'm trying not to think about the money that's being drained."

"Alessandro's right," Angelo continues. "We're hemorrhaging money from the attacks, and each day costs us more. The simplest path is to give Lorenzo what he wants. Let him have the Horizon project, and all this will blow over."

"But this is Lorenzo!" I snap, unable to keep the anger from seeping into my tone.

"So?" Stefano retorts.

"So we can't just give in—not after everything he's done." My voice rises, frustration giving way to fury. "Giving in means letting him walk all over us."

"It doesn't matter." Stefano's tone is dismissive. "The past is the past. Move on."

"When did this family become so willing to yield?" My voice is quiet, but the question hangs heavily in the air, unchallenged.

My resolve hardens. "I'm not letting Lorenzo have his way."

"For the love of—"

"Listen to me, son." Matteo, who's been uncharacteristically silent, finally speaks. "This isn't the road to go down. Let this go. Let's all go home. Let things go back to normal."

I stare at the wall, memories flashing—David's lifeless eyes, Charlie bleeding outside my office, the child she nearly lost. Her kidnapping from the hospital haunts me like a scar that will never fade.

"No, Uncle." My voice is low, controlled, but each word feels like a hammer. "I can't let this go."

A collective sigh echoes from the speaker. Uncle Stefano mutters, "Insolent child," before the line goes dead, him and Matteo gone.

"Dante," Angelo's voice softens, almost pleading. "Think about it. The money, the respect we're losing every day. If we don't resolve this, other families will see us as weak. They'll circle, looking for any piece they can take. This isn't just about us; it's about our family's future."

I don't respond. I can't. Each word digs into me, testing the walls around my resolve. When the silence stretches on, Angelo speaks again.

"Just... think it over, Dante. Goodbye."

"Goodbye," Alessandro murmurs in the background before the line dies.

The silence that follows is thick, almost suffocating. I stand there for a long time, staring at the blank wall, memories flashing like specters before me.

Finally, I turn away. I don't know what I expected from my uncles, but it wasn't this. Part of me wants to believe they're right, that yielding would bring peace, but the deeper part of me—the part that knows what this fight has cost—refuses.

Out of the corner of my eye, I see Charlie by the pool, her figure relaxed, her book open in her hands. She's a vision of calm against the waning orange glow.

Without thinking, I walk to the sliding doors and step outside. The sky fades to deep blue, stars piercing the dusk.

She looks up as I approach, her gaze softening with quiet understanding. "That bad, huh?"

I nod, unable to put the weight of it into words.

"Come here." She pats the spot beside her.

I sit down in the pool chair next to hers, but before I know it, my head finds its way into her lap. Her fingers slide through my hair, a simple gesture that brings a wave of calm over me. She doesn't say anything, just goes back to her book, her hand idly stroking my hair.

We sit like that as the last traces of light slip away, wrapped in quiet comfort. With her touch grounding me, the weight of my family's expectations, Lorenzo's threats, and the unyielding path I've chosen don't seem as impossible.

For now, that's enough.

27

CHARLIE

I lean back in my chair, stretching as I take a break from the computer screen. My hand drifts to my belly, resting on the small but unmistakable bump that's become impossible to ignore. Not too long ago, I stood in front of the mirror, turning this way and that, trying to match the sight with the reality of that pregnancy test. Now, there's no more wondering. I'm carrying a part of him—of us.

Dante's voice pulls me out of my thoughts. "Do you want anything else?" he asks, glancing over from the kitchen.

I shake my head, a soft smile curving my lips. "I'm good, thanks."

He'd offered to bring my meal to me, but I insisted on sitting here with him. I didn't tell him the real reason: I just like being close to him, knowing he's here, both of us sharing this quiet moment. There's a strange comfort in this new normal we've found.

Turning back to the computer, I scroll through the legal documents on my screen. I've been piecing together clues that have nagged at me for days, following a faint thread that feels like it could lead somewhere bigger.

"You should leave that and focus on your food," Dante says, his tone playful but insistent.

"Just five more minutes," I reply, glancing up with a pleading smile.

He raises an eyebrow, unimpressed. "You said that five minutes ago." Leaning over, he gently pushes the laptop aside.

I open my mouth to protest, but his determined look makes me relent. With a sigh, I pick up my plate and fork and start eating.

"It's already cold," he remarks with a smirk.

I roll my eyes, swallowing my first bite. "It's not cold. Just because it's not scalding hot like you prefer doesn't make it cold."

Dante shrugs with exaggerated seriousness. "No steam, no heat."

I huff, pretending to ignore him as I focus on my food, savoring each bite. Despite myself, a sigh escapes.

"You like it, huh?" Dante asks, his voice coming from somewhere behind me.

"It's delicious," I admit, almost grudgingly. "But yes, you'd probably think it tastes better hot."

"Oh, you have no idea." He grins, and I can't help but smile back, shaking my head at his persistence.

The next few minutes pass in companionable silence as we focus on our plates. I don't know what he made—and I'm too busy savoring each bite to ask—but it seems like some kind of chicken dish with an absurdly good sauce. I make a mental note to ask him about the recipe later—if he's willing to teach me.

Dante's been uncharacteristically nurturing since we

arrived at the villa. Last night, he rubbed my feet until I fell asleep, and it was the best rest I've had in ages. It's moments like these that show me the softer side he reserves just for me.

Then, my laptop beeps, startling me. I glance up at Dante, who's watching me with a knowing look.

"It has to be important," I say, reaching for the laptop. "Just one quick check."

He sighs, stepping back as I pull the computer closer and tap the screen to life. My heart skips as I see the notification—a message from Katie. I begin reading, and as the words sink in, a knot forms in my stomach.

"Oh no..."

"What is it?" Dante's voice sharpens, concern flickering in his eyes.

Without a word, I turn the laptop toward him. He leans forward, reading the message in silence, and I watch as his expression shifts subtly—the hardening of his gaze, the tightening of his jaw.

He finally looks up, his gaze dark. "Did you see the pictures?"

I nod, not trusting my voice.

Katie's message, forwarded from her FBI-agent boyfriend Micah, contains a few photos. And in one of them, unmistakably, is Dante's Uncle Matteo—at a party hosted by Lorenzo. Micah sent this, assuming it would be of interest. And judging by Dante's reaction, Micah was right.

"So it's true?" I ask quietly. "That's your uncle?"

"Yeah, that's Uncle Matteo." Dante's voice is low, heavy with a mix of anger and disbelief. He leans back, staring at nothing in particular.

"If he's there, there's no way Uncle Stefano doesn't know about it," he says finally. "Matteo does nothing without Stefano. And if Stefano knows... Uncle Emiliano's probably involved too. He usually does whatever those two want." He sighs, a raw, wounded sound that breaks my heart.

His shoulders slump slightly, the sadness evident even if he tries to hide it. To anyone else, he might look as impassive as ever, but I can see it—the hurt, the betrayal simmering just beneath the surface.

"I'm so sorry," I whisper, reaching out to him. I want to say something that will make it better, but words feel useless.

He waves a hand as if brushing off my sympathy, but I know he doesn't mean it.

"They always disagreed," he murmurs, almost to himself.

"Disagreed?" I prompt, sensing he needs to talk about it.

He nods. "My father had his way of running things, but they always wanted to do things differently." His voice is distant, reflective. "No matter how successful he was, they never seemed satisfied. There was always tension between them."

He pauses, his gaze distant, as though seeing a memory I can't. "They'd argue, sometimes loud enough that I'd hear them from a floor away. But I thought it was normal—just family arguments, all in good faith." He shakes his head slowly. "Or so I thought."

He lets out a soft, bitter laugh that makes my chest ache. There's a hollow sadness in his eyes, a look of someone who's realizing that trust was misplaced, that loyalty wasn't what he thought it was.

I rise to my feet, walking over to his side. Gently, I pull him into an embrace, and he rests his head against my belly. The connection feels intimate, grounding both of us. I wonder what it must be like for him, seeing his family turn away, choosing the man who's been his enemy.

"I'm here," I whisper, brushing a hand through his hair.

For a moment, he doesn't respond. Then his arms come around me, holding me close, as if drawing strength from the simple act of being together.

After a long pause, he speaks again, his voice muffled. "It's one thing to have enemies. But when family sides with them... it's different. It's like the ground beneath you isn't steady."

I hold him tighter, wishing I could take away some of the pain he's carrying. "You don't have to go through this alone. I'm not going anywhere."

He lifts his head, looking up at me with an intensity that sends a shiver down my spine. "You and this baby... you're the only family that matters now."

The words hit me hard, a reminder of how much has changed. This life, this future we're building—it's fragile, precious. I run my fingers through his hair, offering him a small, comforting smile.

"I love you, Dante," I say softly. It's a truth that feels both simple and monumental, grounding me in a way I hadn't expected.

A faint smile tugs at his lips. "I love you too, Charlie."

We stay like that, wrapped in each other's arms, and for a moment, the weight of betrayal, of family discord, feels manageable. The world outside might be fractured, but here, we're whole.

I linger in Dante's embrace, letting the warmth of his arms ground me. This life we're building together, the future I can feel moving and shifting within me, feels so precarious in moments like this. The knowledge that his own family might be conspiring with Lorenzo to undermine him—us—sends a fresh wave of uncertainty through me.

After a long silence, Dante pulls back slightly, his hands still resting on my shoulders. There's an intensity in his gaze, a fierce determination I know well but which still manages to take my breath away.

"I'll take care of this," he says, his voice low, words weighted with a promise. "My uncles may think they can stand by Lorenzo without consequence, but they're wrong. I won't let them jeopardize everything we've fought for."

I nod, feeling the weight of his resolve, even as a chill runs through me. I know how much family has meant to Dante, how much he's sacrificed to protect them, even when they didn't deserve it. Now, to see him ready to sever those bonds—to cut off the ties he's held so close—makes me realize how deep this betrayal has cut him.

"They'll regret choosing him over you," I say softly, a fierce edge to my own voice I barely recognize. "And they'll realize it too late."

Dante's gaze softens, and for a moment, the anger fades, replaced by something gentler. "Thank you, Charlie. For standing by me, no matter what."

"I'll always stand by you," I reply, the words coming from a place deeper than simple loyalty. This is love. It's commitment. And it's knowing that, whatever happens, we're in this together.

He reaches out, brushing a hand over my cheek, and I lean into his touch. The quiet intimacy of the moment lingers, holding us in its grasp, until a faint buzzing breaks the silence. His phone, vibrating on the table, pulls us both back to the present.

Dante's jaw tightens as he glances at the screen. "It's

Gabe," he murmurs, sliding his phone off the table and swiping to answer. "What's going on?"

I can only hear one side of the conversation, but Dante's expression shifts from irritation to grim focus as Gabe speaks. After a moment, Dante's gaze flicks to me, his brow furrowing.

"When?" he asks, his voice tense. "Where did you last see them?"

I feel a pang of dread rise in my chest. Dante's grip tightens on the phone, his knuckles going white as Gabe continues to speak.

"All right. I'll be in touch soon," he says finally, and hangs up, his expression hardening as he sets the phone down.

"What is it?" I ask, my stomach twisting at the look on his face.

Dante's eyes meet mine, dark and stormy. "My uncles have gone off the radar. Gabe's men were keeping tabs on Matteo and Stefano, but they've slipped surveillance. No one knows where they went or who they're with."

A cold shiver runs down my spine. "Do you think…?"

Dante nods, his expression grim. "They're with Lorenzo. I'd bet my life on it. The fact they're moving now means he's about to make a play. This isn't just a quiet betrayal—they're plotting something big."

I swallow, my hand instinctively moving to my belly. "What does this mean for us?"

"It means I need to act, and fast." Dante's jaw is set, a look of steely resolve overtaking the vulnerability I saw just moments ago. "They've forced my hand. If Lorenzo's calling them in, he's ready to make his move. And if my uncles have chosen to stand with him, then they're my enemies now, too."

The finality in his voice sends a pang through me. For Dante, family has always been more than just a word. I can only imagine the toll this is taking on him, even if he refuses to show it.

"What will you do?" I ask quietly, searching his face.

Dante's gaze meets mine, steady and unflinching. "I'll do whatever it takes to protect us. To keep you and our child safe."

He takes a deep breath, his hand reaching out to grasp mine, grounding us both. "We need to leave the villa. Staying here is too risky now. If Lorenzo has half the resources I think he does, he'll know we're here before long."

I nod, feeling the weight of his words settle over me. The villa has felt like a sanctuary, a safe haven where we could finally breathe, but now even that is being stripped away. The realization makes my heart ache, but I know he's right. If we stay here, we're vulnerable, exposed.

"Where will we go?" I ask, trying to keep the tremor out of my voice.

Dante squeezes my hand. "I have a place in the mountains. It's more secluded, harder to find. It'll buy us time to figure out our next move."

He pauses, his eyes searching mine. "I know this is hard, Charlie. I hate putting you through this."

I shake my head, tightening my grip on his hand. "You don't have to apologize. I knew what I was signing up for. And I'll go wherever you go."

A flicker of relief passes over his face, and he pulls me into an embrace. We stand like that, holding onto each other as if we can stave off the storm gathering around us.

"When should we leave?" I ask, my voice barely a whisper against his shoulder.

"Tonight," he says, his tone resolute. "I'll make the arrangements."

I pull back to look at him, searching his face. "Dante... promise me something."

"Anything," he replies, his gaze unwavering.

"Promise me that, no matter what happens, we'll keep fighting for this—for us. For our family."

Dante's expression softens, and he cups my face in his hands. "I promise, Charlie. I'll fight until my last breath to keep you safe. To give our child the life we both dreamed of."

His words settle over me like a shield, and for the first time since Gabe's call, a glimmer of hope pierces the dread clouding my thoughts. We'll fight. We'll find a way through this.

But as we make our preparations, packing only what we need and leaving behind the semblance of peace we'd managed to carve out, I can't shake the feeling that this is only the beginning. That whatever Lorenzo and Dante's uncles are planning is far bigger—and more dangerous—than either of us realizes.

As we step outside, the villa looms behind us, a silent witness to the promises, the secrets, and the fragile hope we're carrying with us into the night.

I glance over at Dante, his silhouette strong and unyielding in the dim light, and I tighten my grip on his hand. Whatever lies ahead, I know we'll face it together. But the shadows of betrayal linger, casting a long, dark trail that we can't escape, no matter how far we run.

28

DANTE

In the days since discovering my uncles' betrayal, my focus has been razor-sharp. I've kept myself busy strategizing, planning—refusing to let the weight of family betrayal drag me down. With Lorenzo entrenched in the Horizon City project through Silas Kane, I have no illusions: he won't stop until he has his claws in everything I've built. Silas might be dead, but I'm certain Lorenzo secured his hold on the project long before taking him out. Whatever he's put in place is still grinding forward, and I need to stop it.

I shared as much with Gabe, sending him a set of carefully worded legal agreements for our partners, filled with incentives and subtle safeguards Charlie helped draft. We plan to keep a grip on Horizon City before Lorenzo tightens his. The agreements are rock solid, enticing enough for any business-minded partner.

"I've sent them over to you. Deliver them as planned and let me know how it goes," I tell Gabe, my voice steady.

Gabe hesitates. "Are you sure this will work?"

"It has to—or at least buy us some time." I pause,

hearing Charlie's voice in my head reminding me to stay calm. "Just deliver them. They're too good to refuse, but if they push back... we'll know why."

"I get it," Gabe replies, with a hint of admiration. "Alright. Talk soon."

"Talk soon," I repeat, ending the call.

Quiet settles over me as I slip the phone back into my pocket. I slide the glass door open, stepping out to watch the sun dip lower over the trees. The sky glows in fiery reds and oranges, casting a warm light over the villa's pool. I spot Charlie gliding through the water, her strokes deliberate and unhurried. She's taken to swimming every other day, finding peace in the routine.

A rare, peaceful smile creeps onto my face as I watch her emerge, droplets tracing paths down her skin. She catches my gaze, breaking into a wide smile that eases the relentless edge of my frustration. I wave back, feeling an unexpected calm wash over me.

But the calm is shattered by my phone ringing. My frown returns as I pull it from my pocket, Gabe's name flashing on the screen.

"Hello?"

"Boss, something strange happened," he says, tense and abrupt. "Right after we got off the phone, I sent the documents and followed up, but the responses were... strange."

My brows knit in confusion. "What kind of responses?"

"The first one—Edgar—said the terms were too stringent. He's pulling out."

I shift uncomfortably, suspicion creeping in. "Edgar? That's... odd."

"That's what I thought," Gabe agrees. "The terms are excellent, almost impossible to refuse. But I called the next partner, just to be sure they'd received and read it."

"What did they say?"

"The same thing. Claimed the terms were unreasonable." Gabe's voice dips. "They couldn't have read it all and consulted legal advice that quickly."

A knot forms in my chest, a sense of dread rising. "They didn't read it."

"Exactly. So I called Thomas Rossi—the high-end merchandise guy who used to hang around with Silas Kane?"

I nod, already dreading what's coming next. "And?"

Gabe sighs. "He said he was just about to call us to pull out. Claimed he suddenly realized he was stretched too thin with other investments."

I grit my teeth. "His other investments, sure."

"He 'sends his apologies,'" Gabe adds dryly.

"He can shove his apologies—" I stop, letting out a frustrated breath and trying to hold my anger in check. I close my eyes, trying to think.

When I open them, the world seems dimmer, colder. "This is Lorenzo, isn't it?"

"I think so, yeah," Gabe says, a hint of helpless anger in his voice. "He got every one of them to back out. I can't say how, but they're all using the same lines, like they were handed a script."

"He's not wasting time." I force myself to breathe, each inhale slow and steady. "Send me Thomas's number. Maybe I can talk him down."

"Alright, I'll send it now."

A text arrives with Thomas's number before I've even hung up. Efficient as ever, Gabe.

I dial and wait, the phone ringing. Each second stretches, tension prickling my nerves. Finally, the line clicks open.

"Hello?"

"Hi Thomas, it's Dante." I keep my voice steady, almost casual, though there's an edge I can't hide.

"Oh." The single word drops like a stone, heavy with unspoken tension.

"I heard you're pulling out of the project," I say, keeping my tone even.

"Yes, Dante. I'm sorry, but I realized I'm stretched too thin with my other commitments."

The words sound rehearsed, echoing Gabe's report. I grit my teeth but keep my tone calm. "Thomas, this project is solid. You'll make more here than with those other investments. Whatever you need, you can get credit to cover it."

"I'm sorry, Dante. But I have other obligations. It's just not possible." His words feel hollow, as if he's reading from a script. I let the realization settle.

"I understand," I reply, masking my frustration. "Take care, Thomas."

The line goes dead, leaving only cold, empty silence. I turn back to the villa, anger boiling over as I kick a chair, sending it clattering against the table. The loud noise cuts through the quiet evening air.

Charlie's head jerks up at the sound, her expression startled and concerned. "Dante!" she calls out, swimming to the edge and pulling herself out, wrapping herself in a towel.

She walks over, eyes questioning. "What's going on?"

I slump into a chair beside her, the anger simmering just beneath the surface. "The partners are pulling out," I say, the words bitter on my tongue.

"All of them?" she asks, voice barely a whisper.

"Every last one." I run a hand over my face, exhaustion settling beneath the anger. "Lorenzo has somehow convinced each one to back out. He's tightened his grip on every angle."

Charlie looks at me, bewildered. "Did he threaten them?"

"No, it's worse than that." I almost smile at the absurdity. "They were like Silas, Charlie. They were never real partners. They were Lorenzo's pawns, placeholders set up just to sabotage me."

"Oh my god," she breathes, horror dawning in her eyes.

I can't help but chuckle bitterly, though it's more a release of tension than any real amusement. "I have to give him credit—it's a smart move. He's cornered me perfectly. With the partners gone, everything falls on me. I either watch the project fail or burn myself out trying to keep it afloat." I shake my head. "If I didn't hate him so much, I'd applaud him."

Charlie steps closer, her towel wrapped around her shoulders, water still dripping from her hair. She sits beside me, folding herself into my arms, grounding me in her warmth.

"Dante..." She rests her head on my shoulder, her voice soft but steady. "This isn't the end. We'll figure something out. You're not alone in this."

I hold her close, grateful for her presence. She's become my anchor in this storm. "I just... I trusted these people. I was careful, but he still managed to get to them."

Charlie pulls back slightly, meeting my gaze. "You couldn't have known. Lorenzo's been playing a long game. But you're smart, Dante. You'll find a way to turn this around."

Her faith in me feels like a balm to my pride, and I find myself nodding. "You're right. He may have won this round, but it's far from over."

The sky darkens as the sun dips below the horizon, casting long shadows over the villa grounds. I look out into the fading light, a renewed resolve stirring. "If Lorenzo wants a fight, he'll get one. But he won't win easily."

Charlie smiles, a spark of determination in her eyes that matches my own. "Good," she says, lacing her fingers with mine. "Because we're stronger than he thinks."

For a moment, we sit in silence, watching as the last rays of sunlight disappear, surrendering to the stars that begin to dot the night sky. The weight of betrayal and frustration is still there, but it feels lighter, more manageable with her by my side.

I break the silence, a new plan already forming in my mind. "I'll start by reaching out to some old contacts. People who owe me favors. I may have lost some allies, but I can find others."

Charlie nods. "And I can go through the project's financials and legal documents, see if there's any way to shore things up, create a buffer."

I look at her, admiration swelling in my chest. "You're amazing, you know that?"

She grins, a spark of mischief in her eyes. "I know. Now, let's go inside and start planning."

We rise together, hand in hand, ready to face whatever comes next. Lorenzo may have tried to weaken me, but he's only made me more determined. With Charlie beside me, I know I'm not fighting this battle alone.

As we step back into the villa, the night closes in around us, but I feel a new sense of clarity. Lorenzo may have dealt me a blow, but I'm not defeated. Not by a long shot.

Inside, the villa feels unusually quiet, each step echoing against the walls as we make our way to the living room. The air is cool, almost too still, and it prickles my nerves as I process the weight of what's just happened. Lorenzo's move was ruthless, strategic—he knew exactly where to hit me to hurt the most. But it's also left me with a sense of clarity. If he's trying to isolate me, to turn my own allies against me, then he's underestimating what I'm willing to do to protect what's mine.

I glance at Charlie, who's already powering up her laptop, her expression set and focused. "I'm going to start running numbers," she says, scrolling through various files and documents. "If we can find any areas to cut costs, reroute investments, or sell off minor assets temporarily, it might give us the breathing room we need to keep Horizon City moving."

"Good idea," I reply, already mentally listing a few of my oldest contacts, people who owe me, or those with a long enough history of loyalty. They're not the first people I'd normally turn to, but given the circumstances, it's time to explore every option.

Charlie's fingers fly over the keys, and I can see the tension in her jaw. Her intensity matches my own, and for a moment, I let myself appreciate the strength she's shown, standing by me when any sane person might have walked away. She could be doing anything else with her life, but here she is, neck-deep in a battle I was born into and that she chose. That choice means more to me than I can ever put into words.

The thought gives me an idea—one I haven't dared to pursue in years.

"Charlie," I begin, hesitating slightly, "there's someone I can reach out to, but it's a long shot. He's... someone from my past, not exactly a friend. But if he's willing, he could be an ally strong enough to counter Lorenzo's influence."

She pauses, looking up at me, her eyes wide with

curiosity and concern. "How sure are you that he'd be open to helping?"

I take a deep breath. "Not very. He's as unpredictable as they come. But if there's one person who despises Lorenzo as much as I do, it's him."

Charlie studies my face for a long moment, then nods. "It's worth a try. If we're going to stand a chance, we need every resource we can get."

Without another word, I pick up my phone and scroll to a contact I haven't called in years. The number sits there, an echo of a former life, one I thought I'd left behind. The name brings a bitter taste to my mouth, a reminder of the risks this alliance could carry. But this isn't the time for old grudges; it's a matter of survival.

My thumb hovers over the number before I finally press "call." The phone rings, each tone growing heavier, my heartbeat drumming faster with every second. Part of me wonders if he'll even answer—or if he'll hang up as soon as he hears my voice.

But finally, there's a click, and a familiar voice filters through, smooth and edged with suspicion.

"Dante," he says, his tone guarded. "Didn't think I'd ever hear from you again."

I force myself to keep my voice steady, matching his wariness. "Believe me, I didn't think you would, either. But circumstances change. I have a proposition—one that could benefit us both... if you're interested."

A silence stretches between us, weighted and tense, before he finally replies. "I'm listening."

As I lay out my proposal, detailing Lorenzo's moves and how our interests might align, I feel a mixture of dread and relief. This alliance is fragile, and if it goes wrong, I could end up deeper in the pit Lorenzo's digging. But it's a risk I'm willing to take—because if it works, it'll give us the firepower we need to not only survive but to hit Lorenzo back where it hurts.

As I finish explaining, he chuckles, low and sardonic. "I have to admit, Dante, I didn't expect you to come crawling to me. But I like what I'm hearing. Let's just say I've got some scores to settle with Lorenzo myself."

"Then we're in agreement?"

"For now," he replies, a hint of warning in his tone. "But remember, Dante, this partnership benefits me as much as it does you. Cross me, and I'll have no problem letting you fall with him."

"Understood." I don't flinch. "We both know this isn't about trust—it's about taking down a common enemy."

"Good." He pauses, and I can almost picture the sharp grin on his face. "Then let's make this interesting."

As the call ends, I set the phone down, feeling a flicker of hope despite the storm we're facing. Charlie watches me, curiosity mixed with relief in her gaze.

"Do you think he'll follow through?" she asks quietly.

I nod, though uncertainty lingers. "As long as it serves his purpose, yes. It's a dangerous alliance, but if it works… Lorenzo won't see it coming."

Charlie reaches over, taking my hand, her grip firm and steady. "Then we're ready. Whatever comes next, we're not backing down."

And for the first time, with her beside me, I truly believe it.

29

CHARLIE

Dante's anger radiates beside me, heat rolling off him as tension knots through the muscles of his arms. His jaw is tight, eyes distant, carrying the weight of betrayal and fury. I can feel his resolve hardening, and in an instant, he moves to rise.

"I'll find him," he mutters, voice dark, almost to himself. "And I'll put an end to this."

Without thinking, I reach out, grabbing his hand to keep him here with me. "That sounds like a terrible idea, Dante. How would you even find him?"

Dante's gaze locks on mine, and a shiver runs down my spine. It's not the usual thrill he stirs in me, but something colder—a chill born from the fierce, ruthless determination in his eyes.

"That part is easy," he replies evenly, his tone calm and unhesitating. I know he could do it if he set his mind to it. He's told me before—he can find anyone if he really wants to. But finding Lorenzo isn't the end of it, and I take a different approach, hoping to steer him from this dangerous path.

"And then what?" I ask, my voice barely a whisper, laced with worry.

Dante pauses, caught between getting up and staying here with me. My grip on his arm tightens, unwilling to let go, afraid that if I do, he'll slip through my fingers and plunge into a storm he can't return from.

"I'll put an end to all of this," he growls, voice taut with suppressed rage.

"How?" I press, holding his gaze. "You mean... kill him?" His only response is a slight shrug, as if it's the most natural answer in the world.

"Then what?" I counter, desperation creeping into my voice. "You know as well as I do that killing him doesn't mean it all stops. There's always someone ready to take his place, someone who will pick up where he left off."

Dante's expression shifts, a flicker of uncertainty breaking through his hardened exterior. I can feel him listening, feel his resolve wavering, so I push a little further.

"This isn't just about him. If you kill him, it might satisfy you for a moment, but it won't guarantee our safety. It's more important to make him powerless, Dante. To take away his ability to touch you, to touch us." My voice softens as I add the last words, the weight of what "us" now means grounding me.

He looks at me, his eyes shadowed in the fading light, the sky behind him streaked with the rich colors of the setting sun. The tension between us feels as tangible as his hand in mine. Finally, he exhales, a sigh heavy with unspoken emotion, and sinks back into the chair beside me.

The tension eases from my shoulders as he settles, and we sit closely, wrapped around each other. I feel his warmth, his solid presence beside me, grounding me amid the chaos that has infiltrated our lives.

I'm about to say something, anything, to break the silence when a flutter stirs in my belly. I gasp, my free hand flying to my stomach.

"Oh my God," I murmur, wide-eyed. My other hand tightens around Dante's.

"What is it?" he asks, distracted, his gaze still clouded with remnants of rage.

"Dante..." I say, barely able to keep the excitement from my voice. "The baby..."

He sighs, misinterpreting my reaction. "I get it. You've made your point. I can't go off after Lorenzo because of you and the baby—"

"No, you idiot," I laugh, rolling my eyes at him. "The baby kicked!"

Dante's face changes instantly, his eyes snapping to my belly and then back to my face, the anger evaporating in a heartbeat. Without another word, I take his hand and press it against my stomach. We sit in silence, waiting. The world seems to hold its breath, even the birds pausing their chirping. And then, there it is—a tiny kick, just a flutter, but unmistakable. Dante's eyes go wide, his mouth parting in awe.

"You felt it!" I exclaim, beaming.

He nods, speechless, his usually composed expression transformed with wonder. I can't help but giggle at the sight. Dante, always so in control, now looks completely stunned, a rare, unguarded look that makes my heart swell.

"Wow," he murmurs, sounding more like a little boy discovering something magical than the powerful man he is. He glances at me, then leans down, resting his face gently against my belly.

"Hello there," he whispers, his voice soft as he presses a kiss to my stomach. "I can't wait to meet you." His words send a shiver through me, curling my toes and igniting a warmth that spreads all the way to my heart.

When he finally looks up, the anger that had darkened his features earlier is gone, replaced by a serene expression. He catches me staring, and a small smile tugs at his lips.

"What?" he asks, his voice gentle.

"Nothing," I reply, shaking my head. I wouldn't even know how to put into words the mixture of love and relief I feel.

We sit there a few moments longer, waiting, but the baby doesn't kick again. Settling against each other, we sink into a comfortable silence, snuggled closer than before.

"We need to be sensible about this," Dante says, breaking the quiet. I nod against his chest, knowing he's referring to our situation with Lorenzo.

"I get it, Dante. But it must be hard to realize he's been playing this game from the beginning. That he was there, orchestrating things right under your nose." I can hear the frustration simmering in his voice.

I rub his arm gently, offering what comfort I can. "You're seeing it now. That's what matters. We'll be careful, and we'll beat him."

Dante's tone hardens, the steel back in his voice. "Sensible, but not passive. He won't get away with this."

I nod, keeping my voice level. "First, we need to reclaim control of your company. That's the face of your organization and the legitimate link you have to the Horizon City project. It's our foundation. To protect it, we'll need a solid plan."

Dante nods, understanding, and together we dive into a serious discussion about what steps to take. We spend the next half hour trading ideas, weighing the risks and potential outcomes, adjusting and refining until we're left with a plan we both feel confident in.

As the evening deepens, our conversation shifts into thoughtful pauses, each of us considering the road ahead. The air grows cool around us, and the lights flicker on, casting a soft orange glow over the yard and reflecting off the rippling surface of the pool. The setting feels almost surreal, a moment of calm amid the storm brewing in our lives.

Finally, after a stretch of silence, I break the quiet. "Despite everything, I'm glad we have this—this time together, this moment to breathe."

Dante's expression softens, and he nods. "Me too. I wouldn't trade it for anything." He reaches out, brushing a strand of hair away from my face, his touch light and tender.

By the time we rise from our shared chair to head inside, we have the bones of a plan, something we can build on, something we believe in. I can see the determination etched in Dante's features, the fire in his eyes rekindled, not with blind rage, but with purpose. He's ready, and so am I.

Lorenzo has been taking his shots, maneuvering us into a corner. But he's underestimated us, underestimated the strength we've found in each other and the resilience that grows with every challenge he throws our way.

As we walk back to the villa, hand in hand, I feel a surge of confidence swelling inside me. Lorenzo may think he's won this battle, but he doesn't know us, doesn't realize that together, we're unbreakable.

For now, it's enough to know we have each other, that we're not alone in this fight. And as Dante's grip tightens around my hand, I know we're ready to take our shot.

This isn't just his war; it's ours. And it's far from over.

As we step into the quiet of the villa, the hum of the

air conditioner and the soft click of our footsteps are the only sounds filling the space. But the silence feels charged, a readiness humming just beneath the surface. Dante's hand is warm in mine, his fingers interlocked tightly with mine as if anchoring us both to what's coming.

He guides me to the kitchen, where he begins preparing coffee, his movements methodical, almost calming. I settle onto a stool across the counter, watching him. It feels like we're gathering strength in these small routines, a moment of quiet before we plunge into the chaos Lorenzo has unleashed.

Dante slides a mug across to me, his eyes softening as he studies my face. "I know this isn't what you signed up for," he says quietly, his voice threaded with something I rarely hear in him—vulnerability.

I take a sip, letting the warmth of the coffee settle me before responding. "Dante, I didn't just sign up for the easy parts of your life. I signed up for all of it, and I wouldn't change a thing. We're in this together." My words come out steady, carrying a conviction that surprises even me.

A faint smile touches his lips, and he reaches out, brushing his hand over mine. "Together, then," he murmurs, his eyes holding mine, as if drawing strength from them.

As the quiet stretches between us, his gaze shifts to the papers stacked on the counter—documents related to Horizon City, financial records, and a thick folder marked with Lorenzo's name. He flips it open, scanning the pages, his expression sharpening with every line.

"You know," he says finally, his voice a low rumble, "Lorenzo has made himself appear untouchable, like he's built this empire around himself that no one can pierce." He shakes his head, a gleam of challenge sparking in his eyes.

"But everyone has weaknesses, even him. We just need to find where he's most vulnerable."

I lean forward, drawn into the fierce determination that radiates from him. "And I have a feeling he's underestimated what we're capable of."

A thoughtful silence stretches between us as we pore over the information. Dante's fingers trace the lines of documents, graphs, and numbers, connecting dots with an intensity that's almost mesmerizing.

After a while, he sits back, a smirk playing on his lips. "He doesn't see us coming," he says, his voice low, almost a whisper. "He thinks he's already won, that he's cornered me, but he has no idea what we're about to do."

I feel a thrill of confidence sweep through me, knowing that this man, so often consumed by duty and control, is ready to push back with everything he has. For the first time since Lorenzo's threats began closing in, I feel a glimmer of excitement—a reminder that we're not helpless, that we can take back control.

"Tomorrow," Dante says, his eyes glinting with a determined fire, "we start making moves. We'll contact allies, pull together resources, and get this plan in motion. Lorenzo may have positioned himself well, but he's far from invincible."

I nod, my own resolve mirroring his. "He's not prepared for us to fight back. This isn't just about defending what's ours; it's about reclaiming everything he's taken."

Dante's hand finds mine across the counter, a silent promise exchanged. We're not alone in this battle—we're a team, and together, we're stronger than anything Lorenzo can throw at us.

As the last trace of light fades from the sky outside, plunging the villa into a stillness that feels almost sacred, I realize we're poised at the edge of something monumental. This is our moment to strike back, to show Lorenzo he miscalculated in ever thinking he could control us.

Dante lifts his coffee mug, a determined smile playing on his lips. "To the beginning of the end—for him."

I clink my mug against his, feeling the spark of anticipation in my chest as we share this quiet toast to our unspoken vow.

Tomorrow, everything changes.

30

DANTE

Chapter 30: Dante

The shower's hot spray had done little to wash away the tension coiled in my muscles. My reflection stares back at me from the fogged mirror, the weariness etched deeper than I'd like to admit. I run a hand through my damp hair, exhaling sharply. Every move Lorenzo makes seems designed to chip away at what's left of my empire, testing the limits of my patience and my control.

I shrug into a shirt, buttoning it as I step into the quiet of the bedroom. It's late, the kind of late where the world outside falls still, yet my thoughts refuse to follow suit. Charlie's light is still on in the study, spilling a faint glow into the hallway. She's been working tirelessly alongside me, her determination as unyielding as my own.

A buzzing vibration breaks the silence. My phone. I glance at the screen: **Uncle Emiliano**. The name alone is enough to stir a mix of suspicion and curiosity.

"Uncle Emi," I greet cautiously, keeping my tone neutral.

His voice is urgent, almost frantic. "Dante! I wasn't sure I'd reach you."

The undercurrent of tension in his words sends my instincts into high alert. "What's going on?"

There's a pause, filled with the faint murmur of voices in the background. "I'm in Italy," he admits. "Meeting with Lorenzo's backers."

I tighten my grip on the phone, a cold clarity sharpening my focus. "Why?"

"To broker peace," he replies, his tone almost pleading. "Dante, I never wanted to take sides, but the pressure... it's mounting. Lorenzo's making promises, deals that some of us couldn't refuse."

"Some of you," I repeat, my voice flat. "But not you?"

A heavy sigh crackles through the line. "No. Not me. That's why I'm calling. There's more at stake here than you realize, and I can't stand by any longer."

I want to believe him. There's a sincerity in his voice that's hard to fake, but trust isn't something I offer lightly—especially now. "What are you saying, Uncle?"

"I'm saying I can help you," he whispers. "But you'll have to trust me."

The weight of his words settles over me. Trust. It's a fragile thing, and in this world, even family can shatter it without hesitation.

After a beat, I respond. "What kind of help?"

"Lorenzo's network is larger than you think. He's using Horizon City as a linchpin for something bigger—money laundering, smuggling operations, you name it. If you're going to take him down, you need leverage. I can get you that leverage."

Silence stretches between us, each second filled with unspoken implications. Finally, I ask the question that's been burning in my mind. "Why now? Why reach out to me after all this time?"

"Because it's the right thing to do," he says quietly.

I want to laugh at the simplicity of his answer, but something in his tone stops me. He sounds... sincere.

"Alright," I say finally. "But if this is a setup—"

"It's not," he interrupts. "I swear to you, Dante. I'll prove it."

The line clicks dead before I can respond. I lower the phone, my thoughts racing. If Emiliano's telling the truth, this could be the break we've been waiting for. But if he's lying...

A soft knock at the door pulls me from my thoughts. I glance up to find Charlie standing in the doorway, her expression equal parts curiosity and concern.

"Who was that?" she asks, stepping into the room.

"Uncle Emiliano," I reply, watching her reaction.

Her brow furrows, and she crosses her arms. "And?"

"He says he wants to help," I explain, recounting the conversation. As I speak, I can see her mind working, analyzing every word, weighing the possibilities.

"Do you believe him?" she asks when I finish.

"I don't know," I admit. "But if he's telling the truth, this could change everything."

She nods slowly, her gaze thoughtful. "And if he's not?"

"Then we'll deal with it," I say, my voice firm.

The room falls silent, the weight of the situation pressing down on both of us. Finally, she steps closer, her hand brushing against mine.

"We'll figure this out," she says softly.

Her touch grounds me, the warmth of her palm a stark contrast to the cold calculations swirling in my mind. I turn to face her fully, my hand closing over hers.

"Charlie," I begin, my voice low. "I need you to know something."

She looks up at me, her eyes searching mine.

"I've spent my entire life building walls," I continue, the words tumbling out before I can stop them. "Walls to keep people out. To protect myself. But you…" I pause, swallowing hard. "You've broken through them in ways I never thought possible."

Her breath catches, and for a moment, the world narrows to just the two of us.

My hands cup her face as I lean in, kissing her with all the vulnerability and need I've held back. She melts against me, her fingers gripping my shirt. The kiss deepens as years of restraint crumble between us.

I pull her closer, one hand tangling in her hair while the other wraps around her waist. Her soft gasp when my lips find her neck sends fire through my veins.

"I need you," I breathe against her skin. "More than I've ever needed anyone."

She arches into me, her body molding perfectly against mine. "Then have me," she whispers, pulling me back to her lips.

The kiss turns desperate, passionate, filled with everything we've left unsaid. Her touch anchors me as the walls I've built finally shatter completely.

"I'm scared," she admits, her voice barely above a whisper.

I reach up, brushing a strand of hair from her face. "I know," I say softly. "But I promise you, Charlie, I'll do everything in my power to keep you safe."

Her eyes glisten with unshed tears, and she nods, leaning into my touch. "I believe you," she murmurs.

The moment stretches, charged with an unspoken

understanding. And for the first time in weeks, I feel a flicker of hope.

But the moment is shattered by the sharp buzz of her phone. She steps back, her expression apologetic as she glances at the screen.

"It's Emiliano," she says, her brow furrowing as she reads the message.

"What does it say?" I ask, my voice tightening.

"He says he's ready to meet," she replies, looking up at me. "But he has one condition—he needs to see you face-to-face."

My jaw tightens, the flicker of hope replaced by the cold weight of reality. "Then we give him what he wants," I say, my voice steady. "But on our terms."

She nods, her resolve matching mine. Together, we'll face whatever comes next.

As I watch her return to the study, I feel a renewed sense of determination. Emiliano's offer is a risk, but it's one I'm willing to take. For Charlie. For us.

Because failure is not an option.

31

CHARLIE

The view from the back of the house is unexpectedly soothing, calming me in a way I didn't know I needed. I wonder if Dante bought or built this place, if he imagined it exactly like this—and if he ever pictured he'd share it with me. The thought stirs warmth in my chest, and I let out a slow, contented sigh, watching the late afternoon light dance on the water, the trees framing the scenery perfectly. It's almost too perfect, like a fleeting moment I want to hold onto.

The sliding doors open behind me, and I already know it's Dante. His presence fills the space before he even touches me, his hand landing lightly on my shoulder. If it were anyone else, I might have tensed, but with him, there's only peace. A small smile tugs at my lips as he steps closer.

"Hey," he says softly, his voice warm and familiar.

"Hey," I reply, a quiet intimacy settling between us.

We stand together, silent, immersed in the view and each other. I imagine Dante just as captivated as I am, though perhaps for different reasons. Finally, he breaks the silence.

"What are you doing?" His gaze drifts to the laptop on the table in front of me.

"Just sending an email to Micah," I reply, closing the screen. There's a pause before I notice him studying me with that familiar, intense look.

He nods, a hint of approval in his expression. "He'll be useful."

When his gaze softens, I place a hand over my stomach instinctively. "How's the little one?" he asks, his tone dropping to a gentle murmur.

A smile pulls at my lips. "You want to ask?" I raise an eyebrow, feeling a flutter of happiness I hadn't expected.

Without another word, Dante kneels before me, his hands landing on my belly. He leans close, whispering, "Hello, little one. How's it going in there?" His breath tickles, and he looks up, catching my gaze. "Your mother's been getting a bit antsy, even if she tries to hide it."

I blink, surprised at his insight. I hadn't realized he saw past the walls I'd put up. "I just... there's a lot to worry about," I murmur, barely above a whisper.

"I know, amore mio." He presses a warm kiss to my belly, grounding me, easing my worries just for this moment. "Mama has plenty to worry about, but we'll try not to trouble her too much, right?" He turns his attention back to our child. "Let's keep her happy." He looks up at me, mouthing, "It's a promise."

I chuckle softly. "You're silly," I say.

He grins, kissing my belly again. "I'll be whatever you need me to be." His gaze lifts, carrying that familiar intensity.

Dante trails gentle kisses up my stomach, stopping at the place where my bump begins to curve inward. My breath hitches, anticipation thickening the air between us. His warm breath skims over my skin, and I squirm, nudging him playfully with my foot.

Then, in that husky tone I know so well, he says, "Kiss me."

I lean forward, our lips meeting in a soft, lingering kiss. He tastes faintly sweet, and I savor it, letting the kiss deepen. My hands slip up to his shoulders, grounding myself, yet there's something else simmering beneath—my own worries, secrets I haven't shared.

Breaking the kiss, I pause, catching my breath, reluctant to pull away. Dante, sensing my hesitation, rises to his feet, cupping my face gently, his eyes dark with desire.

"I want you," he whispers, a vulnerability in his gaze that surprises me. Even now, when I feel heavier each day? My hand drifts to my belly, almost unconsciously, feeling its roundness, its weight. The thought of him wanting me like this makes me wonder if he sees me differently.

"Now," he says, as though he knows exactly what I'm thinking.

I pull him closer, fingers curling in his shirt as I press my lips to his with renewed hunger. His hands find my body, his touch sending shivers through me as he eases his hands up to my chest, thumbing over sensitive skin through the thin fabric of my shirt. We lose ourselves in each other, his hands sliding under my skirt, reaching higher until he hooks his fingers into my underwear.

Rising slightly, I allow him to slide them down my legs. As I step out of them, his eyes trace every curve of me, a familiar spark igniting between us. I reach for him, feeling the heat and hardness of him through his clothes, and guide him to sit. Straddling him, I take my time, savoring the moment, a shared gasp passing between us as we come together.

There's an easy rhythm as we move in sync, a quiet surrender to each other. With each slow rise and fall, his hands clasping mine from behind, I feel both the joy and the weight of everything we've built together. He whispers words of encouragement, of love, guiding me to a place where all tension dissolves.

Afterward, we sit together in a peaceful daze, his arms wrapped around me, grounding me once more. His lips brush against my neck, making me shiver despite the warmth. For a moment, I almost forget everything—the lingering worries, the doubts, the life just beyond our view.

"Wanna go again?" he murmurs, his voice playful against my skin.

I nod, letting out a soft laugh. He nudges me gently, rising to his feet and leading me back inside. Just as we step into the house, my laptop beeps from the table. I glance back, feeling a pull—curiosity, and a small, nagging dread that I can't ignore.

It's a message from my bank. I pause, my heart thudding as I open it. A notification about a deposit... and then the amount—a figure with more zeros than I've ever seen. I swallow, realization dawning, and the world around me narrows. I know exactly who sent this and why.

Lorenzo. He's trying to buy my silence, to make me walk away from Dante.

Dante's voice calls from inside, a soft, "Amore mio?" followed by his face appearing in the doorway, his expectant smile warming me. I freeze, heart racing as I consider telling him, confessing everything right here. But then I see his smile, that familiar warmth, and the words die on my lips.

"Coming!" I manage a smile, closing the laptop. I slip back into the room, taking his outstretched hand. As he guides me to the bedroom, I try to push the deposit and everything it implies from my mind. Its weight presses against me, a reminder of secrets held and choices I'm not ready to face. But here, in Dante's arms, it's easy—just for a while—to let it all fade into the background.

For the rest of the evening, I lose myself in his quiet presence, in our laughter and gentle touches. But in the back of my mind, that deposit lingers, a quiet promise of everything I stand to lose.

As I settle into the warmth of Dante's arms, I try to ignore the way my thoughts keep drifting back to that bank notification. The weight of it sits like a stone in my stomach, refusing to let me forget. For now, though, I focus on the man beside me, his soft breath against my shoulder, his hand resting protectively over my belly. There's so much comfort in him, a safety I don't want to lose. Yet, that nagging thought refuses to rest.

I take a deep breath, savoring his familiar scent, pushing the worry down, hoping it will stay buried long enough for me to enjoy this moment.

"You're quiet," he murmurs, his voice low and drowsy, like he's somewhere between wakefulness and sleep.

I force a smile, smoothing my hand over his. "Just... thinking."

Dante shifts, propping himself up on one elbow to look at me. Even in the dim light, his gaze is piercing, as though he can see right through the mask I'm trying to keep in place. "About?" he prompts gently, searching my expression.

I hesitate, feeling my heart beat just a little faster. My instinct is to reassure him, to brush it off, but I know Dante too well. He won't settle for a lie, not when he senses something's off. Still, I can't bring myself to tell him —not yet.

"Just everything... the baby, the future," I reply, my

words carefully chosen. They're true, even if they're not the whole truth.

He gives a slow nod, his gaze softening. "We'll handle it, amore mio," he murmurs, brushing a strand of hair from my face. "Whatever comes, we'll face it together."

His words steady me, reminding me of what's real. Yet, even as I lean into his touch, the thought of that deposit claws its way back into my mind, refusing to be silenced. I wonder if he'll say the same thing when he finds out what I've been hiding—that someone is trying to buy me off, to push me out of his life.

I close my eyes, burying my face in his shoulder, letting his presence fill me, if only for a moment. Dante is my refuge, my constant—but how long can I keep this secret

Eventually, Dante drifts off, his breathing evening out, but I lie awake, staring into the shadows of the room, feeling the weight of what I'm keeping from him settle heavy on my chest.

As the night stretches on, my resolve hardens. I know this can't stay hidden forever. Sooner or later, Dante will have to know. But right now, here in the darkness with him beside me, I cling to the last moments of peace, even as I sense the storm looming on the horizon, ready to tear everything apart.

Dante's breathing eventually slows, deepening as he drifts into sleep, his arm still protectively draped over me. But I lie awake, staring at the ceiling, the weight of Lorenzo's bribe pressing against my chest like a stone I can't shake. I try to focus on Dante's warmth, his presence, and the calm he brings. But my mind keeps circling back, picking apart every unspoken question and choice that now lies before me.

How long can I keep pretending this doesn't matter?

How much longer can I keep this from him, hiding it in the shadows of moments like this?

In the darkness, the quiet feels almost too loud, my resolve slipping away piece by piece. I tighten my grip on Dante, as if holding him close could somehow keep the storm at bay, keep the secrets buried. But even as I cling to him, I know this moment of peace is borrowed, fragile.

Sooner or later, this will shatter. And when it does, everything—our love, our life, our future—might crumble with it.

32

DANTE

I stand quietly, staring up at the Villa that has been our sanctuary for months. It's strange—this place began as an escape, but over time, it became something more. A haven. Now, with every passing second, it feels more like a cage. A loud car horn blares behind me, making me jump, snapping me out of my thoughts.

"I'm coming! Oh my God!" I call back over my shoulder. Charlie's in the passenger seat, gaze fixed forward, her jaw set in a tight line.

"So impatient," I mutter, knowing she'll hear me.

She sighs, eyes still on the Villa. "I just need to get out of here."

I slide into the driver's seat, glancing back at the building. I feel the urge to say something, give this place a proper goodbye, but then I catch Charlie watching me from the corner of her eye. She starts to say something, then stops, and silence hangs heavy between us.

"I don't know when we'll be back," I say, glancing at the Villa again, hoping for some shared sentiment.

She shrugs, almost dismissively. "Good."

Her bluntness surprises me. "We've been here for months," I reply, unable to keep the question from my voice.

Charlie turns to me, her gaze steady. "What do you want from me?"

I raise my hands in silent surrender, starting the car. "Alright, alright." She sighs, sinking back into her seat, her hand resting protectively over her swollen belly.

"I'm going to miss it... I think," she admits finally. "But not as much as you, apparently," she adds with a touch of sarcasm. "I just feel uncomfortable and stressed."

"Are you okay?" I ask, immediately concerned. I glance pointedly at her belly. She's close to her due date—one of the main reasons for our move back. Her belly is full and round, a visible reminder that our lives are about to change forever.

She doesn't answer, and I take it as enough. I drive us the short distance to the airfield, where a helicopter waits, blades already whirring, ready to take us back to the city. I exhale, looking around the airfield, struck by how long it's been since we stepped outside the Villa.

What started as a forced getaway became months of careful planning. We'd talked to Gabe every day, setting things up down to the last detail. We couldn't afford mistakes—not with Charlie in her condition. The plan was simple: meet our security at the airport, then head straight to the safehouse. Straightforward on paper. But I can't shake the feeling that "simple" rarely goes as planned.

As the chopper takes off, I glance at Charlie staring out the window, her expression a mix of longing and anxiety. I study her, then refocus, running through the plan one last time in my mind. We would land at a private airport, where a convoy would be waiting to take us to safety. No room for error. I can't let anything go wrong—not with Charlie and our child at risk.

When the airport comes into view, I spot the line of black SUVs parked by the hangar—a reassuring sight. I feel some of the tension leave me. Everything looks exactly as arranged.

Charlie reaches for my hand, and I give hers a comforting squeeze. The pilot brings us down smoothly, and as the chopper touches the ground, I'm out in a flash, extending a hand to help Charlie down. The wind from the blades still whips around us, but she grips my hand, stepping carefully from the helicopter.

"We made it!" she shouts with a grin, though she winces as she steadies herself, one hand pressing against her belly.

"Let's get you home!" I call back, nodding toward the line of SUVs. She nods, catching my meaning, her grip tightening on my hand.

Five black SUVs stand in a row, each with two guards—one beside the driver's door and another standing with a gun in hand. Three men break from the line, jogging over to assist us.

"Welcome back, boss!" one of them shouts over the noise of the helicopter. I glance back, noticing the pilot still hasn't shut off the engine. Odd, but I push the thought aside.

"Thanks!" I reply, just as loudly. The guard nods respectfully at Charlie, his eyes briefly flicking to her belly. Swiftly, he reaches into the helicopter for our luggage, passing bags to his teammates, who jog them back to the SUV.

"Ride with me, sir?" he asks, and I nod, wracking my brain for his name. "Freddy," I say, relieved when he grins, confirming I got it right.

We're just about to head to the vehicles when, suddenly,

one of the guards spins on his heel, raising his weapon. The man beside him mirrors the action. In the split second it takes for my brain to register danger, a bullet pings off the helicopter's side.

"Charlie, get down!" I shout, reaching for the gun tucked into my waistband, scanning the horizon. Three vehicles speed toward us across the tarmac, with figures leaning out the windows, guns already blazing.

"Move, move, move!" I yell, grabbing Charlie's arm, pushing her toward the SUV.

She screams as bullets continue to ping off the chopper, and dread tightens my chest. I pull open the SUV's back door, shoving her inside, shielding her as I fire a few rounds toward the approaching cars.

"Freddy! Get us out of here!" I shout over the roar of gunfire. Above us, the helicopter lifts off, the pilot abandoning the scene. I slam the back door shut, turning just in time to see Freddy's crumpled body a few feet away, blood pooling around his neck.

My stomach clenches. Dammit. No time to mourn. I sprint to the driver's door, heart pounding as I pray he left the keys in the ignition. My fingers close around them, and I nearly pump my fist in relief. I twist the key, bringing the SUV roaring to life.

"Strap in!" I shout, not waiting for a response before slamming the gas and peeling out of line.

The other SUVs fall in behind us, engaging in shootouts with the ambushers. As we speed forward, I catch a good look at the attackers—a trio of SUVs, each filled with shooters armed with various guns. They're here for us. Whoever sent them knew our every move.

I spot a chain-wrapped mesh gate up ahead and make a split-second decision not to slow down.

"Grab onto something!" I yell to Charlie.

I hear her muttering under her breath—a prayer, perhaps—and I grip the wheel tighter, needing all the luck we can get.

We slam through the gate at full speed, a jolt shuddering through the car as metal crunches and sparks fly. But we burst through, veering onto a narrow access road leading to the highway. I finally exhale, checking the rearview mirror to see our convoy following, managing to keep up despite the bullets flying around us.

A pained groan from the backseat sets off alarm bells. "Are you okay?!" I try to keep the panic from my voice. Has she been hit?

The groan comes again, her breaths quick and shallow. "Charlie!" I call, this time unable to hide my fear.

"Dante... I think the baby's coming," she gasps, her voice tight with pain. My heart drops. Now?

"Okay," I manage, forcing calm into my voice. "We'll get you home soon."

I swerve into traffic, earning angry honks and shouts from other drivers, but I don't care. My focus is on getting us to safety. Another ambush could be waiting, especially if they knew we'd be here. They were already on the grounds when we landed—someone close fed them our plans.

"It's okay. You're okay," I say, glancing back to see her face pale and covered in sweat. I wish I felt as confident as I sound.

The convoy follows, and I see the attackers still on our tail. The road ahead stretches out—a blur of concrete, traffic, and distant buildings. Safety feels like a mirage. In this moment, the only thing that matters is getting Charlie and our child out of danger.

As we merge onto the highway, I push the SUV as fast as

it will go, weaving between cars, trying to lose our pursuers. I glance in the rearview mirror, seeing the determination in the eyes of the men leaning out of windows, guns raised, aimed at us.

Another contraction hits Charlie, and she doubles over with a cry of pain. "Breathe, Charlie. Just breathe," I say, helplessly. "We're almost there. Just a little longer."

A bullet hits the back of the SUV with a sudden jolt, and my heart lodges in my throat. I swerve, dodging more gunfire, the city skyline finally coming into view. Safety—or what passes for it in our world—is close.

But as I look in the mirror at Charlie, clutching her belly, face twisted in pain, I know this fight is far from over. And with every mile closer to home, one thing becomes clear: we're out of hiding, and whoever's after us isn't letting go.

The baby is coming. And so is the storm.

I grip the wheel harder, my knuckles white as I weave through traffic. Each second stretches painfully long, and each glance at Charlie reminds me of what's at stake. She's doubled over in the backseat, breathing in shallow, frantic bursts. Seeing her in pain—knowing I can't stop, can't give her comfort—feels like a knife twisting in my gut.

"Dante..." Her voice is a weak whisper, laced with pain. "I... I don't know how much longer I can hold on."

"Just a little longer, Charlie. I promise," I say, my voice rough, betraying my own fear. "We're close. We'll be safe soon."

The words feel hollow, more desperate hope than certainty. The gunfire behind us is relentless, and with every bullet pinging against the car, I'm reminded just how exposed we are. The city's outskirts rise ahead, close yet feeling miles away.

Another contraction hits, and she lets out a pained cry. I

glance in the rearview mirror, seeing her pale, sweat-covered face. She's fighting, holding on as best as she can, but I can see the toll each wave of pain is taking on her.

I push the gas pedal to the floor, desperate to gain distance. The road narrows briefly as we pass an overpass, forcing me to slow down, and in that moment, the attackers close in. One of their SUVs pulls up beside us, the passenger leaning out, gun aimed directly at us. My heart pounds as I swerve, trying to shake him, but he keeps pace, gun locked on us.

"Get down, Charlie!" I yell, voice sharp with fear. She ducks as best as she can, clutching her belly protectively.

The gunman fires, and I feel the shudder as a bullet slams into the SUV's side. I lean out just enough to return fire, squeezing off a few rounds. The driver swerves, forcing the gunman to lose his aim, but they're relentless.

Another contraction hits, and Charlie's scream is raw, filled with pain. "Dante, please... I can't..."

The sound of her agony pushes every ounce of rage and fear to the surface. I glance back, seeing tears on her cheeks. This can't go on.

Up ahead, I spot an exit ramp veering into a less congested part of the city. A narrow alley sits just beyond it —a chance to lose them, or at least buy a few moments. I make a snap decision, yanking the wheel, forcing our SUV onto the exit.

The tires squeal as we take the turn, and I grip the wheel, barely keeping control as we shoot down the ramp. The sudden change throws the attackers off; one of their SUVs misses the turn entirely, screeching past and disappearing. But the other two follow, engines roaring.

I spot the alley just ahead, narrow and winding. I steer us into it, hoping the tight space will slow them down. The

SUV barely fits, side mirrors scraping the brick walls, but I keep going, determined. The echo of gunfire fades, the walls closing around us, dampening the chase.

For a brief moment, it feels like we've lost them.

I glance back at Charlie. Her eyes meet mine, wide with pain and fear, and something in her gaze steadies me. We're not safe yet. But we're together, and as long as we keep moving, we have a chance.

"Just a bit longer, Charlie. We're going to make it," I promise, gripping her hand tightly, hoping my strength can hold us both steady in the storm.

33

CHARLIE

The car swerves, and I cry out—not from the jolt, but from a wave of pain tearing through me. My hands clench the seat as I try to breathe, beads of sweat breaking out on my forehead.

"Sorry!" Dante shouts from the front. I grit my teeth, squeezing my eyes shut and riding out the pain. When it finally ebbs, I catch my breath and open my eyes to see Dante glancing back, worry etched on his face.

"Watch the road!" I yell, and he quickly refocuses on driving. What good would it do if he crashed us into a ditch? I mutter under my breath, letting irritation distract me from the relentless ache. The baby is making a dramatic entrance, and this is not where I pictured it happening.

"We're almost there, sweetheart," Dante says, his voice unusually soft, as if trying to soothe a frightened child. He keeps one eye on the road and one on the rearview mirror. I want to smack him for the overprotective tone but swallow the urge, breathing through my mouth as I fight to hold it together.

Suddenly, the SUV jolts sharply, as if something

rammed into us from the side. The weight of the impact ripples through my body, sending a fresh spike of pain through my abdomen.

"Bastard!" Dante growls, tightening his grip on the wheel. The SUV accelerates, and I hear him fumble with a device, his voice sharp as he yells, "Get them off me!"

He tosses the walkie-talkie aside, his knuckles white on the wheel. Behind us, there's a crunch of metal on metal, and I twist enough to see through the rear windshield. A black SUV—like ours—is locked in a brutal push against a smaller car, its front fender barely hanging on.

"Oh my God." My breath catches as the reality of our situation sharpens. They're really after us, and they're not holding back. Panic bubbles in my chest, but I grit my teeth and place a trembling hand on Dante's seat. "Hurry, please."

Dante glances back, and whatever he sees in my face makes him press down on the gas. The SUV surges forward, each bump and lurch sending shockwaves through me. My body tenses, then I feel a trickle down my leg. My heart skips as I realize what's happening.

"Dante, my water just broke."

"Of course it did," he mutters, his tone between resignation and determination.

"Are they still after us?" I ask, though I'm almost afraid of the answer.

His eyes flick to the side mirror before he replies, "Yes."

A sharp wave of pain crashes through me, and I cry out, clawing at the back of his seat for something—anything—to hold onto. But there's only unyielding leather, and my hands slip off. I'm helpless against the pain and frustration building within me.

"We're almost there," he repeats, his tone tense. "The doctor's waiting."

I nod, gritting my teeth, clinging to his words rather than the fear rising inside me. My mind holds to that thin thread of reassurance: We're almost there.

As we veer off the main road, I can tell we're moving onto less-traveled paths. The tires hum against dirt, and for a moment, calm settles, as if the world is holding its breath. Dante grabs the walkie-talkie again, his voice tense. "Open the gate. We're coming in hot. And get the doctor ready!"

I brace as the iron gate comes into view, slowly sliding open. It looks sturdier than the one at the airfield, but Dante isn't slowing down. My heart pounds as I squeeze my eyes shut, praying we'll make it through.

The SUV slips through the gate just as it opens wide enough, and Dante spins the wheel sharply, bringing the vehicle to a screeching stop inside the small compound. Another wave of pain hits, and I lean forward, clutching my stomach. I want to be anywhere but here—safe and far from this chaos.

I sit up, catching a glimpse of two black SUVs speeding in behind us. Lorenzo's men, closing in fast.

Dante jumps out, his voice slicing through the air. "Close that gate! Close it!" He turns to a driver climbing out of another SUV. "Where are the others?"

"There were five SUVs when we landed," I murmur, mostly to myself. Now only three remain.

One of Dante's men steps forward, his voice low. "Tommy led a few of them away to throw off the tail. Ray and Doug... didn't make it."

Dante's face hardens, but there's no time for anything else. The gate slams shut just as Lorenzo's men reach it, the heavy iron a barrier between us and certain death. A thick silence fills the air, broken only by muffled engine sounds on the other side.

For a long moment, there's nothing. No movement, no voices—just the eerie calm of a temporary sanctuary. I let out a shaky breath, the weight of it pressing on my lungs. Then silence shatters, the metallic rattle of bullets clanging against the gate echoing around us.

Dante looks back at me, his face calm but his eyes intense. "It'll hold... for now." He raises his voice. "Get her inside!"

Two men with guns dangling at their sides step forward to help, and just as they reach me, I see a woman rushing toward us. She seems out of place here, but I realize she must be the doctor Dante arranged.

"Hi, I'm Martha," she says breathlessly, her voice soothing even amidst the chaos. "What's your name?"

"Charlie," I manage.

"Well, Charlie, looks like you're about to have a baby." Her tone is brisk but gentle as she checks my pulse, her hands moving with practiced speed. "Don't worry, mama. We'll take care of you."

Another spray of bullets slams against the gate, and I flinch, clutching Martha's arm instinctively.

"Let's get you inside," Dante orders, his voice tense. Martha hooks her arm through mine, guiding me toward the house, the two guards flanking us.

"Wait!" I gasp, panic rising. "My purse!"

One of the men dashes back to the SUV, retrieves my purse, and hands it to me with a baffled look, but I don't care. I clutch it to my chest, feeling a strange reassurance from its weight.

Inside, Martha guides us to a small room that seems hastily prepared. The walls are bare, the bed covered in a clean sheet. It's not the sanctuary I dreamed of, but right now, it feels like a lifeline. I barely make it to the bed before another contraction hits, and I double over, gasping.

"Breathe, Charlie. Just breathe," Martha murmurs, rubbing circles on my back. Her touch is grounding, and I cling to it like a lifeline.

"They're getting closer together," I gasp between breaths.

"That's normal, mama. You're doing great." Martha helps me lie down, her hands firm. She glances at the two guards standing awkwardly nearby, giving them a stern look. "I'll need extra towels and water. Now, please."

They nod, visibly relieved to have something to do. Martha lifts my legs, checking under my skirt with a swift, clinical touch.

"Alright, Charlie, we're almost there. Are you ready to push when I tell you?"

The gunfire outside grows louder, and I flinch, but Martha's voice brings me back to the room. "Focus on me. You're safe here, and we're going to get through this together. Ready?"

I nod, my body aching to be done with this ordeal. I want it over, want to hold my baby and feel something besides fear.

When Martha finally tells me to push, I'm swept into an entirely new state of existence. Everything narrows to this single, all-consuming effort, my mind blank as I become the conduit for this new life. Images flash in the corners of my vision—Dante at the bar when I met him, then his face when I learned his true name. Moments of our life together, brief but filled with love.

Tears spill over, dampening my cheeks, but I barely register them as I push with everything I have. Martha's voice is the only anchor in the storm, guiding me, steadying me. "You're doing amazing, Charlie. Just a little more."

Another push, and then I hear it—a high, sharp cry that cuts through the room like a beacon. I collapse back, my body drained, but a flood of relief and overwhelming love rushes in.

"Congratulations, Charlie. It's a boy." Martha's face is beaming as she wraps the baby in a soft cloth, placing him gently in my arms.

I stare down at the tiny face nestled against me, his features barely visible. My heart swells, and a tear slips down my cheek. Relief washes over me, tempered by exhaustion and the distant sound of gunfire.

"We're all cleaned up," Martha says. Her voice is calm, but there's a shadow in her eyes. "But now we need to get you out of here."

"What?" Panic jolts me back into the present. "We can't go now!"

"It's the boss's orders," she says, referring to Dante with a firmness that leaves no room for argument. "They've breached the compound. We're barricaded in here, but we need to move."

"Where's my purse?" I blurt, struggling to sit up. I can feel the blood rushing to my head, a strange determination overriding the fatigue.

"Here," someone says, placing it in my hand. I rummage through, my fingers finally closing around the cold metal object I'd been holding onto.

A familiar voice calls from outside. "Hello, Dante! Long time no see!" Lorenzo. My breath catches, fear slicing through the joy of holding my son.

I press a button on the pager hidden in my purse, praying I'm not too late. The device remains silent, and a sense of dread tightens in my chest. I press it again, repeatedly, refusing to accept failure as an option.

Holding my son closer, I steel myself, hoping this one small signal will bring us the help we desperately need.

Martha catches my eye, her expression fierce. "We're moving as soon as it's clear," she whispers, her hand resting on my shoulder. "I won't let anything happen to you or your baby."

In that moment, I feel a flicker of strength return. I nod, my grip tightening on my son, and brace myself for whatever comes next. The door rattles, a gunshot rings out, and then silence hangs, heavy and foreboding, on the other side.

34

DANTE

"Come out, Dante!" Lorenzo's voice blares through a loudspeaker, sharp and mocking. "I don't mind coming in, but you can save us both some trouble."

I clench my jaw. "Stay away from the windows!" I snap at the men around me. "They're reinforced, but let's not take any chances."

Before I can react, someone grabs my shirt, pulling me deeper into the room. "Doors too, boss. We can't risk anything."

I nod, letting myself be pulled back. I'm surrounded by heavily armed men, all looking at me, waiting for direction. They believe I'm the answer to their survival. I can't let them see my hesitation.

One of them, the one who dragged me away from the door, speaks up. "Now what, sir?"

Before I respond, Lorenzo's voice cuts through the silence, oozing with smugness. "Let me tell you a fun story, Dante," he croons, his tone almost playful. "Do you want to know how I found you?"

A chill settles in the room. I don't respond. I won't give him the satisfaction.

"I'll tell you anyway." Lorenzo's laugh rings out. "It took an admittedly large sum of money wired into the right account. I don't like parting with cash, but knowing I've got you? Worth every penny." His laughter crackles through the speaker, sending a ripple of unease through my men.

I stay silent. My silence is a shield, one I need to keep up.

"Oh, come on, Dante. Don't you want to know who betrayed you?" Lorenzo's voice drips with malice, meant to stir doubt. I feel the men's eyes shift to me, silent questions swirling, but I ignore them all.

Then he twists the knife further. "Hi, Charlie," he says sweetly, mockingly. "I hope you're not foolish enough to be there with him."

Around me, tension rises, whispers spreading. Eyes widen, brows furrow, as they wait for my reaction, but I refuse to let him bait me.

Finally, Lorenzo's voice returns, sharp and dangerous. "Dante, I'm getting bored. Let's end this game. Either you come out at the count of five, or I come in."

The loudspeaker cuts off, leaving a vacuum of silence. Everyone tenses, waiting. It feels as if the room itself is holding its breath.

"One!" Lorenzo's voice barks, final and unyielding.

A few men shift nervously, exchanging glances. I remain completely still.

"Two!"

More start edging closer, anxious. "Boss, what's the plan?"

"Three!"

I keep my gaze steady, pretending calm, while my mind races through contingencies.

"Boss..." Panic sneaks into their voices.

"Four!"

I look up, meeting their eyes with a steely calm. But I don't have to answer. A crash rips through the compound as gunfire erupts outside, bullets ricocheting against walls. My men look around wildly, confusion and panic taking over. I remain unmoved, already expecting this.

I glance at my watch. Perfect timing.

"Everyone to the south exit," I command. "Get there and wait, but don't open it yet." I scan the faces around me. "Charlie—what room is she in?"

A hand gestures toward the far end of the hall. I ordered her evacuation, but I need to confirm it myself. I move quickly through the chaos, ignoring the gunfire and shouting.

The door bursts open just as I approach. Charlie's two assigned men wheel her out in a rush. I catch my breath at the sight of her holding our newborn son, his tiny face wrapped in a soft blanket. Despite the chaos, she looks up and smiles, calm and steady.

"Hello," she says softly.

I swallow hard. "Hello." My voice comes out rougher than I'd like, but she doesn't seem to notice.

I nod at the man nearest me, gesturing toward the south exit. "Get her there. Now."

He nods, and they wheel her away. I look down at my watch. Any minute now.

The crackling sound of gunfire fills the compound, louder and closer. I force myself to stand steady, feeling every second stretch, dragging out in agonizing beats.

"Boss! Boss!" A man rushes over, tense. "Someone just knocked on the south exit."

"Let them in. Quickly."

He runs, and I follow closely, my pulse hammering. The entrance has to be opened from the inside—an intentional design to prevent ambushes or breaches from multiple sides. I steel myself as they input the code, the mechanisms whirring before the door swings open.

Bright light floods in, illuminating the figures at the door. I squint until Gabe's familiar outline steps forward, his expression mirroring my own mix of relief and tension.

"Took your sweet time," I mutter, but relief seeps into my voice despite my best efforts.

Gabe strides over, pulling me into a quick hug before stepping back. A cheer rises from the gathered men, faces lighting up as they recognize our allies. Gabe's arrival shifts the air, turning our fear into hope.

He exchanges a quick smile with Charlie before turning to me. "Come on, let's get everyone out of here."

One by one, we file out into the sunlight. Armed men surround us, providing a perimeter of protection. The sounds of gunfire from the compound fade as we retreat, putting distance between us and Lorenzo's threats.

Charlie slips her hand into mine, and I squeeze it, feeling the warmth of her presence beside me. Her men give her curious looks, but I ignore them. They'll have time to wonder later.

Trucks await us, and we split up, climbing into the reinforced vehicles. Charlie, the doctor, her two bodyguards, Gabe, and I settle into one. As we leave the safe house behind, a phone rings, jarring us out of the silence.

"It's mine," Charlie murmurs, reaching into her purse. She listens for a moment, then slips it back in, turning to me with a slight smile. "Micah says it's done."

Relief flows through me, easing the weight of our long weeks of planning. Micah, Katie's boyfriend in the FBI, had been the cornerstone of our plan, and knowing he came through lifts a weight off my shoulders.

Gabe catches my eye, giving an apologetic shrug. "We couldn't move in until we were certain they'd engaged Lorenzo's men. We needed the distraction."

I nod. It was part of the plan, and Gabe did exactly what was needed. I glance at Charlie's bodyguards, watching questions flicker in their eyes as they glance from her to me.

"Wait, this was all part of some plan?" one of them asks, incredulous.

A grin tugs at my lips as I nod, but I keep quiet. Let them piece it together.

One of them clears his throat. "What about the... betrayal?" He hesitates, his voice lowering, unsure if it's even safe to mention.

I glance at Charlie as our truck jolts over uneven ground. "What did Lorenzo say about that money?"

Charlie's grin matches mine. "He said I could keep it."

I can't help but chuckle, satisfaction settling in my chest. Lorenzo had just funded my latest project without realizing it. The Horizon City development—the one Lorenzo wanted to sabotage—was now fully funded by his own desperation. When Charlie showed me the figures, I almost laughed. He must have really wanted my head.

After weeks of hiding, Lorenzo grew anxious. An enemy you can't see is the most dangerous. Uncle Emi spread subtle rumors, hinting that Charlie was with me and her loyalty was for sale. In his desperation, Lorenzo took the bait.

Meanwhile, Uncle Emi sold the contents of my warehouses to Lorenzo's partners—without Lorenzo knowing the products were mine. The FBI tracked every transaction, each one inching Lorenzo closer to his end. All of it evidence, all ammunition.

I glance back at the compound receding in the distance. I wonder if Lorenzo survived the chaos or allowed himself to be taken by the feds. Either way, his reckoning is near.

We soon reach an open field. A helicopter waits on the grass, blades whirring softly under the sunlight.

Gabe grins as we approach. "Thought this would be faster."

As we pile out of the truck and head to the chopper, my phone rings again. I pull it out, a familiar voice greeting me.

"Uncle Emi."

"They're rounding up the others," he says, sounding nervous but resolute.

"You're safe," I reassure him. "Nothing implicates you."

He lets out a breath. "So it's finally over?"

"It is," I reply, feeling the truth settle into my bones.

"How's Charlie?"

"She's fine. The baby too." I can't help the smile that sneaks onto my face.

"A boy!" Uncle Emi's voice bursts with excitement. "Congratulations! What's his name?"

I pause, realizing I hadn't thought of that yet. "We haven't decided."

He chuckles. "Another Romano. Let me know when you do, yes?"

"Of course," I say, my smile widening.

I glance over to where everyone else is seated in the helicopter, waiting for me. Uncle Emi's voice comes through again, softer. "Will you come to the wedding?"

A laugh escapes me. "When is it?"

"Whenever you decide to propose," he teases.

"Then yes, Uncle. You'll be there."

He laughs warmly. "Goodbye, Dante."

I slip the phone into my pocket and climb into the chopper, feeling a release I haven't known in months. Finally, the weight lifts.

Charlie scoots closer, resting her head on my shoulder as the chopper takes off. I glance down at our newborn son, swaddled so snugly that only his peaceful face peeks out. Despite the roar of the helicopter, he sleeps soundly.

He's a Romano, alright.

The last few months have been a storm, but I have everything that matters beside me—my son, my future wife, and a path to a new life.

EPILOGUE

The sunlight filters through the tall windows of our penthouse, painting the room in warm, golden hues. It's been six months since the chaos of Lorenzo's downfall, six months since Charlie and I have finally found a semblance of peace. I never imagined I'd find solace here, with her, and now, with him—our son, Mateo, sleeping soundly in his crib across the room.

The Horizon City project is in full swing. Lorenzo's fortune, the one he so desperately funneled to take me down, is now driving the rise of a community center, schools, and affordable housing across the city's south side. It's ironic that, in his end, Lorenzo is helping rebuild the very city he tried to tear apart.

A soft sound catches my attention, and I look over to see Charlie standing by the window, gazing down at the skyline below. She looks serene, her hair tumbling over her shoulders, a small smile playing on her lips as she cradles a cup of tea.

"You're awake early," I murmur, moving up behind her and wrapping my arms around her waist.

She leans back into my chest, sighing contentedly. "It's nice to just... be," she says, her voice barely a whisper. "After everything, sometimes I still can't believe it. I can't believe we're here, safe, and... happy."

There's a wistful edge in her tone, a reminder of the battles we've fought, the lives we left behind. I press a kiss to her temple. "You're safe now. We all are. No one is coming after us."

She turns to face me, her eyes filled with that fire I've come to love, a spark that refuses to be dimmed, no matter how much she's endured. "You really believe that?"

"I do." I nod, my voice firm. I've worked too hard to make this life for us, this new chapter. Lorenzo's empire has crumbled, and anyone who once answered to him is either in hiding or under lock and key. I made sure of it.

Charlie takes a breath, her hand resting on my chest. "It's strange... The life I had before you feels like it happened to someone else. I feel like I've lived two lives."

"You have," I say, brushing a lock of hair from her face. "You're not the same person you were then. And neither am I."

Her gaze softens, and I see the hint of a smile. "I like this version of us."

I pull her closer. "So do I." Just as I'm about to lean down and kiss her, a small, demanding cry echoes from across the room. We both turn, chuckling softly.

"Looks like someone else is awake," I say, letting her go as she moves over to the crib. I watch her as she lifts Mateo, her face lighting up with a love that fills the room, warming every corner. It's a sight I never get tired of.

Charlie carries Mateo over to me, her eyes glinting with that playful look she gets when she's about to challenge me. "Your turn," she says, handing him over with a smirk.

I take my son into my arms, feeling the weight of him, the life we created together. Mateo's tiny hand wraps around my finger, and he looks up at me, his eyes wide and curious. I still feel a surge of awe every time I hold him. This little life is part of me, part of her, a testament to everything we've been through and survived.

Charlie sits beside me, leaning her head on my shoulder as we both look down at our son. "Do you ever wonder what he'll be like when he grows up?" she whispers, her voice filled with wonder.

I nod, a hint of protectiveness curling in my chest. "Strong. Resilient. Fierce. Just like his mother."

Charlie rolls her eyes, a small laugh escaping her. "And maybe a little stubborn like his father?"

"Maybe," I admit, grinning. "But he'll be surrounded by family. He'll know love. He'll know loyalty. He'll know what it means to stand up for what's right." My voice grows serious. "I'm going to make sure he never has to see the things we've seen."

Her hand finds mine, giving it a squeeze. "You already have. You've given him this life." She glances around our home, her eyes lingering on the framed photos that line the walls. Images of us in quieter moments—our wedding day, the three of us at the beach, Mateo's first laugh. Each picture a promise, a reminder of the life we've built together.

The sun climbs higher, casting long rays through the glass, and for a while, we just sit there in silence, holding each other close, holding onto this life we've made.

By afternoon, the family begins to arrive. Uncle Emi is first, his arms laden with gifts for Mateo. He kisses Charlie's cheek and clasps my shoulder in that old, familiar way, a proud gleam in his eye. For as long as I've known him, he's been my mentor, the one who guided me through the darkest parts of my life, but now, I see the peace in him, too. The relief.

"Look at him," he says, peering over Mateo, who's gurgling happily in his playpen. "A true Romano. Already commanding the room."

Charlie laughs, the sound light and musical, as she and Uncle Emi share a knowing look. "He's definitely got the Romano spirit," she agrees, winking at me.

Soon, Gabe arrives, bringing an armful of flowers for Charlie and a bottle of vintage whiskey for me. "A gift for all your sacrifices," he says with a grin, slapping me on the back as we share a warm embrace.

We gather around, our family, the people who helped us survive, who stood by us. The conversation flows, the laughter fills the room, and I feel the bond between us strengthen, forged by battles fought and won together.

Uncle Emi watches us, a small smile playing on his lips. "You know, Dante," he says, his voice soft but steady, "it's strange, isn't it? You spent all those years building your empire, fighting for power, and yet this…" He gestures to the room, to the laughter, to Mateo playing on the floor. "This is what you were fighting for."

I nod, a deep understanding settling within me. "It was always about family. The power, the money… none of it meant anything without this."

He pats my shoulder, pride shining in his eyes. "You've done well, Dante. Your father would be proud."

It's a rare moment, hearing him speak of my father, but I feel the truth of his words. I built this life to protect the people I love, to ensure their safety, and I succeeded. This is the legacy I'll pass on to my son.

. . .

As night falls and the family drifts home, leaving us with a quiet house, I find myself standing by the window, gazing out at the city lights below. Charlie comes up behind me, wrapping her arms around my waist.

"What are you thinking?" she asks, her voice soft.

I take a breath, my gaze focused on the city I once ruled with an iron fist. "That it's strange... to be free of it all. The deals, the alliances, the threats."

She tilts her head to look at me, her expression tender. "It's not strange, Dante. You've earned it. We've earned it."

I nod, pulling her closer. "I still feel like I'm adjusting, like there's a part of me that's waiting for the other shoe to drop."

She smiles, understanding. "We've been through a lot. It'll take time to let go."

I turn to face her, holding her close, feeling the warmth of her body against mine. "But I want this. I want to be here, with you, with Mateo. I want to build something that lasts, something that's untouched by the past."

Charlie's fingers trail up to my cheek, her touch grounding me. "You already have, Dante. Look around you. Look at what you've created."

I glance around, taking in the life we've built together, the love we share, the child we brought into the world. "You're right," I say, my voice steady. "This is our future."

She smiles, leaning up to press a soft kiss to my lips, a promise of all the tomorrows we'll share.

The weeks blend into a rhythm of quiet mornings and joyful moments with Mateo, shared dinners with family and friends, and late-night talks with Charlie about our dreams, our plans. Slowly, I feel myself relax, the tension I've carried for so long finally melting away.

One night, as we sit on the terrace overlooking the city, Charlie rests her head on my shoulder, her hand entwined with mine. The stars are bright above us, casting a soft glow over the world.

"Do you think Mateo will ever know the life we came from?" she asks, her voice filled with wonder.

I shake my head. "No. He'll know a different world, a safer one. And if he ever asks, we'll tell him about where we came from, about the choices we made to protect him."

She smiles, her gaze on the stars. "And one day, he'll make his own choices. He'll create his own path."

I nod, my heart swelling with pride and hope for the life we're giving him. "He'll have that chance, thanks to you."

Charlie looks at me, her eyes shining. "Thanks to us, Dante. We did this together."

I pull her close, pressing a kiss to her forehead, feeling the depth of my love for her, for our son, for this life we've built. The shadows of the past may linger, but they no longer have power over us. We're free.

And as I hold her close, the city lights stretching out below us, I know with certainty that this is only the beginning. The legacy of the Romano name is no longer about power and dominance—it's about love, loyalty, and the family we fought so hard to protect.

In this moment, with the world quiet and peaceful around us, I know we've finally found what we were searching for all along: a future worth fighting for.

The End

. . .

DID YOU LIKE THIS BOOK? Then you'll LOVE <u>Seduced by the Grumpy Mafia Boss: A Secret Baby Enemies to Lovers Romance</u>

I'm the new Mafia Boss, thrust into power by my brother's untimely death. His last words haunt me: "Protect Gwen. She has the key." Little did I know, she'd become the key to my heart as well.

Gwen is my dead brother's Ex and therapist and the guardian of his secrets. I captured her, determined to uncover the truth that could secure my empire. But this curvy temptress with emerald eyes becomes my own forbidden obsession.

Our interrogations ignite a dangerous dance of desire. Each heated glance, each "accidental" touch sparks a fire I can't control. Her intoxicating scent, her lips begging to be claimed—we know it's wrong, but our attraction is undeniable.

One scorching night of passion changes everything. Before I can unravel the mystery, she vanishes, taking her secrets—and my heart—with her.

As I tear through the city's underworld, my enemies kidnap Gwen, unaware she carries my child.

Now, I'll risk it all to reclaim what's mine: my empire, my woman, and our unborn baby

CLICK HERE NOW TO GET, Seduced by the Grumpy Mafia Boss: A Secret Baby Enemies to Lovers Romance

35
SNEAK PEEK

Chapter 1
Brent

A bullet narrowly misses me, burning a part of my sleeve in its path, and pierces through the upholstery of our chair. Tobias shoots me a quizzical look as he slowly leaves the cellar.

"What was that?" The whiskey in his glass reverberates as he speaks. Even with the softness in his tone, he still sounds intimidating.

A sharp crack pierces the air, followed by the sickening sound of shattering glass. Instinctively, I throw myself to the floor, my heart pounding as adrenaline courses through my veins. Tobias quickly throws himself beside me, his eyes wide with alarm as we take cover behind the nearest piece of furniture.

"What the hell is going on?" I shout over the gunfire, my voice tight with tension.

Tobias doesn't answer, his attention fixed on something

beyond my sight. I follow his gaze and spot movement on the neighbouring house's roof. A hooded figure obscured by shadows has an instrument strategically placed before him.

"It's them," Tobias's voice is grim. "The bastards finally found us."

The realization hits me like a punch to the gut. The Hooded Vipers have tracked us down, and now they're coming for blood.

I fumble for my binoculars, my hands trembling in fear and fury as I bring it to my eyes. Adjusting the focus, I zoom in on the figure on the rooftop and see what I hate the most in all my years as the right-hand man in a Mafia group—a sniper.

"Son of a bitch," I mutter under my breath, clenching my jaw in anger. "We need to get out of here."

"Are the boys situated at the entrance?" Tobias pours the rest of the whiskey down his throat after lifting himself from the ground.

"They should be. They're always at the entrance whenever we're brainstorming."

"Good. That'll buy us some time."

Time? It's a luxury right now because we don't have it for anything else but to exit this condo immediately. But Tobias moves in a different direction from where I'm headed to escape.

His footsteps echo the increasing chaos as he dashes back toward his room. The gunshots are louder now. The sniper used silencers, so that must mean foot soldiers are coming for us.

"What are you doing?" I demand, my voice rising with frustration. "We can't stay here!"

But he doesn't listen. "I need to find something."

"Is it important right now? This place is clean! We don't have any traces here..."

"Gwen's photos," he cuts me off, his voice distant and urgent. "I have to get Gwen's photos."

I halt in my tracks. Amid a bloody ambush, he's thinking about his damn ex-girlfriend's pictures? Does he have none on his phone, even if he needed something to jerk off to?

"Are you kidding me?" I snap, my patience wearing thin. "Forget about the damn photos! We need to survive!"

He's already disappearing down the hallway before I finish, his figure fading into the darkness. I want to go after him, but I watch more bullets slice through the curtains we have just moved away from.

"Tobias!" I scream in frustration and duck, avoiding a bullet that hits the painting above me. I hear more gunshots, but one is suddenly followed by a strangled cry of pain.

Time seems to slow as I rush after him, and my heart hammers my chest. When I reach his room, Tobias is on the floor, a pool of blood spreading beneath him.

I'm frozen in shock, helpless to do anything as I watch him bleed. My brother is holding his wounded chest, and I couldn't do a damn thing to stop him from being shot.

I rush to his side, unsure what to do. I am a bundle of nerves and pure agitation. Every shot I hear makes me cringe, ramping up my agitation tenfold.

"Fuck! Fuck! FUCK!" I don't know what to do. I can hear Tobias's breath, but it does not sound good.

"Help! HELP!" I yell back down the hall. The sounds of bullets crashing through the glass and into the wooden panels of the walls answer back.

I rush to Tobias's side and try to staunch the bleeding. I have no idea what I am doing.

"HELP!" I yell back down the hall, praying for help in a storm and hoping against hope.

"Alonso!" I called for one of the guys who was supposed to be in the other room, hoping someone was still alive.

"Stay with me, man, stay with me," Tobias is looking progressively worse.

A bullet whizzes over my head and smashes into the wall behind me, making me flinch hard.

"Stay with me, bro, please," I can feel myself coming apart. This is not me. My body feels like a vessel I am not a part of, experiencing emotions I do not feel. I am watching myself go through this. I would like to know if this is what shock is.

I glance around — my hands are doing little to stop the flow of blood pumping out of Tobias's chest. I run to a door with a lovely bright yellow curtain across it. I grab the curtain with my bloodstained hands and yank on it hard. The force rips it from its place across the mouth of the door and down to the floor in a clatter of broken metal.

I rush back to my brother's side — he is moving less and less now, and his breathing is becoming more and more laboured — and bunch up the curtain, then proceed to shove it at his chest, pressing it against the leaking wound. A groan of pain escapes him at my actions.

"I'm sorry, I'm sorry, I'm sorry," I mumble over and over. I don't know what to do or what I am doing wrong. All I know is that the red life leaking out of him should be inside, and I am trying to stop that.

Tobias groans again.

"ALONSO!" I yell out of desperation. The shots are still smashing through the house, although if I was not so agitated, I would have noticed they have lessened in intensity.

"B—Brent," my brother mumbles.

"Yes! Yes!" I lean in closer to him. "Stay with me, brother."

"Brent," he breathes. His words are barely words now. They seem more like gasps. It looks like a lot of effort on his part to get them out.

"Save your strength," I notice the reduction in the frequency of the shots ripping through the house. Either Alonso and the guys are down, or they managed to drive off those bastards. We will know which soon enough.

"You hear that?" I muster a peppiness I do not feel in my tone. "No more shots." One chooses that exact moment to ring through the condo. "Well, almost no more shots." My grin does not go beyond the grimace etched on my face.

With blood smearing my cheeks from my hands touching my face, I wonder what I look like in the moment.

"No shots, Toby," I say, nearly mad with frantic energy. "We will soon be out of here. You'll be safe. You'll be fine."

I hear footsteps. "You hear that? Alonso and the guys are on their way." I hope it is Alonso and the guys.

It won't matter if it isn't, I think grimly to myself, but I don't say that last part out loud.

Tobias breathes heavily, his chest pumping weakly against my blood-soaked hands.

"Brent," he manages.

"Yes, Toby?"

"Brent," he calls my name again. He looks about, his eyes looking for me as if I'm not inches away from his face.

"Toby, I am right here. Right here, Toby," I stammer. I let go of the repurposed curtain with one hand and grabbed his hand with the other, clasping it as we have done a million times in our years together.

"I am here, brother," my voice is choked.

"Brent," he gasps. Both his hands grab mine as if finally finding something long lost.

"Brent," he repeats.

"I am here, brother," I repeat too.

"It is all in your hands now," he says.

What?!

"No, no, what do you mean?"

"Everything," he manages through heavy breaths. "Everything is in your hands."

"What does that mean, Toby?!" A part of me does, but I refuse to accept it.

"It is yours now," my brother repeats. His eyes seem to be losing their sharpness. He is looking at me, but I am unsure if he sees me.

"Toby!" I shake him. In my hands, he feels unlike my brother—light and quickly moved. My heart drops inside me.

Presently, Tobias comes to, his grip on my hand still held in his tightening. Renewed hope flares within me.

"Br-Brent?" He says.

"Here, brother. I'm not going anywhere," I answer quickly.

The footsteps are getting closer. They are almost on us. The shots tearing through the house have stopped entirely. I hope the footsteps belong to friends.

One thing I know for sure is that I am not leaving my brother.

He brings his other hand up, and it is then that I notice what it has been grasping all this while. Even as his grip on life slipped slowly away, he held on to his.

He brings the hand and its content around, surprisingly devoid of blood but for a few drops and an edge that must have laid in the pool on the floor.

Toby presses the picture into my hand. It looks like the type is meant to be housed in a frame. An edge is missing, and I get the picture of it being ripped out of a frame and getting caught.

I wipe bloodstained hands on the curtain still gripped in them — doing little by way of cleaning the blood — then accept the photo from my brother with the tips of my fingers, trying to get as little blood on it as possible.

Bodies barrel into the hall behind me. I glance over my shoulder and am slightly relieved to see it is Alonso and the guys.

They rush forward, Alonso sliding to his knees beside me, cussing violently.

He turns and looks over his shoulder.

"Call an ambulance!" He yells at one of those standing behind us, looking distraught. Their guns are out, and their eyes scanning everywhere.

Two of the five men who now occupy the hallway, excluding Tobias, Alonso, and me, peek into each doorway in turn, ascertaining there is no one else present and making sure there isn't anything else that can prove a danger.

One of those left standing whips out his phone and starts dialing.

"Too late," Tobias mumbles. Alonso and I snap back to him.

My brother's hand tightens weakly in mine. His other hand, now free of the photo held in its grip, comes around and holds my hand in a two-handed grip.

"It's too late," he intones. He is trying to impress the reality onto me. I resist forcibly.

"Everything," he begins but stops to gulp. His eyes sharpen for a moment. "Everything... Is yours."

I feel Alonso glance sideways at me. I ignore him.

"Toby—" I begin, but he cuts me off.

He lifts himself off the floor slightly, seemingly intent on impressing the importance of his following words on me.

His grip on my hand, still holding the now thoroughly red curtain in place, tightens ever so slightly. His eyes catch mine and keep them in a death grip. I feel my vision blurring.

This is not happening.

"Find her."

For a second, I am confused. Find who?

"Find her," Tobias repeats. Oh, the girl. A flare of rage wells up within me.

Tobias is still speaking. "Find her," he gulps, "and keep her safe."

I start to protest.

"She is important," he says. His eyes are beginning to lose focus. "She has the key..."

"Ambulance is on the way," the man tasked with calling them speaks over my shoulder.

I nod, but I know it is futile. It is too late.

"Keep her safe," Tobias repeats.

I nod.

"Pr–" he breaks into a wretched coughing fit that seems to sap whatever strength was left in his body.

"Promise..." His eyes are glossy in the hallway's light.

"I promise," I mumble shakily.

A sigh escapes his lips.

"Toby," his eyes are drifting closed. His grip on my hand slackens.

"Toby," my vision grows blurry. Wetness runs down my cheek.

"Toby..." I cannot believe this is happening. My brother...

"We have to go," Alonso says, standing up and at the end of the hallway. When did he get there?

He walks back towards me.

"Brent," he says. "We have to go."

I barely hear him. My eyes are on my brother. His chest is no longer moving under my hand.

His face is still, blood-smeared, but somewhat at peace. His eyes are in slits, like those of someone stuck somewhere between waking and sleep.

"We have to go," Alonso repeats. "Those shots... Cops will be here soon. If the Vipers don't come back to finish what they started. We can't stay here," he finishes.

I know he is right.

I raise the arm not gripped in my brother's now lifeless ones and wipe my eyes on my sleeve.

As I do so, I notice the photograph still pinched between my fingers. The smiling face on it, the laughing eyes, and the full lips... A wave of anger surges over me, rage that turns my vision from blurry to red.

"We have to go. Now!" Alonso yells.

I loosen my hand from my brother's grip and, with two fingers, close his eyes the rest of the way.

I rise to my feet slowly. There is a silence in the hallway. Unnatural for a place populated by seven breathing bodies.

It is as if a stillness is brought on by recognition of a significant moment.

I turn around to face the men arrayed in the hallway behind me. Their eyes are all on me.

I wipe my face with my sleeve once again, no doubt smearing some more blood onto it.

"Let's go," my tone is clipped.

"You heard! Move!" Alonso intones.

They filed out with quick, cautious steps, making for the

entrance and the garage below where our vehicles were parked.

As we move, they form a protective ring around me, their guns ready, scanning our surroundings.

Some people poke their heads out of their doors, curiosity getting the best of them. They are quickly dissuaded from further investigation by the sight of seven armed men, one of them his face and shirt smeared with blood.

As we descend the levels crammed into an elevator together, Alonso nudges my arm, shaking me out of the daze I was slowly slipping into. I look down to see what he is stretching at me. It is a handkerchief.

I look up at him, not understanding.

He moves towards my face. I glance at the mirrored walls of the box we are in, and I am quite a sight.

"Let's not scare people off or draw more attention to ourselves," Alonso says.

I silently accept the proffered piece of fabric, seeing the wisdom of his words. I imagine I look like something out of a child's nightmares.

After wiping my face and removing some of the now dry blood from my hands, the handkerchief was red—as red as the bottom portion of my shirt.

Alonso sees me looking at it.

"You should have a shirt in your car, yes?" He raises an eyebrow.

I nod dumbly. He is right. I always carry extra clothing. I never thought I would need one because of my brother's blood.

An image of Tobias's prone, lifeless body flashes before my eyes. I shake my head to clear it.

The elevator stops, and we file out. We are in the basement garage under the building.

The men spread out as soon as the doors opened, taking up positions to the left and the right, guns out and pointed forward. So far, we have not seen any indication that the Vipers are still in the vicinity.

"They seem to be gone," I hear Alonso mutter beside me, echoing my thoughts. His eyes flit around the quiet garage, the cars sitting under the fluorescent lights our only companions.

We move forward as a whole, exercising extreme care all the way.

We are parked together, so it is just a matter of reaching the place.

"My vision is slowly starting to clear. The fog that has enveloped my mind is gradually beginning to lift. Its recession is courtesy of the red-blind anger bubbling beneath the surface.

I just watched my brother die.

The thought plays over and over in my head, a broken record stuck on a hated song.

I saw the light in his eyes dim and die, and there was nothing I could do.

We creep forward quietly, ever vigilant. We can see the cars where they are parked, and I am sure the temptation is as strong in them as it is in me, but we resist it, maintaining our cautious pace.

A few feet from the car, we break apart.

There are four vehicles parked together.

Two SUVs are the men split up and hop in. One is my luxury 2-door sports car low to the ground, and the third is Tobias's more sensible 4-door Jaguar. I turn my face away from it.

Alonso pauses beside it.

"We don't have the key," I say gruffly. With everything happening and how we exited the condo, no one had thought to take Toby's keys. If they are still here, I'll have someone come pick them up later.

When I push the button, I fish out my keys and am rewarded by a beep from the automobile.

I can see the uncertainty on Alonso's face. I can see him contemplating asking me if I should be driving. I pull open the door to forestall all arguments and slip inside. Alonso opens the passenger door and sits next to me. I glance at him for a moment before shutting my door.

"Where to, boss?" Alonso asks.

I finger the photograph still held in my hand. The nonchalant smile... Unknowing and unconcerned about what just happened...

"Do you know where she is?" I ask Alonso, turning the photo to face him.

He leans into peer at the image, his face immediately brightening.

"Oh! I don't," he says.

I am just about to sigh when he adds. "But I can find out in five minutes."

I say nothing but push the start button and the car purrs.

Alonso has his phone to his ear, talking into it. I block him out — I block everything out. All except the buzzing in my ears and behind my eyes. The sound of blood thudding in the back of my head.

I pull out of the parking spot and head toward the entrance to the parking lot. Alonso raises a hand from the window above the car, waving it at the men in the other two cars to follow us.

He reclaims his seat as I speed out of the lot and over a ramp.

"Okay, thanks," he takes the phone away from his ear and looks at me.

"I got it," he says.

It takes me a moment to push through my cloudy mind to remember what he is on about.

"You found her?" I ask.

"Yes," he replies. "Tobias keeps—kept," he clears his throat, and I try to ignore the significance of what just happened. "Tobias kept active track of her whereabouts, and one of the guys knew it. It's not even far from here." he finishes.

"Where is it?" The words come out through clenched teeth.

The address is barely out of Alonso's mouth when I gun the engine.

I assume the SUVs are behind me, but I don't even look to confirm. My mind is on one goal and one goal only.

Tobias died gripping her photo. He died getting to it. His last words were about her.

My thoughts are not coherent enough to blame her for his death. Still, she has been a significant factor in everything that has happened over the past two hours, and I am getting to the bottom of this.

Alonso, pressed back into the seat beside me by the g-forces, says nothing. I notice him look at me from the corner of my eyes and then back out the windshield.

Good. Right now, I am not in the mood for conversation.

Traffic is light, and swerving between lanes is not tricky. We soon begin to approach the area.

My eyes scan the buildings on either side, taking it all in

seconds. It looks like a suburban neighbourhood with houses lined up on either side of a small street.

I have barely let off the gas since I came off the highway.

This, and the barreling speed I was already going at, are probably why I didn't see the woman trying to cross the street until the very last minute.

I slam on the brakes, pulling the roaring car to a halt in a cloud of smoke and burning tires.

There is a thud on the car's hood and a moment of silence, during which Alonso and I exchange looks.

I pull open my door and step outside. The SUVs arrive behind me, each pulling to a halt.

I walk around the car to see what has happened. I see a woman lying prone on the asphalt.

Did I kill her? The thought flashes through my mind.

I lean down to press a finger to her throat. She gasps loudly, coming awake suddenly and winding into a sitting position all in one motion.

The suddenness of the action startles me somewhat.

She is breathing quickly.

"Oh my God... Oh my God... Oh my God..." She goes on and on.

"You're okay," I tell her absently. I don't have time for any of this. I scan the buildings nearby, looking for thirty-seven, as that is where Alonso said Gwen—the woman in the photo—lived.

I notice immediately that we are right in front of thirty-seven. I may have passed it if I hadn't almost hit this woman. I look back at her, remembering I almost hit someone, but stop immediately.

For some reason, I thought she'd been a middle-aged woman. But that was far from true. She is a young woman, beautiful, her hair now loose, falling in cascading waves down her shoulders. Her eyes are agitated, and she is looking about her, staring up into the front fender of my car in shock. She swivels on the floor and looks up at me, taking me in as I do her. Her face is stunning... And identical to the one in the picture gripped in my hand.

"Gwen?" I manage.

She looks up at me in surprise as if seeing me for the first time.

What the hell?

CLICK HERE NOW TO GET, **Seduced by the Grumpy Mafia Boss: A Secret Baby Enemies to Lovers Romance**

Printed in Great Britain
by Amazon